The Wedding Promise

**Center Point
Large Print**

Also by Thomas Kinkade and Katherine Spencer
and available from Center Point Large Print:

The Inn at Angel Island

**This Large Print Book carries the
Seal of Approval of N.A.V.H.**

The Wedding Promise

An Angel Island Novel

THOMAS KINKADE
& Katherine Spencer

CENTER POINT PUBLISHING
THORNDIKE, MAINE

This Center Point Large Print edition
is published in the year 2011 by arrangement with
The Berkley Publishing Group,
a member of Penguin Group (USA) Inc.

The text of this Large Print edition is unabridged.
In other aspects, this book may vary
from the original edition.
Printed in the United States of America
on permanent paper.
Set in 16-point Times New Roman type.

ISBN: 978-1-61173-069-2

Library of Congress Cataloging-in-Publication Data

Kinkade, Thomas, 1958–
The wedding promise : an Angel Island novel / Thomas Kinkade and Katherine Spencer.
p. cm.
ISBN 978-1-61173-069-2 (library binding : alk. paper)
1. Taverns (Inns)—Fiction. 2. Hotelkeepers—Fiction.
3. Weddings—Planning—Fiction. 4. Islands—New England—Fiction.
5. Domestic fiction. 6. Large type books. I. Spencer, Katherine, 1955– II. Title.
PS3561.I534W43 2011b
813'.54—dc22

2011001601

Dear Friends,

It is always a pleasure to return to a place we have enjoyed visiting before. And it certainly gives me and Katherine Spencer great joy that you have decided to come back to the Inn at Angel Island.

To me, the inn represents a place of peace and harmony, a warm and homey place filled with the soothing aroma of homemade muffins fresh from the oven. It is a haven that looks out at one of God's greatest creations: the sea.

But even in this blessed spot, doubt and fear and negativity can find a way in. Even when our hearts are filled with love and joy, as they are on the occasion of a wedding, we may still have to fight off the feelings that keep us from happiness and grace.

Jennifer and Kyle are in love and eager to marry. Their fondest hope is to be married at the Inn at Angel Island, but that wonderful decision sets off ripples of fear in Liza Martin, the innkeeper. Can she handle the job? Will she fail? And how can she be totally happy for the couple when she sometimes fears that she will never experience the love she herself longs for?

And what about the bride and groom? They are happily in love, but no love ever goes untested. Will their love be strong enough to weather the dark storms that are approaching?

There is no greater miracle than love—and in a place like Angel Island, it seems as if God Himself has carved that miracle into the sheltering cliffs and traced it on the shoreline like footsteps in the sand.

Let's follow them. . . .

Please join us at the wedding. You are always our most welcome guest.

Share the Light,
Thomas Kinkade

Chapter One

THE Hobarts were the last guests to leave the Inn at Angel Island on Monday morning. Kate Hobart came down the steps just ahead of her husband and handed Liza the room key.

"Everything was perfect, Liza. I wish we could stay the rest of the week. Or two."

"I wish you could, too." Liza placed the key in the cubbyhole of the oak secretary.

The Hobarts had been at the inn for the past four days, celebrating their anniversary. Two other couples had checked in during the weekend, but the Hobarts had stayed the longest and Liza had come to know them the best.

"Come back anytime. Beach weather is on the way," she promised.

It was the second week in May, and a wave of warm weather over the weekend had given everyone a taste of summer.

"We're thinking about a stay in July, with the rest of the family," Kate said, slipping a brochure into her purse. "Do you have any adjoining rooms?"

"There's a suite on the third floor. Two bedrooms with a private bath. Ocean view," Liza added.

Liza did not add that those particular rooms were far from renovated. If the Hobarts made a reservation, the suite would jump to the top of Liza's to-do list.

"I'll check our calendar and get back to you," Kate said. "It was only a few days, but it's so peaceful here. It's going to be hard to get back to real life again, right, Tom?"

Kate glanced at her husband, who was coming down the stairs with their bags.

"I'm planning on a slow reentry, honey. With a stop along the road for one last lobster roll."

The half-dreaming, half-scheming look on his face made Liza laugh.

"Sorry, pal," Kate replied. "I've already gone overboard on that awesome breakfast. Which was worth every calorie."

Liza was glad to hear that. The rooms weren't perfect yet, but all the guests were quickly won over by the meals—by Claire North's cooking, to be precise.

Liza answered a few questions about directions and wished the Hobarts a safe trip back to Connecticut. Then she stood on the porch and watched them drive away.

The Inn at Angel Island had been officially open since the first week in April, just a little more than a month. Though she'd only entertained a handful of guests so far, Liza already knew she would always feel the same exhilarated rush when her guests arrived, and always feel sorry to see them go, as if she were saying good-bye to dear friends.

Most of the guests had come on the weekends, arriving Friday and leaving Sunday morning. A few, like the Hobarts, had stayed longer, from Thursday or Friday night through to Monday. No one had come yet for a solid week. But she hoped to see far fewer blank spots in the reservation book once the warm weather and vacation season arrived. And it was just on the horizon, Liza reminded herself.

She had considered placing advertisements in local travel magazines or even the newspapers. She'd been in the advertising business before moving to the island and knew that a well-designed, well-placed ad worked. But she didn't have the extra money right now. The inn still needed loads of repairs, and her priority was to keep the renovation going. Right now, there were only a few rooms to offer on the second floor, and one totally refinished bathroom.

No point in advertising when she couldn't accommodate a flood of customers. Or even a steady stream.

"Are the Hobarts gone?"

"They just left." Liza turned at the sound of Claire's voice. As usual, Claire had come up so quietly, Liza hadn't realized she was there. "They said they're coming back in July. Mainly for some more of that baked French toast thing you served this morning."

"Cinnamon Raisin Strata," Claire quietly

corrected her. "I'll copy down the recipe. You can send it to Mrs. Hobart."

"That's very thoughtful, Claire. But why would I do that? It's the perfect bait to get them back." Liza was partly joking—and partly serious. "We don't have any bookings until Memorial Day weekend. Only one reservation in June, and July is a big blank," she reported. "Let's not even turn the page to August."

"Don't turn the page and don't worry. The calls will come," Claire said decidedly. She'd set down a large basket of freshly laundered linens on the wicker table and now began to fold the towels and sheets in her calm, methodical way. The laundry looked so perfectly smooth when she was finished, you'd think a folding machine had done the task.

"I know it's too soon to worry. I'm just feeling restless. I'm going to check the old registration books and send out more reminder cards. Maybe I can stir up some business."

"Good idea. People may have heard that your aunt passed away and assume the place is closed." Claire snapped a fresh white pillowcase in the breeze. "Your aunt Elizabeth used to fret about the same thing this time of year. But most folks haven't even stuck their noses out the door and realized that summer's almost here."

Liza knew that was true. New England winters were long and harsh. It took most of the hardy residents in the area a while to thaw out and accept that the warm weather had arrived. Then suddenly, the long, hot days of summer rolled in.

As usual, something about Claire's quiet, certain tone soothed Liza's anxiety. Claire had a way of looking at the world that made life seem easy and uncomplicated.

The housekeeper and cook had worked for Liza's aunt Elizabeth for many years—as both an employee and a companion. Claire had also taken care of Aunt Elizabeth in her final months last winter when she fell sick with pneumonia and never recovered.

When Liza arrived and took over, she discovered that Claire more or less came with the property—which was at first worrisome but soon turned out to be a blessing in disguise. A great blessing, Liza knew now. She wouldn't have survived more than a week on her own without Claire's help.

"Guess I'll go up and put away these linens." Claire lifted the heavy basket with ease and headed for the door. Liza rushed ahead to open it for her. "I did want to tell you, the sink in the laundry room is backed up. Looks like the tree roots again."

Liza's heart sank. Another unexpected repair? Was that really possible? And what was this about the tree roots *again?* She was afraid to ask.

11

"What do you mean? Do the roots get into the pipes somehow?"

"Every few years. Always in the spring. The new shoots work themselves right through the metal. Nature is amazing, isn't it? So . . . persistent," Claire added with a wistful smile.

Liza forced a smile in answer but didn't feel half so awed by the natural wonder . . . wondering more what this clog was going to cost.

"It always hits that sink first. Low spot on the building. We need to take care of it before the rest of the works get backed up," Claire warned.

"Yes, of course. There's a number in the book, I guess?"

Liza had quickly learned that no matter what the crisis, there was always a number in her aunt's battered old phone book.

So far, there was no repair crisis the big, old house had not seen before.

"Joe Lindstadt. He's the one. But you might try *D* for drains . . . or *C* for clogs. Your aunt had an odd way of categorizing her phone numbers."

"So I've noticed," Liza agreed.

Aunt Elizabeth had her own way of doing things, artistic soul that she was. Her phone book was the least of it.

Claire took her basket of laundry and went inside. Liza rose but did not follow. She stared out at the startling blue sky and the wide ocean, silently calculating. The profits from the guests who had stayed over the weekend could have pushed her accounts into the black this month. But now those clogged pipes would wipe out any profits, and then some.

When she looked at the inn's budget, the income and outlay, she wondered how she would stay in business at all. But you just got started, she reminded herself. You need to have patience. Isn't that what Claire always tells you? Patience and faith.

It had taken a huge leap of faith to quit her job and move here from Boston, taking on the inn without any experience at all at running a hotel. Except for spending summers here with her aunt and uncle, watching them run the place.

The change had been exhilarating at first. But now that reality had set in, along with invading tree roots and a list of other unexpected crises, Liza sometimes wondered what she had gotten into. But in her heart, she knew she'd made the right choice. The daring choice, but the perfect choice for her.

She would quickly look past her worries and out at the world around her—the tender blue sky and sparkling sea that greeted her every morning. The long curving stretch of sandy beach below the cliffs, just across from the inn's front door. The garden her aunt had planted so long ago, green stems slowly pushing through the earth, peonies and early roses bursting into bloom. The sight calmed her heart and restored her spirit.

She was so grateful to live here, surrounded by beauty every day in every season, and grateful to have the freedom of running her own business. The freedom to create a life for herself that felt authentic and true to her spirit and values.

If the pipes got clogged and the gutters drooped . . . well, it was an old building and one that had been neglected for years. Liza knew she had to step back and focus on the big picture. Things were slowly but surely falling into place, getting a little bit better every day. She had made a big change in her life to be here, but she felt it had been the right one. She felt right being here, as if she was in the place she was meant to be, doing what she had always been meant to do.

Liza gave the ocean one last lingering look, then entered the inn, intending to search through her aunt's phone book and call Joe Lindstadt—then had the impulse to call Daniel Merritt instead.

She knew Daniel couldn't fix this problem, though his skills seemed to cover just about everything else under the inn's roof. But she did know she'd feel better just hearing his deep, calm voice. He had a way of making her laugh about even the worst catastrophe.

Daniel, a local carpenter and jack-of-all-trades, had also come with the property and had also proven to be another blessing in her life. Her aunt

Elizabeth had relied on Daniel for everything from a squeaky hinge to a shaky chimney.

Liza was far more self-reliant, willing to try her hand at most jobs that didn't require great skill, just basic know-how and grunt work. When she made a mess, as she often did, Daniel would step in and show her the proper way to do things. They would usually wind up doing the job together, which Liza always enjoyed. That was how they had first gotten to know each other and become friends.

Now it seemed there was something more between them, though it was hard to say exactly what. Liza didn't worry about it. She was very newly divorced and had not yet begun dating. She wasn't sure if she was ready for a new relationship—even with a man as attractive as Daniel. All she did know was that she always looked forward to seeing him and always laughed with him. She always felt better just being around him. That seemed enough for now.

Finally, Liza decided not to bother Daniel and instead, under *D* for drains, found Joe's number. Daniel might run over even though he couldn't fix it, and she didn't want to waste his time.

Later that morning, Liza stood beside Joe Lindstadt in the dank, dingy basement, peering over his shoulder as he searched for the trap on the main line.

Joe stood up, clicked off his flashlight, and

sighed. "I'm sorry, Ms. Martin," he said, and named a price that was twice as high as what she'd expected. "I can usually do a job like this for less," he went on. "But for one thing, these pipes are old. We have to handle them with care. And that new water heater has blocked the trap. So I have to cut a new trap somewhere. If we have to dig—"

"I understand," Liza replied evenly. She could tell it was a fair price for the work involved, just a lot more than she had anticipated. But what could she do?

"I can start today. Or maybe you'd like to think about it?" he offered in a kind tone.

Liza knew he was giving her a chance to call around for another estimate. But choices were limited on the island and most of the repairmen came from the town of Cape Light, on the mainland. Joe had come over to the island quickly and now that he was there, it was best to just let him get started on the work.

"You go ahead, Joe. If you can start today, that would be great."

"I can start right now," he said cheerfully. "I just need to go back out to the truck."

Liza climbed up the steps to the first floor and Joe followed. When they reached the foyer, he slipped out the front door, leaving it ajar. "I'll be right back with my tools."

"No problem," Liza told him. She turned to

Claire, who walked out of the kitchen to meet her.

"It's the roots, just like you thought," Liza told her. "Aunt Elizabeth hadn't taken care of it for a while, so it's worse than usual. And the new water heater is blocking the trap or something. In short, the bill is going to be a whopper," Liza concluded. "I don't know. Sometimes, this inn seems like a disaster just waiting to happen. Sometimes I feel like the entire place is just about to fall down around me. . . ."

Liza noticed the look on Claire's face and realized someone had entered the inn and was standing right behind her.

She heard a polite cough and felt her face flush.

There was someone here, a potential guest perhaps, and here she was, going on and on about how the inn was a falling-down mess.

Great marketing strategy.

Claire sailed past the tongue-tied Liza with a smile. "Good morning. May I help you?" she asked in a warm, polite, and totally sane tone.

"I'm looking for Mrs. Dunne . . . Elizabeth Dunne . . . Is she still here?"

"Not any longer, dear," Claire explained. "Elizabeth Dunne passed away a few months back, in February."

Liza felt relieved that Claire had stepped in to relay that news. It still pained her to tell anyone about her aunt's passing. She took a calming breath and turned slowly.

She saw a young woman in her early twenties, standing at the open door. The light breeze lifted the long hair that hung past her shoulders in gentle waves, a rich shade of auburn with golden streaks of blond. Natural highlights, Liza could see, not the kind from a beauty salon.

Everything about her looked very natural and unstudied. She wore a flowered sundress and a dark blue sweater that complemented her wide blue eyes and dark brown lashes. A khaki green canvas bag was slung over one shoulder. It was big and battered enough to be a backpack but was probably a purse. She was very pretty, Liza thought; strikingly pretty, without a bit of makeup. And she didn't even seem to realize it.

"Oh, I'm sorry to hear that. I knew her, a little. She was so nice. A really interesting person," the young woman said sincerely. "Was she a relative of yours?" she asked Claire.

"We weren't related. Just friends. I've worked here a long time." Claire turned to Liza. "This is Ms. Liza Martin, Elizabeth's niece. She owns the inn now."

"Oh, you're the new innkeeper?" The young woman looked at Liza, clearly cheered to learn that someone had taken over.

Liza met the young woman's gaze and smiled. "Yes, I am. Can I help you with something?"

"I hope so. . . . I'd like to have my wedding here." The girl smiled as if she'd just informed

Liza she had won some sort of sweepstakes. The grand prize, in fact.

When Liza didn't immediately react, the girl looked at her curiously. "You do weddings here, don't you?"

Liza stared back, still dumbstruck. "You want to have your wedding *here?*"

I've barely mastered serving breakfast, Liza nearly confessed.

Before Liza could say more, Claire jumped into the conversation. "Oh, there have been some lovely weddings here. We even have pictures around somewhere. Such a romantic setting, especially in the summer. . . . Would anyone care for a cup of tea? I just put the kettle on."

"I'd like some tea," the young woman said. "By the way, my name is Jennifer Bennet."

"Hello, Jennifer. Nice to meet you," Liza said.

"Nice to meet you, Jennifer. I'm Claire North," the housekeeper introduced herself as she headed back to the kitchen. "Why don't you two go into the sitting room. I'll serve the tea in a minute."

Claire's easy, gracious ways made Liza remember her own manners. "Please come in, Jennifer. We can talk more comfortably in here," she added, leading the way to the large sitting room.

Liza couldn't imagine what she would say to this girl. Had she really come here hoping to plan her wedding? The idea was simply . . .

impossible. But something in Jennifer Bennet's gentle manner and hopeful expression made Liza reluctant to disappoint her.

When they entered the sitting room, Jennifer slowly looked around, seeming pleased by what she saw. She settled on the chintz-covered sofa as Liza chose a nearby armchair.

"It looks the same, almost exactly. Kyle will be glad to hear that," Jennifer announced. "I mean, it's been painted and all. But not that much has been changed."

"I haven't changed much in these rooms so far," Liza replied. Partly because she didn't have the funds yet to redecorate. But also because there was something warm and familiar in the rooms just the way they were. Her aunt and uncle had both been artists and had exquisite taste and style.

Liza assumed Kyle was Jennifer's fiancé, but before she could ask, Jennifer smiled and pointed to the big bay window that framed a view of the ocean. "I remember those curtains, with the birds. They're so pretty."

"My aunt designed them and made them herself. She was a wonder with a sewing machine."

The silk fringed curtains with their remarkable fabric had held up well. Liza had considered putting them away, as a memento, but it turned out that they had only needed a good cleaning to make the colors bright again. Liza was pleased to rehang them. The curtains seemed to carry some of Elizabeth's vivacious spirit in their style.

"When were you here last, Jennifer?" Liza asked, curious about how well the girl had known her aunt.

"Oh, about six years ago, I guess," Jennifer replied.

The answer surprised Liza, but before she could ask more questions, Jennifer began to explain.

"My boyfriend, Kyle, and I . . . Well, he's my fiancé now," Jennifer corrected herself. "We met on the beach just down the path, across the road from the inn. We were in high school. Kyle is a little older than me, two years. I'd seen him around school, but I never had the nerve to talk to him.

"I came to the island for the day with some friends," Jennifer continued, "just to hang out on the beach. I got bored and decided to take a walk, and there was Kyle. He was fly-fishing with his brother, but he said hello when I walked by and we started talking. He'd noticed me around school, too, and had been trying to meet me. He told me that later," she added with a laugh. "We just hit it off, and we spent the rest of the day together. When we finally left the beach, we came up here, to the inn. Your aunt was so sweet. She brought us cold lemonade and cookies, and we sat up on the porch in the shade and talked to her for a long time."

Liza could see it all happening. Her aunt must have spotted the budding romance and decided to encourage it along.

"She showed us some of her artwork," Jennifer went on. "And when we finally left, she told us to come back and visit her. We did come back a few times. We liked to bike ride on the island or come to this beach. We started thinking of it as our beach," she added. "We always stopped to say hello to your aunt. She told me once that she was sure Kyle and I were a perfect match and felt sure we'd get married someday," Jennifer confided with a small smile. "I asked if we could get married here, at the inn, and I remember exactly what she did. She sat back and clapped her hands and said, 'My dear, that would make my heart sing.' "

Liza smiled. That was Aunt Elizabeth. Her heart could sing, quite beautifully. And she could make other hearts sing, too.

Liza heard the rattle of china and flatware and saw Claire coming into the sitting room with a tray that held a teapot and cups and a dish with slices of fragrant lemon poppy-seed cake.

Claire set the tray on the table. "The tea has been steeping in the kitchen. I think it's ready to pour."

"Thank you, Claire," Liza said. "Would you like some tea and cake, Jennifer?"

"Yes, please. I really shouldn't have the cake,

now that I need to shop for a wedding dress. But it looks delicious," she admitted.

"Oh, a small piece couldn't hurt," Liza assured her. She was grateful for the small break in the conversation. Talking about her aunt brought back memories. Liza did miss her.

"So, you visited my aunt often while you were in high school but haven't been back in a while?" Liza asked.

"Around the time Kyle started college, we stopped coming to the island. Not enough time, I guess." Jennifer shrugged. "But we never forgot this place. We always imagined having our wedding here someday. It's just so special to us, almost . . . magical or something." Jennifer's bright eyes sparkled. "Your aunt told us the legend of the island, too."

Liza smiled ruefully, not at all surprised. "The legend, yes, of course. My aunt loved that story. I made her tell it almost every night when I was a little girl and stayed here during the summers."

Aunt Elizabeth never minded telling it over again—unlike some adults who balked at repeating a bedtime story—even though Liza knew it by heart and could have easily told it to herself.

In the mid-1600s, English colonists came to the area and founded the town of Cape Light. During their second winter, a highly contagious illness ravaged the village. None of the usual cures, herbs, or even bleeding, could help, and most of those who became ill did not survive. The village authorities decided quarantine was necessary to control the outbreak. The sick were brought to the island, and very few of the colonists were brave enough or selfless enough to come out and help them.

There would be weekly visits with food and water and other necessities but not much more than that. Sometimes storms washed out the land bridge and made it impossible to reach the island by boat. In the winter, the island was practically inaccessible to the villagers, even if they wanted to come.

That winter was particularly brutal with ice storms and high snow. For months, no one could get to the island to visit the sick villagers, and no one believed they would survive. It was spring when a group from the town finally made it out to the island, bracing themselves for a grim sight. But the truth was even more shocking than they could have imagined. The quarantined islanders had not only survived the harsh winter but were restored to full health.

They claimed that a group of very able, gentle people had come and nursed them through the winter. But no one could say exactly where those helping hands were from.

Of course, they wanted to thank their rescuers.

After they all returned to the mainland, some of the survivors traveled around, searching for the ones who had answered their prayers. But they could never find a nearby town or anyone who knew about the quarantine. Or who would admit to having gone to the island that winter.

A number of the survivors concluded that they had been saved by the healing touch of angels disguised in human form. It was said that their spiritual healing presence could be felt and experienced on the island forever after. Those who believed even pointed to the shape of the island's cliffs that jutted out like angels' wings.

The unnamed island became known as Angel Island, and locals still debated the truth of its history.

"I heard different versions of the story growing up," Jennifer said. "But your aunt made it sound so . . . convincing."

"Yes, she did." Liza had to agree.

"What do you think? Do you believe the legend?" Jennifer asked curiously.

"I guess I've gone through phases, believing and not believing," Liza said honestly. "Right now, I suppose I'm in an 'anything's possible' stage," she added with a smile.

"Me, too. I do think that anything's possible." Jennifer's expression became more serious. "Your aunt told us that when couples married on the island, the angels watched over them for the rest of their lives. She said the partnership is forever blessed and protected."

"I've never heard that before," Liza admitted, "but it's a lovely thought." And romantic and spiritual, too, just like Elizabeth. Now that Liza knew her aunt had been in the picture, it made it even harder to refuse Jennifer's request.

But she couldn't do a wedding here. There had to be some way to let the girl down easy. To make her see that, despite her lovely memories and daydreams, the inn in its present state would never live up to her fantasies.

"It sounds as if you and Kyle are a perfect match," Liza said sincerely. "I understand why the inn has such meaning for you, but I just don't think it's possible to do a wedding party here. Not at this time," she quickly added.

"But your helper . . . Claire . . . She just said that you do weddings." Jennifer looked stunned and suddenly so sad.

"I know she did. I think she meant that there were weddings here in the past—when my aunt and uncle ran the inn and were up to the task. But that was years ago. And I just took over in March," she added.

"Oh . . . I see." Jennifer sighed and looked down at her hands a moment, twisting her diamond engagement ring on her finger—a sparkling round stone in a plain gold setting.

She suddenly looked at Liza again. "Does that

mean you haven't had the opportunity to do a wedding? Or you just don't want to do one? Because this isn't going to be a very big wedding," she continued. "Not big at all. Just our immediate family and a few friends. I mean, if you do any sort of parties here, it wouldn't be much more complicated. And if you want to just try a wedding, it would be a good place to start."

Liza couldn't help smiling at the girl's persuasive manner and persistence. Jennifer had seemed a bit shy at the door but was clearly no pushover.

"Frankly, I haven't given weddings much thought, one way or the other," Liza said honestly. "We have so much repair work to do. After my uncle died, my aunt wasn't able to keep the inn up, and now we need some major renovations, inside and out."

"You seemed to be talking about that just before I came in. I overheard a little from the porch."

Liza's face flushed, recalling her exact words— a disaster waiting to happen—but she tried to maintain a professional manner. "It's not quite as bad as it sounded. I was feeling a little frustrated about something."

"Well, that's good to hear," Jennifer said quickly.

"But the inn really is a work in progress," Liza insisted.

"That's okay. As long as it's presentable."

27

"Presentable?" Liza echoed. Jennifer nodded.

Didn't brides want to be married in picture-perfect, jaw-droppingly beautiful sites? Like castles and chateaus? Vineyards and grand estates?

The inn was far from that standard.

Liza was starting to feel backed into a corner. No matter how many pitfalls she pointed out to having a wedding here, Jennifer had some solution.

She decided to change the subject entirely.

"So tell me a little about yourself, Jennifer. Are you in school?" Liza thought she looked about college age.

"I just graduated," Jennifer replied. "I went to Boston University. I grew up in Cape Light. My family still lives there. They didn't want me to go too far away and it worked out fine."

"What did you study?"

"I have a degree in education," Jennifer said proudly, "but I decided to put off looking for a job until Kyle and I are married. Teaching jobs are so hard to find right now, and it seemed a lot to do along with planning the wedding."

"That would be a lot to handle." Liza paused. They were back to the wedding again. No avoiding it. "Have you and your fiancé picked a date?"

"We'd like to be married as soon as possible. In a month or so. Certainly by July." Liza could see that Jennifer was watching her expression, waiting for her reaction. "Would that be a problem for you? I mean, it sounds as if you don't have any other big parties planned here."

"No . . . I don't . . . but that's because I don't do big parties," Liza clarified, reminding herself of the fact again. "I mean, I don't do them yet. And a month or so . . . well, that's not much time to plan a wedding, don't you think? I mean, for anyone to pull it together."

"That's what my mother keeps telling me. If you need a bit longer, that would be all right. But not too much. I don't want to have one of those long, drawn-out engagements. Kyle and I just want to be married. We don't need to make a project out of it. We're not that type of couple. Know what I mean?"

"Yes, I do." Liza smiled at her. So often it seemed that couples—especially the brides— were so focused on the wedding day, planning it for a year or even two, that they forgot about the days after, the rest of their married lives together. But Jennifer seemed to have the right focus.

"Is this the first place you've visited?" Liza asked curiously.

"Yes, it is. And the last. I really don't plan on visiting any place else. Honestly." Jennifer's expression was completely calm and certain, as if Liza had not just told her point-blank, several times, that she didn't do weddings.

"I thought brides liked to look around and compare their options. Maybe if you looked at some other inns or restaurants, you'd be surprised—and pleased," Liza suggested.

She had a feeling this inn would not seem nearly as appealing compared to other possibilities, local choices like the Cape Light Country Club or the Newburyport Yacht Club, both just a short distance away on the mainland.

Jennifer sat back and smiled. "Oh, I don't need to go through all that. It would be a waste of time. Kyle and I have our hearts set on the inn. We really do. It would mean so much to us. And we wouldn't be fussy at all, I absolutely promise. The inn is so charming and unique. Even if it's not in perfect condition, it really has character. Could you just please think about it, Liza?"

Jennifer stared at her with wide blue eyes. Liza didn't know what to say.

She had been touched by Jennifer's romantic story and hearing that her aunt had known the young couple. That part had hooked her, for sure. It wouldn't be good for her business reputation, either, if she just dashed this girl's hopes to bits and seemed unfeeling and abrupt.

"Yes, I will definitely consider it. But I'm not promising anything," she hurriedly added when she saw the sun come out again in Jennifer's lovely face. "I have to warn you, I think the answer will still be that I'd love to do it, but the circumstances here aren't ideal."

"But you'll think about it?" Jennifer replied quickly. "I mean, you really will think it through?"

Liza sighed, then nodded. "Yes, I will. I promise."

"Great." Jennifer practically bounced in place on the old sofa. "As I mentioned, we aren't planning on a large party at all, only thirty to, say, fifty guests at most." She gazed at Liza quickly to check her reaction. Liza was about to explain that it was premature for any details like that, but Jennifer rushed on and Liza couldn't get a word in edgewise.

". . . and we would like the ceremony here, too. Maybe out in the garden in back. I remember there was a beautiful garden, with all these roses and all kinds of flowers in the summertime."

"I'm not really sure what's left of the garden. My aunt wasn't able to do any outdoor work as she got older."

That was another item on her to-do list. Liza loved to garden and had begun working around the property as the warm weather set in. But the large beds of perennials, in the back especially, needed serious attention—a new garden design and a truckload of new plants.

"The gardens need some work," Liza said briefly.

"Oh, we won't worry about that. We'll bring in

flowers. That's what florists are for," Jennifer cut in again. "And don't worry about a lot of fancy food either. Honestly, the food thing is so overdone at all the weddings I go to lately."

Liza had to agree with that. There was usually a lavish cocktail hour with hundreds of appetizers. Just when you thought you couldn't eat another bite, the guests were led into another room for a long dinner with several courses followed by an elaborate array of desserts.

"We want something different. Something fun but simple. Maybe just champagne and hors d'oeuvres."

"That sounds simple and elegant, too," Liza had to agree. She liked parties like that. Maybe with live music, a trio of some kind in the corner. Flowers, of course. Yes, she could see it.

Jennifer looked pleased at her reply, and Liza caught herself before saying anything more.

Whoa, what was going on here? She was letting this girl get her carried away, like a riptide. Getting her all involved in these wedding plans when tomorrow Liza knew she would have to tell Jennifer in a diplomatic but final way that she could not have her wedding here.

This conversation was only getting the girl's hopes up. That wasn't right. "What I meant to say is, it sounds like a simple, very tasteful wedding. The type of party you could have anywhere," she added quickly.

"I'm glad you think it sounds easy. All the more reason to have it here, right?" Jennifer grabbed her big bag and stood up. "It was so great to meet you, Liza. Thank you so much for taking time to talk with me."

Jennifer leaned over and grabbed Liza in a quick, warm hug.

She felt almost embarrassed by Jennifer's effusive gratitude. Especially since she knew what her answer would be.

"I enjoyed meeting you, too, very much," Liza replied sincerely. There was something about Jennifer that was truly refreshing. She was earnest and straightforward but not in a pushy, overly assertive way. She was also so sweet.

Jennifer smiled and briefly squeezed Liza's hand. "I'll call you tomorrow. Or maybe you should call me?" she asked brightly.

"I'll call you," Liza said, wondering what she'd gotten herself into. Jennifer quickly scrawled her phone number on a piece of paper and handed it to Liza. She stared down at the number. She was really just postponing the inevitable, wasn't she?

But maybe it was best to give this girl the bad news over the phone. When she didn't have to look right into those big blue eyes and see that brilliant smile unravel.

"The morning is probably the best time to reach me," Jennifer said. "But please, take your time.

Think this through. Maybe you should jot down a few notes—just so we can talk when we get together again. The guest list will be very small, and the ceremony on the premises, remember?"

Liza nodded. She did remember everything Jennifer had told her, but she wondered now if this girl had heard a word she'd said.

"I will call you tomorrow. I promise."

Joe Lindstadt appeared in the foyer, a metal bucket full of rags in one hand and a power drill in the other.

"How's it going, Joe?" Liza asked.

"Okay, I guess," Joe answered in his typical laconic tone. "I'm almost done with the new trap."

"Sounds good," Liza replied as he walked out to his truck again.

"I can see you're busy here. I'd better go. So long." Jennifer departed with a little wave and Liza waved back, watching her head down the porch steps.

"Bye, Jennifer. Have a good day," Liza added, though she normally didn't use that trite postscript.

What she really wanted to say was, "Have a good life, dear."

She felt a sudden rush of protective feelings for the girl. Maybe because Jennifer was so buoyant and hopeful and so much in love.

Liza suddenly wished she could have Jennifer's

wedding at the inn and could make the girl's dream come true. But it didn't seem possible, however small and simple the party. It was just out of the question.

Wasn't it?

Chapter Two

I
S the bride gone?" Liza heard Claire's voice and turned from the front door to find the housekeeper standing a few steps behind her in the foyer.

"Yes, she is." Liza shut the door with a snap.

"How did you leave it?"

"What do you mean?" Liza asked, though she knew perfectly well what Claire was asking. "We can't have a wedding here, Claire. You of all people should know that. I'm not saying never. Someday in the future, when the place is in better shape—and I have some vague idea of what I'm doing—it might even be fun."

"Oh, I see. But I thought I heard her say she was going to speak to you tomorrow. What would that be about?" Claire asked curiously.

Liza felt a little embarrassed. Obviously, Claire had overheard more than she'd let on. "Well, I tried to tell her we couldn't do the wedding. But she just wouldn't take no for an answer. She made me promise that I'd think it over. So now I have to call her tomorrow and tell her the same thing I said today and hope that it sinks in."

Claire stared at her a moment. "Persistent, was she?"

"Was she ever." Liza rolled her eyes. "The guest list would be small, they didn't need a fancy meal, they would get married in the garden . . . and the garden doesn't even need to have flowers."

"Sounds as if Jennifer has a real vision," Claire remarked.

"She does, a very clear one. But putting together a wedding is never that simple. There are a zillion details. And I'm not even a party planner."

"That's all true. But it's nice to be around a bride, don't you think? She just radiates hope and love. All love comes from God above, of course, and a bride seems to bring a little bit of heaven wherever she goes, like a messenger of love," Claire reflected.

"Jennifer does seem to have a certain . . . glow," Liza had to agree. "But it will take divine intervention to pull off a wedding here. I mean, what about the condition of this building? Has anyone thought of that?"

Liza stared at Claire but she didn't answer. In fact, she seemed to be looking somewhere over Liza's shoulder. Liza turned, expecting to see Joe's puzzled expression. Instead, she saw Daniel walking in.

"I've given that question a great deal of thought, and I'd say this building was coming along remarkably well. You must have found a darned good carpenter, ma'am. The guy must be a genius."

Liza looked up at him, his handsome face set in a serious expression, his eyes quietly laughing at her.

I found a good one, all right, she wanted to reply. Instead she decided to ask his opinion.

"You're just in time to help us out here, Daniel. What do you think—isn't it too soon for me to have a wedding?"

Daniel stared at her a moment. "I'm not sure. It all depends on who's getting married. Are congratulations in order, Liza? I had no idea."

He was teasing her, as usual. Though it was often hard to tell.

"Of course not." She waved her hand at him. "What are you doing here anyway? I didn't expect you until tomorrow."

"Now, there's a warm welcome. Has your future husband seen this bossy side? He might get cold feet."

"He loves me. Unequivocally. Cold feet and all," she replied, not missing a beat. "But what do you think, really? A young woman stopped in this morning. Her name is Jennifer Bennet. A lovely girl, fresh out of college. She insists that she wants to have her wedding here. Her heart is set on it. She wouldn't take no for an answer."

"She was very persistent . . . in a sweet way," Claire added.

Daniel glanced at Claire, then turned back to Liza. "Okay, let's start from the beginning. I feel a little lost," he admitted. "A girl named Jennifer is getting married?"

"Yes, she wants to be married here. The ceremony, the reception, the works . . ."

While Liza told the story from start to finish, Claire poured Daniel a cup of coffee. He sipped, listening until she was done.

"So what do you think?" Liza asked finally. "I can't put on a wedding here. Can I?"

"Well, it sounds to me like it could be great . . . or it could be a total disaster," he said finally.

"Thanks a lot. That's no help," Liza said honestly. "I already know that."

Claire laughed and shook her head. "I'm going to finish upstairs. You two talk it out. Let me know if you come to any new conclusions."

"Well, there are pluses and minuses," Daniel went on. "I did some work at the yacht club in Newburyport last year, and from what I heard there, the wedding business can be very profitable. Especially when you consider there aren't too many spots in the area as scenic as the inn."

"That's probably all true," Liza allowed. "I'm not saying I'll never do a wedding—just not this one. Not this soon. Jennifer wants to have it in a month or two. Even if I could make all the arrangements by then, what about the building? I know it's coming along," she added quickly, "and I know I have an excellent man on the job. But we're just not working that fast, are we?"

"It won't look much different a few weeks from now. But if the couple getting married isn't worried about it, why should you be?"

"Oh, maybe because I can imagine the wedding guests telling all their friends the food was good but the place was a wreck."

Daniel shrugged. "I think that, as the owner, you see the inn differently. Most people don't notice as much as you think they do. They notice if they're having fun and enjoying the band. They're not thinking too much about the crown molding in the foyer."

That was something a man would say. But he had a point. Still, she wasn't convinced. "Maybe . . . but I'd notice it."

He smiled at her, a certain smile that made her heart jump. "I know you would, Liza. Because this place is special to you, and you put your heart and soul into rescuing it. But there is a point when a person needs to look past the peeling wallpaper of life and focus on the party."

He was right. Maybe she was looking at this from the wrong perspective. Seeing the lemon seeds instead of the lemonade . . . or something like that?

"I'm sorry. I'm not helping you figure this out at all, am I?" he asked.

"No, you are. Go on," she encouraged him.

"I don't know that I have more to say on the subject. I'm not exactly an expert on weddings."

Daniel had told her he'd never been married, only engaged. It had not worked out, though he'd never told her why.

They were both quiet a moment, but not in an uncomfortable way. That was another thing she liked about being with him. They didn't have to talk all the time. Daniel wasn't afraid of silence and neither was she. She felt comfortable and calm around him and happy at the same time.

"Listen, there is one more thing that occurred to me," he said suddenly. He glanced at her, then looked away. "Never mind. Forget I said that."

"No, go on. What did you want to say?"

Daniel still hesitated, then met her gaze again. "I don't want to make you feel bad, Liza. That's not why I'm saying this. But you told me that this girl, Jennifer, knew your aunt?"

"Yes, she did. A little." Liza explained how the friendship began, then added, "Elizabeth told her she had a feeling the romance would last and they would be married someday. Jennifer even asked if they could get married at the inn. Of course, my aunt was delighted."

Daniel smiled. Liza could tell he was recalling

his own memories of Elizabeth, whom he'd also known well. "I can see that. She had a real romantic soul."

"Yes, she did."

"Well, I was just thinking that if Elizabeth were still here, she wouldn't think twice about this girl's request. She'd be excited about helping them and throwing a party."

"She did love a party," Liza had to agree.

"No matter what the place looked like," he added. "If the whole inn fell down during the reception, Elizabeth would have turned up the music and acted as if that was part of the festivities. Like a fireworks display or something."

His exaggeration made Liza smile, but she also knew that what he said was true.

"That's exactly the way she was." She meant to sound bright but couldn't keep the melancholy from her voice.

He reached over and covered her hand with his own. "I'm sorry. . . . I didn't mean to make you sad. I should have kept that thought to myself. That was stupid."

"No, it wasn't. I'm glad you reminded me." Liza sighed. Jennifer was right. She did have some thinking to do about this question.

Daniel finished his coffee in a big gulp, then headed outside to work on the gutters. Liza cleared the table and tried to remember what she planned to be doing this morning, before the tree roots and Jennifer Bennet had thrown her entirely off course.

She returned to her desk. It was tucked away in a corner of the sitting room and usually hidden behind a painted screen. Right now, she felt the need to see the ocean view framed in the sitting room windows, so she pushed the screen aside.

She sifted through her bills and correspondence, then pulled out an old register. She had started to put a list of past guests and their addresses on the computer and now continued that task. The list would help her send out a new round of postcards, announcing the inn's new ownership and reopening.

She worked carefully and efficiently, but all the while Aunt Elizabeth hovered in her thoughts.

Elizabeth had been a spontaneous soul. She was the type who used the good china and sterling every day, who wore her best hat while digging in the garden if she felt like it.

If Elizabeth had met Jennifer on her doorstep this morning, she would have been thrilled that these two lovebirds wanted to be wed at the inn. She would have just jumped right in and made a party, and worried later if the leak in the downstairs powder room ceiling was repaired.

Or not worried at all, Liza reflected.

Part of the reason she had decided to take over the inn had been to carry on Elizabeth's way, her spirit and tradition of making the inn a unique place in the world, a restful, healing haven. Liza knew that if Jennifer had come here, explaining to her aunt how her heart was set on this place, Elizabeth never would have refused her.

Still, Liza had her qualms. Even if she overlooked the disrepair of the building, who was she to take on a project as big and important as someone's wedding day?

Maybe Daniel was right and there was good money in it, but Liza couldn't just jump in for the profit and hope for the best. That wouldn't be fair to the bride and groom or their families.

No, it wasn't the right thing to do, she decided finally. She would have to call Jennifer Bennet tomorrow and give her the news, and hope she would understand.

Claire passed by and stopped at the desk. "I'm just going out to the market. I left you a sandwich in the fridge for lunch. I had mine earlier. I didn't want to disturb you."

"Thanks, Claire. I'll take a break in a little while." Liza sat back and stretched.

Claire peered down at her. "Any more thoughts about the wedding?"

"I have thought it over, and some part of me would love to say yes. But it's not for me. Not right now. I'm going to tell her tomorrow that I'm sorry but we can't do it."

Claire gazed at Liza with understanding. "As

long as you feel you gave it some thought. That's all you promised her. By the way, I found that old register book you were looking for. I was putting away some blankets in the cedar chest, and I saw it up in the attic, just sitting there."

Claire placed the long, heavy ledger on Liza's desk. Liza rested her hand on the dusty cover. "Thanks, Claire. I'm almost finished with the last one. This will come in handy."

"I'm sure it will. You get back to work. I won't be very long." Claire left the sitting room, and Liza soon heard the front door snap shut.

Liza sat back and opened up the ledger, reading the handwritten names and addresses of past guests and their comments. You could tell that some of these entries had been written with real ink, from a fountain pen; the book was that old. Liza marveled at the sight. People had such nice penmanship in those days, she thought. Then again, they had lots of practice, writing letters and lists. No one had a computer or e-mail.

She turned a brittle page and a photograph slipped out. The color was faded, and there was a large crease down the middle. But Liza could still see it was a picture of a summer wedding party, taken behind the inn during the days when Aunt Elizabeth and Uncle Clive ran the place. Not a very large party but an elegant, joyous affair. The bride and groom looked jubilant. Her aunt looked beautiful and her uncle very dapper. The gardens

44

were in full bloom, and everyone seemed to be having a wonderful time.

Liza turned it over and read the note on the back. *Bernadette and James, Happily Wed 6/30/55.* Liza recognized her aunt's handwriting immediately. Then she remembered what Claire had told Jennifer.

"There were many weddings here, back in the day. Lovely ones, too," Claire had said.

Had Claire slipped the photo in the book for Liza to see?

Liza doubted that. Claire was so forthright; if she'd found the photo, she would have just handed it over.

Liza was sure Claire hadn't planted it. But it was one of those meaningful coincidences Claire was often the first to notice. Once she did point them out, Liza found it hard, if not impossible, to see the situation any other way.

Now she stared at the photo a moment longer, then propped it up on the desk. If a picture spoke a thousand words, this one was speaking ten thousand to her.

A short time later, Liza had pushed aside her accounts and sat surfing the web, searching terms like "wedding planning checklist" and "wedding planning tools."

For some odd reason, she felt a little guilty doing this research, since she had so adamantly opposed the idea. Liza told herself this online exploration didn't mean she had changed her mind. She was just curious to see how a small, simple but elegant wedding might be put together. For future reference . . . when she was ready.

But as she scrolled through information and hopped from site to site, even printing out pages here and there, Liza knew she was catching the bug.

The old photo on her desk urged her on, too. Aunt Elizabeth's smile beamed out at her, her very expression seeming to say, "Look how easy this is, Liza. Don't be such a scaredy-cat. Of course you can do it."

By the time Claire returned from shopping in the town of Cape Light, Liza had printed out an entire pile of wedding information. She knew Claire would notice as she passed the desk, but she didn't try to hide it from her.

The first thing Claire noticed, however, was the photo. "Goodness, where did you find that?"

"It was in that guest ledger you brought down. It fell out when I turned a page." Liza glanced at Claire, noting her honest surprise.

Claire reached out and picked up the photograph. "Everyone's having such a good time. I love the expression on your aunt's face. Did it give you any ideas?" she asked curiously.

"I guess it did. I started checking out some wedding sites," Liza explained. "If Jennifer really wants something simple and the guest list will be small, maybe we could pull it off. I can at least make a few notes and tell her my ideas."

Claire did not seem surprised. She did seem pleased, though, and rested her string bag of groceries on the desk.

"For some reason, Jennifer Bennet has her heart set on this place. All you can do is try your best to help her," Claire said. "What else are we here for?"

By "here," Liza had the feeling that Claire didn't just mean at the inn, or even on the island. But here on earth, living their lives. That was a good question, Liza thought. The kind Claire often came up with.

"I met Emily Warwick in town today. She asked about you, Jennifer." Jennifer's mother, Sylvia, raised an eyebrow as she helped herself to some green salad. "She didn't even know you were engaged."

Jennifer's father laughed at his wife's shocked tone. Jennifer just rolled her eyes.

"Mayor Warwick is a busy person, Sylvia," her father said between bites of his dinner. "She doesn't have time to keep up on all the social news."

Her mother never called Emily by her title, Jennifer noticed. It wasn't because they were good friends. They actually weren't. It was more because they had gone to school together, and Sylvia just couldn't defer to an old schoolmate that way.

"I was just surprised, that's all. I announced it in church just last week. I guess she didn't remember. She asked if you and Kyle had set a date. I didn't know what to say."

"Really?" Jennifer's father looked up from his plate. "How did that feel, dear?" he asked his wife.

Sylvia didn't notice the quip. But Jennifer did. Her father glanced at her and winked.

"We have set a date, Mom. Sort of. It's going to be very soon, in a month or so. You know that's our plan."

"It's fine to tell me 'that's our plan,' Jennifer. But putting a wedding together involves a lot of work. Not just picking some random date—an impossible deadline at that. I really don't know what you're thinking sometimes. What in the world is the rush?"

"Kyle and I want to start our life together. We've known each other forever and we're ready," Jennifer replied, a touch of impatience in her voice. How many times did she have to explain this to her mother?

"Oh, let's not get into this again," Mr. Bennet said. "Sylvia, the kids have decided. There's no sense dragging our heels. You don't want to see them run off and elope, do you?"

Sylvia looked suddenly alarmed. "You wouldn't do that to me, would you?" she asked her daughter.

The idea had occurred to Jennifer and Kyle. They'd even discussed it secretly. But not seriously.

Jennifer knew she was not the eloping type. She had always imagined herself in a long white gown, walking down the aisle on her father's arm, surrounded by family and friends.

"Don't worry, Mom. I'm not about to run off and get married up at town hall, in between people paying parking tickets. Even if Mayor Warwick could perform the ceremony," she added. "But we want to get married in a few weeks. Definitely by the end of June. Can we agree on that much?"

Her mother glanced at her, then fiddled with her fork, not really eating the baked salmon that Jennifer had cooked. Since she was home from school now and didn't have much to do, Jennifer liked to help out by cooking. She enjoyed it, knowing it was practice for when she had her own home.

"Even if I did agree, what about the rest of it?" her mother asked. "What about a bridal gown and dresses for bridesmaids? Those take months to order."

"There are tons of dresses on the Internet, Mom. Lots of really nice ones," Jennifer added, feeling she was finally making some headway.

"A dress from the Internet—to wear down the aisle on your wedding day? Oh, Jennifer, please . . . we might as well have the reception at McDonald's."

Jennifer started laughing. "Good idea. The guests can drive by the window and get their own food. We can put a favor in the bags, along with the fries."

"Okay, now you're getting silly." Her father looked over at her. Jennifer could see he wanted to laugh, but her mother was clearly not amused. "There are stores for dresses. I'm sure Jen can find something. What else do we need to worry about?" he asked.

"A place to hold the reception. Have you called any restaurants or caterers?" her mother challenged her. "How are we going to find a suitable place on such short notice? There aren't many choices—the yacht club in Newburyport, the Spoon Harbor Inn, Lilac Hall, but there you need special permission from the Warwicks and your own caterer."

Frank Bennet's eyebrows rose in amusement. "So you've already looked into this, Sylvia? Is that what you're saying?"

Her mother rose and carried away her father's empty dinner dish. "I looked into it a little. The best places are all booked for the summer and into next year."

"Well, we could have the wedding here," Mr. Bennet suggested. "The house isn't very large, but we could put a tent in the backyard or something."

"Oh, I don't want to do that," her mother said quickly. "It would seem so . . . patched together. And those tents always leak if it rains. We don't have the type of house for a big party. And I would have to do some redecorating—paint the living room and dining room at least."

Jennifer's father looked about to argue with her, then stopped himself. He glanced at Jennifer. "What do you think, sweetie? You're the bride."

"Kyle and I already know where we want to have the wedding. We've had the place picked out for years."

"You have?" Sylvia stared at her daughter. "Why didn't you say anything?"

Jennifer shrugged. "I wanted to handle it on my own. I was there today, in fact. I stopped in and asked some questions." Jennifer braced herself. She knew what her mother would ask next and could also guess her reaction to the answer.

"Excellent." Her father seemed encouraged and glanced at Sylvia. "She's a grown woman now. Of course she can plan her own wedding. So, what did you find out? Any openings in their calendar?"

"It doesn't look like the date will be a problem. The woman I spoke to, Liza—she owns the place—she said they usually don't do big parties, but she would think about it. I'm not sure why, but I think she'll say yes."

"What do you mean, they usually don't do big parties, dear?" her mother asked carefully. "Where is this place? Do we know it?"

"Yes, Jen, is it around here? We don't want the guests to have to drive too far."

"It's very close. The Inn at Angel Island," she told them. "It's the absolute perfect place for our wedding. Kyle and I totally agree. We don't want to get married anywhere else."

Her father looked confused. "That old place?"

"That big old mansion when you come across the bridge? I thought it was sold and a builder tore it down. Or maybe it fell down all on its own." Her mother gave her a look, the kind that said she wasn't taking the conversation seriously anymore.

"No one has torn it down. No one intends to," Jennifer informed her parents. "There's a new owner, Liza Martin. She inherited the inn from her aunt and has been renovating everything and just opened for business again about a month ago."

Her mother folded her napkin carefully. "I think I heard something about that. Well, it must have been in terrible shape if the poor woman has to renovate so extensively. Do you really want to get married in a place that's so run-down? That won't reflect well on your father and me. It will look as though we tried to get away cheap, as if we don't care enough to have your wedding at a really nice place."

"Mom, come on. You haven't even seen it. It's not run-down. She's fixed it up."

Jennifer looked at her father, who was usually much more reasonable. But he looked worried, too.

"I'm not sure, Jennifer. I hardly remember that inn. From what you just told us . . . well, I think we would all have to visit before we can agree on this."

"And didn't you just say that this woman who runs the place—"

"The innkeeper's name is Liza Martin," Jennifer cut in.

"Liza, right," her mother said impatiently. "Didn't you just tell us that she doesn't do big parties? And she might not even be able to have a wedding there?"

"She hasn't had the opportunity to do a big party." Jennifer fudged her answer a little, presenting the situation in the best light. "Since our wedding is going to be on the small side, it would be a good place for her to start."

Her mother smiled and tossed her hands in the air. "Oh, well, that changes everything. I'd be so happy to give some strange woman the chance to practice putting on a wedding—my *only daughter's* wedding," Sylvia clarified. "I'm so glad we have this chance to do a good deed."

"Sylvia, let's all relax a minute and talk this out," Jennifer's dad said.

Jennifer could tell her father wasn't thrilled with the idea of the inn, either, but at least he was willing to hear her out.

Her mother took a deep breath and stared straight ahead, her chin set at a stubborn angle.

"Jennifer," her father said, "I'd just like to know something. Why that particular place? Why do you and Kyle have your hearts so set on it?"

"Because it's where we met, Dad. Not at the inn, but on the beach right below. And we went up to the inn later that day and sat with the innkeeper, Elizabeth Dunne, Liza's aunt. She passed away in February," Jennifer explained. "We sat with Elizabeth and she was so nice to us. And we used to go back and visit her all the time and once she told me that she was sure Kyle and I would get married. And I said, 'Maybe we could have the wedding here, at your inn.' And she answered, 'Would you? That would make my heart sing.'" Jennifer smiled at the memory, even though it was the second time that day she'd told the story. "Wasn't that a wonderful thing to say?"

"Very . . . poetic," her father agreed.

"So, you feel an attachment to this place because of that old woman, the one who passed away?" her mother asked. "Is that it?"

"Not exactly. That's not the only reason. It's just our special place. That's where we met, where we had our first date, our first kiss . . ." Jennifer was starting to feel embarrassed now, discussing these personal things with her parents. "We don't care if it's not some fancy, famous place. The Inn at Angel Island has real meaning for us. Those other places have no meaning, no character. This is what we want and if Liza Martin says she'll hold the wedding there, that's where we'll be married." Jennifer had rarely been so insistent with her parents. But she'd rarely felt this strongly about anything in her entire life.

She could see her mother bristle. "No need to raise your voice, Jennifer."

"I wouldn't have to raise my voice if you'd just listen to me. You argue with everything I say. This is my wedding, remember?"

"I'm not sure what we're all debating about." Her father also raised his voice a notch, just to be heard over the two women. "We don't even know if the new innkeeper is willing."

Jennifer knew that was true, but she just couldn't believe that Liza wouldn't come around and change her mind.

"You're right, Frank." Her mother wasn't exactly smiling, but she did look calmer. "How did you leave it with her, Jen?"

Before Jennifer could answer, the phone rang.

"Let the machine get it," Sylvia said. "This is important."

"I just want to listen. It might be Kyle," Jennifer insisted. Kyle usually called on her cell phone, but she wanted to make sure. Besides, she could use an excuse to get up and end the conversation. She could see that her parents weren't going to be persuaded tonight.

Jennifer listened for the message, hoping to hear Kyle. Instead, she heard a woman's voice.

"Hi, Jennifer. It's Liza Martin. I hope I'm not calling too late. . . ."

Jennifer stood rooted to the spot, listening.

"—I just want you to know that I've given our conversation some thought, and I have some ideas about your wedding. Maybe we can meet in a few days and you can see if I can put together a party that would be right for you."

"Oh, blast!" Her mother groaned, and sat down in a kitchen chair. "I had a feeling this would happen. She probably realized how much money she was turning down."

"Sylvia, let's give the woman a chance," Frank said.

Jennifer dashed to the phone, managing to pick it up before Liza hung up.

"Liza? Hi, it's me, Jen. Thanks for calling back so quickly. I just heard your message. I'm so happy you decided to do it." Jennifer's heart was pounding. She could hardly speak.

"Well, I'm not entirely sure I'm the woman for the job, but you can be the judge. Why don't you stop by later this week and we'll try to figure it out," Liza suggested.

"Tell me a good time for you. My schedule is totally free."

Jennifer had been hoping to go back to the inn tomorrow. But she didn't want to pressure Liza too much. This call was the answer to her prayers. She was just amazingly grateful.

"Let's see . . . how about Thursday morning, around eleven? Does that work?"

"That would be fine."

"Tell her your mother is coming, too," Sylvia shouted from the next room.

"Of course you'll want your mother with you," Liza said before Jennifer even had time to relay the message. "I look forward to meeting her."

Easy to say that now, Jennifer nearly replied.

Instead, she thanked Liza again and said good night.

As Jennifer hung up the phone, she hoped her mother wouldn't interrogate Liza and criticize every inch of the inn. Liza might decide she didn't want to do the wedding after all.

I'll worry about that when I get to it, Jennifer decided. *At least I have good news for Kyle.*

While her parents continued to discuss what her mother called, "this absurd fixation on that inn,"

57

Jennifer slipped upstairs to her bedroom and closed the door.

She took out her cell phone and quickly called Kyle. She couldn't wait to talk to him. She had tried to reach him a few times after she visited the inn, but he had been in meetings all day.

"Hi, Jen, I was just going to call you," he greeted her. "I just got in from the gym. What's up?"

Jennifer felt breathless, as if she had just run a few laps. "I went to the Inn at Angel Island today. It's still there and it's still open. . . . But Elizabeth Dunne passed away," she added sadly.

"Oh, that's too bad. But I'm glad it's still open. Did she sell it?"

"Her niece runs it now. She's very nice. We had a long talk about the wedding."

Jennifer quickly relayed their meeting—how Liza had at first refused to even consider the idea, then seemed to soften, and finally called tonight to set up an appointment.

"I guess you persuaded her, Jen. It's hard to resist those big blue eyes. Don't I know it . . ." he teased her.

"Kyle, stop. I just told her how much the inn means to us. How we've never imagined being married anywhere else."

"No, we never have," Kyle agreed. "When do you see her again?"

"On Thursday. My mother is coming with me.

She already hates the place and she hasn't even seen it."

"That sounds about right." Kyle laughed. "Your mother never lets the facts get in the way of her opinions, I'll say that for her."

Jennifer didn't answer. She knew her mother could be difficult, though she meant well. But all the advice and opinions had been rubbing Kyle the wrong way lately, and there would probably be a lot more of them before this was all over.

"Just cross your fingers that Liza agrees to do the wedding," Jennifer told him. "I did tell her a few times that all we want is a small, simple party. That seemed to help."

"Good. That is all we want, a nice celebration with our closest family and friends. Nothing over the top," Kyle agreed.

Jennifer was glad they were in tune about their wedding. She had a feeling, though, that her parents—especially her mother—had other, more elaborate ideas. But she couldn't worry about that yet. Getting her parents to agree on the inn was the most important thing right now.

"So how's work?" she asked. "Anything interesting going on?"

"There is, actually. A big project is starting up in New York, and Ted told me a few of us might be sent down to help out." Ted Waters was Kyle's boss. He liked Kyle and often took him into his confidence. "It's a merger, I think, but pretty confidential," Kyle added.

"Oh, cool. New York is fun. For a few days."

"If I have to go, it will be more than a few days," Kyle explained. "And I'll be working every minute. But Ted says it's good to be assigned to the main office, even on a short-term project. All the big executives are down there, and they get to see your work firsthand."

"That would be great, honey. But I hope they don't send you this time. We have so much to do before the wedding," Jen said honestly.

Kyle had a master's in business administration and worked at a branch of an investment firm in Boston with a main office in New York. His office wasn't very far from his apartment on the waterfront, where they planned to live once they were married. Jen had moved some of her belongings there from her dorm when she graduated and couldn't wait to move the rest.

The space had real potential, Jennifer thought, though right now it was decorated in Early Guy, with a lot of dark leather furniture and a big flat-screen TV. She couldn't wait to start fixing it up and had already ordered some furniture, area rugs, and window treatments. She also hoped she and Kyle could do some painting. Which wouldn't be likely if he was stuck in New York until their wedding day.

Jennifer did love the location of their new

apartment. Kyle could walk right across the new highway, past Faneuil Hall, and into the financial district without ever needing a train or a bus.

That was just one of the great things about Boston. You could walk anywhere you wanted, and the city had everything you needed but on a livable scale. Not like New York, which was exhilarating at first and then seemed so crowded and overwhelming.

It really got on Jen's nerves if she was there for more than a weekend; she didn't envy Kyle if he had to work in that main office.

"I wish I had a job, too," she said. "I don't think you should be the only one working while I'm hanging out all summer."

"Give yourself a chance, Jen. You just graduated two weeks ago," he reminded her with a laugh. "Besides, you have plenty of work to do planning our wedding."

"That's not work. That's my dream come true. I can't wait to be married to you," she said softly.

She heard Kyle sigh. "Me, too. I can't wait to be with you twenty-four-seven, three hundred and sixty-five days a year, forever and ever."

Jen didn't answer. She set the words very carefully into a little pocket in her heart, to think about later and help her feel less lonely for him while they were apart.

"Should I pick you up at the station on Friday?" Jennifer asked. Kyle had a car but sometimes left it at his parents' house. He rarely used it during the week; it was annoying to search for parking in Boston. Besides, Jennifer enjoyed picking him up at the train station. It felt as though they were really married.

"You'd better. I left my car at my parents' house last week. Oh, I almost forgot . . . Your dad sent me an e-mail about golf on Saturday. What do you think? We would just play nine holes, and then you and I can go out for dinner Saturday night."

"That would be fine. My mom and I can work on the wedding," Jennifer said agreeably.

Although Jennifer coveted her precious time with Kyle on the weekends, she knew it was important for her parents to have a good relationship with him, too. Kyle got along well with both of them, especially her dad. Jennifer imagined that once they were married, Kyle and her dad would have regular golf outings in Cape Light on the weekends while she and her mother enjoyed some one-on-one time.

She often pictured the way it would be in the summertime. She and Kyle could rent a little cottage in Cape Light or even on Angel Island for the season. She'd have the entire summer off as a schoolteacher, which would be perfect once they had children. It was a great place for kids to spend the summer—just as she and Kyle had growing up. There was so much to look forward to. She couldn't wait to start her new life.

It was all going to work out just fine. If they could just manage to get married.

They talked a bit more before Jennifer ended the call. She felt tired but happy. She went to bed feeling satisfied that she had made some real progress with their plans today.

As she drifted off to sleep, visions of her wedding day filled her head, floating up like satin ribbons against a clear blue sky.

Chapter Three

WHY had she ever told Jennifer Bennet she would give this wedding business a try? On Tuesday morning, Liza regretted the impulse that had taken hold of her the night before.

"I'll put some ideas together for you, Jen. . . . Let's see how it goes." Liza mimicked herself aloud, then stuck out her tongue. Then she dropped her head onto her desktop, amid the pile of wedding checklists, sample menus, glossy bride magazines, and everything else she had found while doing research.

She'd only been at it for a few hours, but it felt like days. There was so much information and so many choices. How did anyone navigate this vast nuptial sea?

Claire peeked into the sitting room. "Any progress?"

"I'm not sure. But I do have a splitting headache." Liza sat back and rubbed a knot of tension at the back of her neck. "Why did I ever say I would try this? I should call her up right now and back out. That would be the sane, humane thing to do."

Claire made a sympathetic sound but totally ignored her question.

"Would you mind going to the General Store for me?" Claire asked. "I've run out of Old Bay. I'd go myself but I'm in the middle of weeding the vegetable patch. I put the chowder on and I can't leave it."

Liza suddenly realized Claire had dirt stains on her hands and knees, and even a little on her cheek. She wore her usual cotton dress but had a bandana tied around her head as well.

"I should help you. It's getting hot out, and there's a lot to do. At least I'd feel productive."

"You can get me some Old Bay," Claire repeated with emphasis. Liza knew the famous seasoning was essential to many of Claire's dishes, and running out of it was unthinkable. "And a few carrots, potatoes, a turnip, and some parsley. That would be productive." Claire smiled gently at her. "Some fresh air might help your headache, too."

The suggestion made Liza smile. She hadn't known Claire very long, but she already knew that the remedy she suggested most often, for most any ailment, was fresh air. The funny thing was, Liza had found, it usually worked.

A short time later, Liza was headed toward the town center on her bike. It was one of many old bicycles she had found in the barn behind the inn. It was heavy, hard to pedal, and the gears slipped. The seat seemed to be made of cast iron, and she could barely walk straight after a long trip. But the bike was the best of the lot and got her where she needed to go.

The views along the road that led from the inn to the town center were so distractingly beautiful that, after the first few minutes, she hardly noticed the discomfort of her ride.

The ocean stretched out on the left side of the road, rolling meadows on the right. A few large old houses built in the late 1800s could be seen nearby. Some were in better condition than the inn and some in worse. Every time Liza took this ride, she tried to judge how the inn compared to its neighbors, now that the renovations were coming along. The inn had definitely improved, moving up a few notches, but it wasn't quite in the top tier yet.

But you have to have goals, Liza reminded herself with a grin.

A farm stood on the property that bordered her own. Liza pedaled past the familiar sign "Gilroy Goat Farm—Organic Herbs, Goat Cheese, Fudge, Soaps & Lavender." She gazed out at the large meadow, trying to catch a glimpse of her friend Audrey Gilroy, who owned the farm with her husband.

Liza checked the barn area and the area around the large white building where the cheese was made. No sign of Audrey working outside. Liza thought she might give her friend a call later, when she got home.

She pedaled farther, passing a few cottages and lots of open land, then finally came to the small commercial center of the island, the place where the two main roads met. There was a small square with benches and a fountain, shaded by tall trees.

The fountain was running today, Liza noticed, and the stone urns were filled with colorful flowers and trailing vines. She hopped off the bike, parked it by a bench, and headed for the General Store.

The store was one of the few commercial buildings on the island. A walk-in medical clinic stood right beside it. A large, first-aid cross, red on a white background, decorated the storefront window.

Daniel and her friend Audrey both volunteered at the clinic. Wondering if either of them was working now, Liza peered in through the window. She saw two people sitting on the hard plastic chairs, waiting for medical attention. A volunteer sat at the reception desk, taking information from another patient. Liza looked around the small room again but didn't see Audrey.

Then she felt a tap on her shoulder and nearly jumped two feet in the air.

"Need some first aid, miss? I'm fully certified."

Liza instantly recognized the voice. She turned and faced Audrey Gilroy, who, before moving to Angel Island, had, in fact, been a registered nurse.

"Glad you asked. I need my head examined," Liza moaned. "Think you can help me?"

Audrey stared at her, trying not to laugh. "What's up, Liza? Anything wrong?"

"Do you have a minute? This could take a while."

"I'm not in a rush. I'm on front desk duty today but I'm early. Let's go over here and talk." Audrey led Liza back to the benches and they sat down. "So . . . does this have anything to do with Daniel?"

Liza gave her a look. "No. What made you think that?"

Audrey shrugged. "I don't know. I was just taking a wild guess. Too bad," she added under her breath.

"What's that supposed to mean?"

"I'm just wondering what's going on with you guys. Don't keep telling me you're just friends," Audrey warned. "I'm not buying."

"We are just friends . . . more or less. Well, more than friends, I guess. But I don't really know what you'd call it, exactly." The question had her stumped. "I wish I knew myself. But I can't even think about that right now. I have a real problem."

"Okay, go ahead. Sorry I distracted you." Audrey sounded contrite, but the twinkle in her eye told Liza she was really not sorry at all and wanted to talk more about Liza's love life—or lack of one. "How can I help?"

"Just listen to what I did and tell me how stupid I am."

"No problem," Audrey promised with a smile.

Liza sighed and quickly told her the whole story—how Jennifer had arrived at the inn out of the blue yesterday, insisting that she had to have her wedding there, telling her romantic story, including the touching memories of Aunt Elizabeth.

And how Liza had first said absolutely no way, but by the evening, had called and told Jennifer she would put together a few ideas for her.

"Wow, a wedding. That's great! I'd love to see a wedding at the inn. Do you need any goat cheese? I'd be happy to contribute to the cause," Audrey offered.

"That's just the problem," Liza admitted. "I don't know the first thing about planning or putting on a wedding. Do I even need goat cheese? I haven't got a clue. I've been researching that very question and many others online all night and this morning and I'm totally in over my head. This girl and her mother are coming on Thursday morning to hear my ideas. Jennifer has her heart set. She won't take no for an answer. I don't know how to get out of it gracefully."

Audrey's big brown eyes lit up and she smiled. "I know the perfect person to help you. Molly Willoughby. She runs this fabulous gourmet food shop and catering business in Cape Light, Willoughby Fine Foods."

"I've gone in there a few times. The food is amazing."

"So is Molly. She's a sweetheart, too. She buys all her goat cheese from us and a lot of other products. Her firm caters weddings and huge parties every weekend. Let me get you guys together. I'm sure she'll give you some good advice."

Before Liza could reply, Audrey whipped out her cell phone and called Molly. Audrey quickly explained the situation, listened a moment, then turned to Liza.

"She's coming to the island this afternoon. She can stop by the inn and talk to you."

"She will? That's great. Tell her to come anytime."

Audrey relayed the message and hung up, then sat back with a satisfied smile. "Any other problems I can solve? Ready to talk more about Daniel now?"

Liza laughed. "I'll let you know when."

Liza had a feeling she would talk to her friend about Daniel sooner or later. Audrey and her husband had been friends with Daniel for a few years, ever since they had settled on the island. But this was not the time for that conversation, Liza knew.

"Thanks for connecting me with Molly. She sounds like she knows her stuff," Liza told her friend.

"Oh, she knows her stuff and she's very plainspoken. If Molly thinks you're crazy, she'll let you know," Audrey promised.

"That's what I need, an honest, straightforward, expert opinion."

Secretly, Liza wondered if Molly would say she was crazy to try it and that the inn was in no shape for a wedding. That would get her off the hook; she could tell Jennifer that she had consulted with a well-known expert.

"Thanks, Audrey, you're a pal. I owe you one."

"Don't worry about it. Next time my goats wander over and start munching on your flower beds, I'll remind you."

"I might ask to borrow a few of them next week so I don't have to mow the lawns."

"Deal."

Liza just smiled. Sometimes it was hard to remember that their friendship only went back a few months, not a few years. She was very lucky to have found such a warm, funny friend on the island. She knew Audrey was a special blessing in her new life.

Audrey got up to report to the clinic for her volunteer shift, and Liza headed into the General Store. The store was wide and low, and the very distinct smell of the place immediately transported her to the long-ago days when she spent summers on the island as a little girl. It was a unique mixture of fresh-brewed coffee, soap powders, fresh donuts, produce, and the wooden floorboards.

Marion Doyle, who ran the store with her husband, Walter, stood behind the counter, wearing a white apron over a short-sleeved red-and-white-checked blouse and baggy khaki pants.

Liza didn't see Walter around. Marion was helping a customer send a package by parcel post, since she also doubled as the island's postmistress. Liza could overhear their long discussion about the rates and the various dates the package could be delivered. By the time the transaction was complete, Marion had learned a lot about the sender, the receiver, the contents of the box, and various other facts about the customer's life.

There was little that happened on the island that Marion did not know. She could have written a newspaper gossip column, she was so well informed. But there was no paper on the island, so most residents relied on chatting with Marion for their local news.

Liza browsed the two short grocery aisles and

the small but well-stocked section of fresh vegetables. Claire had given her a list, and Liza found everything except for the turnip. She was wondering if she could bring back a big yam instead when Marion approached.

"Finding what you need, Liza?" she asked cheerfully.

"Just about. You don't have any turnips today, do you?"

Marion shook her head, her lips pursed. "No, ma'am. We have been out of turnips for a few days. I expect to get more vegetables in tomorrow. There should be some artichokes. It's the season."

"I'll tell Claire. I'm sure she can do wonders with an artichoke."

"She can do wonders in the kitchen with anything cookable," Marion agreed.

Knowing that was true, Liza decided to take the yam. She brought her items up to the register in a little wire basket, and Marion rang them up. "So, I hear there's going to be a wedding soon at the inn," she said cheerfully.

"Who told you that?" Liza asked, though she could already guess.

"The Bennet girl, Jennifer." Marion's tone was innocent. "She told me herself. Just yesterday. Stopped by for a cold drink and we got to talking."

That goes without saying, Liza thought.

"I was admiring her ring. I hadn't seen it yet, though I'd heard in church that she was engaged. I asked her if she had set the date and she told me not exactly, but they really wanted to get married this summer at the inn and she'd just come from talking with you."

Liza nodded. She could see now how Marion had misinterpreted Jennifer's vague but hopeful reply.

Marion just assumed Liza wouldn't turn down the request—or the business. Liza wasn't sure if she should bother clarifying the situation. It wasn't any of Marion's business. Yet, if she didn't put her straight, the story would soon be all over the island and the town of Cape Light. Marion's news had a way of going viral very quickly.

"Kyle is a nice boy," the storekeeper went on. "I know they seem young, but those two have been going together since high school. They should know their minds by now."

"They probably do. Jennifer seems very levelheaded," Liza replied. "And she's a lovely young woman. But nothing is definite about the wedding yet, Marion. The Bennets will probably look at a lot of places."

"Oh, really?" Marion looked disappointed as Liza handed some bills across the counter. "That's too bad. The inn is a beautiful spot. Walter and I have gone to a few weddings there over the years. Your aunt did a lovely job of it."

"Yes, I'm sure she did." Liza wasn't sure why but the conversation was suddenly getting under her skin. She wished everyone would stop reminding her that her aunt had pulled off these events with such ease.

Things were different back then. People didn't have such high expectations. They didn't expect showers of rose petals, elaborate table settings, and PowerPoint presentations set to the couple's favorite songs.

"Here's your change," Marion said mildly, handing Liza back some coins.

"Thanks. I have to run. Nice to see you." Liza grabbed the change and her bag of vegetables, then practically ran to the door. The little bell over the threshold jangled wildly as she yanked it open.

"Don't sweat the small stuff, Liza . . ." Marion called out in her usual way. "And it's all small stuff, you know."

"Right," Liza called back. Marion always said that to her.

Did she look like she was sweating the small stuff? Well, maybe sometimes, she had to admit.

Liza stuck the bag in the basket of her bike and set off for the inn, pedaling at double speed. It was amazing. She hadn't even figured out *if* she could do the wedding, and the news that she would was already all over the island. Now if she didn't do the wedding, it might reflect badly on the inn, as if she'd cancelled or something.

She just hoped that if this didn't work out, Marion Doyle wouldn't put a bad spin on the situation. Oh, she couldn't worry about that now, Liza decided, pedaling even faster. She had to get back to the inn and get ready for her meeting with Molly Willoughby.

"THIS is a great old place," Molly said as she stepped through the inn's front door. "You've really come a long way with it," she added, glancing around the foyer and into the sitting room.

"My brother Sam is really into old houses," Molly went on. "He must have worked on every old house in the village by now. I know these old places are beautiful, but they're also a pain in the neck, like big old divas," she joked. "Maybe that's why I live in a new one. But you miss out on the history and the charm."

Liza led her into the sitting room, and Molly looked around again with an admiring expression. Molly was a very pretty woman, Liza thought, probably in her early forties, with dark curly hair, sparkling eyes, and a very expressive manner. She wasn't model thin but had curves in all the right places. Liza sensed she was a good saleswoman and probably a strict boss.

"Oh, this room is very nice. You could maybe

do a cocktail thing in here if you take out some of the furniture. You'd leave the piano, of course. You can hire some college kid to play standards. Everybody loves that. You might bring in a few pieces, a trio maybe. Or you could put the music outside. You definitely have the room . . . not necessary, of course, if cost is a big issue."

"I'm not sure. The bride didn't really say. She did say she was going to keep it small and simple, a very limited guest list."

Is that really me talking? Liza could hardly believe her own ears. She was suddenly in full wedding-planner mode, even speaking the lingo.

"You know, if you not only provide the site but take on some of the planning details— coordinating the flowers and tablecloths and all of that—the wedding business can be very profitable. And you could have a lot of fun with a small party." Molly's excitement was contagious.

"I could?" Could this really be fun?

"Definitely. Those special touches are much easier for a small group and make the event so memorable."

Special touches—that's what Liza was afraid of.

"How about if I just start with the standard, stripped-down model? Honestly, I think that's all I could manage."

Molly laughed and took a seat in an armchair. "That's cute. Sure, I can give you the lowdown on a no-frills wedding. What do you want to know?"

Liza sat down on one of the love seats. "Everything."

Molly looked as if she might laugh again, then noticed the serious expression on Liza's face.

"No problem. I'll tell you everything I know and believe me, it's not rocket science."

"Do I look like I think it is?"

"Yeah, you do," Molly said bluntly. "That's okay. I felt the same way when I first got into this business and let me tell you, there were some real disasters." She smiled at the memories.

"But you just have to feel the fear and let that box of canaries—which should have been white doves—loose anyway. Know what I mean?"

"I do," Liza replied. "Were they really canaries?"

"Yes, they were. And they were not trained properly and never came back. That was an extra cost we had to swallow." Molly grinned again, then picked up the folder Liza had left on the low table. "So what's this? Some ideas?" Molly started looking at the pages. "Oh, nice. Let's start here. . . ."

The two women talked for more than an hour, with Molly giving Liza a clear idea of what was possible and what was flat-out insane. Liza made notes all the while. They walked through the inn and out to the garden where Jennifer wanted the ceremony and then circled the entire property.

Molly agreed that the inn was a work-in-progress but didn't rule it out as too much of a construction site.

She seemed to take Daniel's position. "Hey, if the bride and groom don't see the drawbacks, why point them out? You know what they say, Liza, 'love is blind.' "

That was true, and Jennifer was definitely in love with the idea of being married here.

Molly made suggestions about where a tent might be set up and how many tables it would hold and where a catering truck might park.

"I'm not saying you have to hire me just because I'm a friend of Audrey's. But I can give you some information on the kind of food we can supply and the cost, and that will give you a ballpark for the bride," she suggested.

"That would be wonderful," Liza said honestly. "I've been to your shop many times. Everything's delicious."

"Well, thanks. But the bride may have another caterer in mind. You said she wants to have the wedding soon?"

"No later than the end of June. About six to seven weeks from now?"

Molly gave a low whistle. "That is fast. But that might be to your advantage," she pointed out. "Every time the family makes an outrageous request, you can say you'd love to do it, but there isn't enough time."

"Good one. I have to remember that line," Liza said.

Molly had spouted more than a few lines Liza wanted to remember. She had turned out to be a wonderful mentor, the kind of coach you really wanted in your corner.

They came inside again through the back door and found Claire in the kitchen, cooking the chowder. "Molly, I thought that was your truck. How are you, dear?" Claire greeted her.

"Very well, thanks. Good to see you, Claire. I was wondering if you were here today," Molly replied as she walked over to the older woman and gave her a quick hug.

"Oh, I'm always here. Liza inherited me with the place," Claire joked.

"One of the many treasures," Liza noted.

"Indeed she is. I've always told her if she ever leaves the inn, she can come cook for me—in a heartbeat." Molly peered over Claire's shoulder to check the soup. "What are you making today, fish chowder?"

Claire nodded. "With yams instead of white potatoes or turnips." She dipped in a spoon and offered Molly a taste.

"What do you think?"

Molly looked skeptical, Liza noticed, but gamely took a taste. Her eyes widened in surprised approval. "Hey, that's really good. What made you think of that combination? Have you been watching those cooking shows, Claire?"

"Oh, you know those TV chefs are not for me. Yams were all Liza could find at the market. I thought I'd give it a try. Just a lucky cooking accident, I guess."

"Some cooks are luckier than others that way," Molly observed wryly.

Claire and Liza just laughed.

Molly left a short time later with instructions from Claire to send greetings to her entire family.

"Thanks so much for all your help today," Liza said as she walked Molly to her truck. "I don't know how to return the favor."

"Don't worry about it, Liza. I had fun. Maybe someday when my in-laws come to town, you can find an empty room. That will keep me on my mother-in-law's good side," she joked. "Good luck. Let me know how it turns out, okay?"

"Oh, I will. I'll give you a full report," Liza promised.

Liza was eager to dig into the wedding plan again and wanted to remember all of Molly's suggestions and tips while they were fresh in her mind. She went back to the kitchen to get her notes and folder, and found Claire was still hovering over the soup pot, the can of Old Bay in her hand as she decided if the soup needed another dash.

"I didn't realize you knew Molly. I would have

brought her back to the kitchen sooner to say hello," Liza apologized.

"Oh, I was all over the house doing things. I would have caught her at some point to say hi. Everyone knows the Willoughbys. They're a big clan and have lived in the area for generations. Since the colonial days, I think." Claire put the seasoning aside and tossed in a handful of chopped parsley instead. "Molly's the live wire in the family."

"I had a feeling about that," Liza said. "She's really fun to talk to."

"She had a hard time for a while. Divorced with two little girls and left to take care of them on her own. She worked very hard—cleaning houses, driving a school bus, waitressing . . . whatever she had to do. Your aunt used to hire her from time to time to help out here when we were busy in the summer. She managed to start her business a few years back and married a very nice man, Dr. Harding. He has a practice in town," Claire added. "They have a lovely family, four girls. Three from their previous marriages and a little one of their own named Betty."

"She has her hands full, doesn't she?" Liza said, even more impressed.

"Molly's what I'd call a tornado-type," Claire agreed. Now she had the pepper mill in hand and ground some fresh pepper into the soup. "I'm sure she wouldn't be happy with any less on her plate. Was she a help to you?"

"Absolutely. She gave me some great tips."

More than that, Molly's can-do spirit was contagious. Or maybe it was her candid confession that making a big party was not exactly rocket science. Liza wasn't sure. She did know that she suddenly felt she could put together a viable wedding plan for Jennifer and her mother, and present herself as someone who could be trusted to carry out that plan.

"I hope the Bennets hire Molly to do the catering," Liza said. "It would be great to work with her on this."

Claire glanced over her shoulder and then turned back to her cooking. "You sound as if you want to do the wedding now."

Liza's eyes widened in surprise. "I do sound like that, don't I."

She didn't know exactly how it had happened, but she really was excited now about this opportunity and wanted to give the wedding a try.

"It would be great for the inn—if I can pull it off," Liza mused. "Jennifer already wants to hold the wedding here, but her parents are the final word. The inn and I still have to pass inspection."

"I think you will," Claire said simply. "I think this wedding is meant to happen here. I just have a feeling."

Liza smiled but didn't say more. She had come to respect Claire's predictions. If her wise friend felt the wedding at the inn would come about, well, that meant she'd better get back to work on her plan.

LIZA worked most of Tuesday night on the wedding plan, taking just a short break for her supper of fish chowder, fresh crusty bread, and a mixed green salad. She worked on Wednesday, too, organizing her plan with a wedding checklist she'd found online, filling in the blanks with all her ideas and sorting out the various pictures she had found of flowers, table settings, favors, the cake, and other important touches.

Molly had shown her how to figure out costs and mark things up so that all the work was worth her while. That was the hard part. Liza felt guilty tacking on her own fee since she was such a raw amateur. But she knew that she was probably asking far less than any of the other places Jennifer might choose, and she would do her best to give the Bennets their money's worth.

Figuring out the presentation was the easy part. Her years as an account executive came in handy. She typed up all the information and used attractive fonts and a simple page design to make the pages professional-looking and easy to read.

She was printing out the entire document at her work space in the sitting room when she saw Daniel's truck turning into the drive.

Liza stared out the window a moment, frozen,

like a small animal caught in car headlights. Then she dashed upstairs to clean herself up. She had been working intensely at her computer the past two days and knew that she looked like a mad scientist.

At least I washed my hair in the shower this morning, she thought. Though she hadn't taken time to blow it out, and it now sprang out around her head in a mass of waves and curls. She twisted it all up in a big clip, then pulled off her baggy, bargain-store T-shirt and searched her closet for something more attractive—or at the very least, free of coffee stains.

Just as she brushed her teeth and smeared on some lip gloss, she heard Claire at the bottom of the stairs, talking to Daniel.

"—I'm not sure. Maybe she's upstairs. I don't think she went out. She was in here working all day. . . . Liza, are you upstairs? Daniel's here," Claire called to her.

"Be down in a sec," Liza called back. She took a few deep breaths on the way down, trying to calm herself after her mad cleanup dash.

"Hi, Liza, how's it going?" Daniel greeted her. His gaze swept over her, taking her in from head to toe. He lingered on her upswept hair, and she realized he had never seen it fixed this way.

"Claire tells me you've been working hard. Have you made any progress in the wedding business?"

"I'm making plenty of progress," she answered brightly. "In fact, my party plan is printing out right now." She strolled over to her printer and checked the pile of pages it had spit out so far.

It was good to have something to do while they spoke, she realized. She loved being with him, but his closeness also made her nervous at times. "I'm meeting with Jennifer and her mother tomorrow morning."

"And you're all set for them?"

"I am." She nodded decisively. "Claire says she has a feeling that the wedding is meant to take place here. But I thought it wouldn't be a bad idea if I gave the Bennets a decent plan."

"I'm sure it's more than decent. It's thick enough, I think," he remarked, watching her tap the pile of pages into an orderly stack.

In the drawer of the big desk where her aunt had stored stationery, Liza found a cream-colored folder with the name of the inn imprinted in blue on the outside. Luckily, it didn't look stained or discolored; it seemed perfect for her needs. "It's not really that much information," she said, gathering some of the photos she'd found in the bridal magazines and online. "But when people are going to give you a lot of money, they like to feel something hefty in their hand. I learned that in advertising," she added.

"Good to remember. Maybe I should give my customers folders, too," he speculated in a teasing tone. "Though there's not too much you can say about replacing a roof or painting a house."

"Oh, you'd be surprised," Liza teased him back. "Some people could think of a lot of things to say. But you're more of the straight-talking, honest type. I can see how the folder approach would be a challenge for you."

"Thanks, I think." He looked puzzled but amused.

It was true. Daniel was the honest type, in business at least. She had never once felt that he was misleading her in any way. Except, when she asked about his past. It wasn't that he seemed deceptive in that area either, only that he hardly ever spoke about it. That door was closed tight and carefully guarded.

Daniel's voice jarred her from her wandering thoughts. "So, now that you've finished this challenging assignment, would you like to go out tonight and celebrate? There's a movie playing in Cape Light I wanted to see. Some mystery—"

"*False Witness*?"

"That's it," Daniel said. "I thought we could go to the early show and then have dinner in the village."

Liza was surprised by the invitation, pleasantly surprised. "Sure . . . I'd like that a lot. I've been wanting to see that one."

"Me, too. I have to run home for a little while,"

he said, checking his watch. "Can you be ready by six?"

"No problem," Liza told him.

"Good." He turned to go, then looked back at her. "I like your hair like that. It suits you."

She felt her face get warm, an instant reaction to his compliment. "Thanks. I couldn't do much with it today," she admitted.

"Some women don't need to do much," he noted with a smile. "See you later."

Liza wasn't sure what to say. But she did know how she'd wear her hair when they went out tonight.

Daniel took off, and Liza stood a moment, wondering what had just happened. Had Daniel just asked her out on a real date? They'd hung out together, shared meals, even visited Daisy Winkler's tearoom in the village center. But those almost-dates had all been by chance, never initiated by a premeditated invitation on Daniel's part—or her own.

Liza was just getting used to the idea of being divorced. She had separated from her husband, Jeff, in the early winter, after discovering he'd been unfaithful to her. Their divorce was finalized in March, about the same time she came to the island to settle her aunt's estate. She'd been confused about nearly everything in her life then, but coming out to the island had helped her see things clearly. Jeff had made one last attempt to get back together, surprising her by showing up at the inn. But Liza knew in her bones that ending their marriage was the right decision for her. And staying on the island had definitely helped heal her battered heart.

Was she ready to date again? Well . . . not just anyone. But Daniel wasn't just anyone, and dinner and a movie didn't seem like such a great leap.

But it was definitely a real date, and Liza felt an unfamiliar excitement, like standing in line for a roller-coaster ride.

THE movie theater in Cape Light was small and old-fashioned looking, complete with a balcony and amber glass light fixtures that slowly dimmed as the film began. Though there were plenty of seats, Liza and Daniel decided to sit in the balcony, just because it was fun.

The story got off to a quick start and was very suspenseful. The main character, living an ordinary life in a small town, had a secret past and finally the criminal ties from his past began to catch up with him.

Liza found herself totally drawn into the story, hardly aware of Daniel sitting so close to her. Well . . . less aware than she thought she would be.

She took a moment to glance at him, secretly studying his shadowed profile. He really was very handsome. But more than that, she just liked who he was inside, his sharp intelligence and quick, warm wit. The way he listened to her. Even the way he teased her. She just liked . . . him.

When he slipped an arm around her shoulders, she easily relaxed against him. It felt good. It felt right. Were they moving into a new stage in their relationship?

Ready or not, she hoped so.

When the film was over they walked down Main Street toward the harbor. There weren't that many choices for dinner in the village, but they both liked the Beanery, a café that had practically scandalized the town years back with its modern coffee bar. But it also served good, simple food and stayed open late. Late for Cape Light, that was, Liza realized as they walked inside.

The place was practically empty, except for a few tables up front, near the coffee bar, where a group of teenagers took up a few tables. They had books and laptop computers out and were probably supposed to be studying but were talking and teasing each other.

"I guess this is one of the few places kids can hang out around here, except for the library," Liza said as they sat down. "It must be hard to grow up in a small town."

"It is," Daniel agreed.

Liza knew he hadn't grown up here, but she didn't know much beyond that.

"What were you like when you were a teenager? I picture you as one of the cool kids, an athlete probably. Right?"

He flashed a smile and shook his head. "I went out for track and cross-country. But I wasn't a real jock. And I wasn't one of the cool kids, whatever that means."

"Ah, a runner. I can picture that." Liza nodded, glancing at her menu, but something in his tone made her wonder if maybe Daniel was still running—though from what, she couldn't guess.

"What were you like, Liza? I'm picturing a very social type. Not in the crowd with the snobby girls, but someone who got along with everyone. School newspaper or the yearbook? Student council?"

She laughed at his perceptive guess. "You're good. I was on the yearbook, art and design. And I did run for class secretary in my junior year. My guidance counselor said it would look good on my college applications."

"Class secretary? I'm impressed."

She laughed at his mocking expression. She could tell he was anything but. "You make it sound so corny. I hung out in the art room, too. That was pretty cool."

"I never said you weren't cool, Liza. I think you're very cool. I was the nerdy type. Big science geek."

"Really? That's surprising. . . . Not that I have

any doubts about your intelligence," she added quickly.

He was, in fact, one of the most intelligent men she'd met in a long time, and she could tell he was well read and knowledgeable about a wide range of subjects.

"But I just don't see you as hanging out in the lab, working on your science-fair project."

"Well, think again. Second prize in my junior year. I probably still have the ribbon and certificate somewhere. Or maybe my dad does," he added with a laugh. "He likes to save all that stuff."

"That's sweet," Liza said. "Do your parents still live up in Maine? I don't think you ever said."

"Not anymore, no," he said, suddenly staring down at his menu. "What are you having? Did you decide yet?"

"I'm going to have the salad with grilled chicken. Maybe I should have guessed about your secret past as a science geek," she added, turning the conversation back to his past again. "I mean, since you volunteer at the medical clinic. Did you ever think of going in that direction for a career?"

He glanced at her, looking uneasy. She sensed she'd hit on a sensitive topic and was suddenly sorry. He quickly shook his head. "Nope, wasn't for me. I didn't like school that much."

His tone was light and joking, but she also heard a note of tension.

Before she could reply, his hand shot up, signaling to their waitress. "Let's order. I'm starved," he said. "How about you, hungry?"

Liza nodded and didn't say anything more.

She was hungry, but even more than that, curious now about what she'd said or done that had broken their relaxed mood. So, he hadn't been interested in college, even though he'd been a self-described science geek in high school. That didn't seem logical, but she sensed that if she asked him more about it right now, he would dodge the question. He was good at that.

Liza suddenly realized that she had a list of things she wanted to ask him. Over the past few weeks she had come to see that it was easy to talk with Daniel about any subject at all—except himself.

While they waited for their order, the conversation moved on to more familiar ground, mainly, the renovations on the inn. Liza knew it was going to take time to get the place back to its former glory, but the possibility of holding a wedding in a month had suddenly raised the stakes.

"I'm worried about what Mrs. Bennet will say when she takes the grand tour tomorrow," Liza admitted as she took a bite of her salad.

"Well, if she points out some problems that really get under her skin, make a list of her priorities and I'll see if we can at least patch things up in time for the big day. I can do some cosmetic sort of fixing. The place only has to look good for a few hours, right? Who cares if a ceiling or two caves in or a few doors fly off their hinges after that, right?"

Liza held back her laughter. "You mean, like tossing all the dirty clothes in the closet when unexpected company comes? That sort of quick fixing?"

"Exactly." Daniel had ordered a large, juicy cheeseburger that came with a pile of thin, crisp fries and another pile of coleslaw. It looked so good, Liza almost regretted her guilt-free salad.

"So, how did you like the movie?" Daniel asked between bites. "As good as the reviews claimed?"

"I thought it was even better. I would have never guessed the ending. I thought the wife was going to turn him in for sure."

"Really? I didn't. I could tell she was the loyal type."

Liza nodded. "Despite the fact that he'd been lying to her for years. But maybe she just wanted to believe him all that time. Even though the signs were there," she added.

"Maybe. The film really didn't make that very clear."

"No, it didn't," Liza agreed. She took another bite of salad. "So, how did you go from science-fair winner to ace carpenter? That seems quite a jump."

He looked surprised by her question, his eyes widening as he bit into his burger. "Oh, I don't know," he managed. "I worked on construction jobs in college, to help my folks with the tuition. So that's how I learned the trade. After I graduated, I tried . . . the more conventional jobs. But that didn't work out for me. So I went back to something I knew and enjoyed doing."

His answer was vague, as usual.

He was an amazing carpenter, and Liza knew that he took pleasure and pride in his work. But she also had a strong feeling that Daniel had started with a different ambition and plan for his life.

"What types of jobs did you try after college? Did you work in an office? A corporate kind of setting?"

He looked across the table at her and didn't answer for a moment. "Not corporate, not exactly. . . . It doesn't really matter, does it?"

She could tell he was annoyed now, pushing her back.

Liza felt a bit stung. "I'm sorry. I didn't mean to pry. It's just that, you seem to know everything about me. Where I grew up, what I did for a living before I came here. You knew my aunt. You met my brother and nephew. You even met my ex-husband," she added with a small laugh, trying to lighten the mood. "But I feel as if I don't know much about you at all, Daniel . . . and I want to," she added.

He glanced across the table at her. He didn't look irritated anymore but still seemed troubled. "I'm sorry. I don't like to talk about myself much. It's just the way I am."

"Sure, I understand." Liza took a sip of her water, thinking that she didn't understand at all.

"Would you like anything else—dessert? Coffee or tea?" he asked.

"I'm fine, thanks." Liza forced a smile. "I'm ready to go if you are. The Bennets are coming pretty early."

"Sure. I'll get the check." Daniel signaled to the waitress, and Liza reached for her sweater, wondering if she had just ruined everything.

THEY drove home in silence, riding across the land bridge that seemed to float on the dark waves of Cape Light harbor, connecting the mainland with Angel Island.

This time, it felt like an uneasy silence, not a comfortable one. Liza knew Daniel was upset. Had she pushed him away just as their relationship was progressing? Her panic at that thought made her realize how much she cared for him and how awful it would be if she'd really messed everything up tonight.

"Well, here we are," Daniel said as he pulled up in front of the inn. He leaned toward her to look at the inn through the window on her side of the truck's cab.

"It looks pretty good in this light," he joked. "Why don't you tell Mrs. Bennet to come after dark?"

"Good idea. Why didn't I think of that?" Liza turned to him, feeling relieved that he'd found his sense of humor again. She smiled at him and he smiled back very slowly.

Then he took her hand and looked down at it held in his own. "I'm sorry we ended the night on a bad note. But I had a great time with you, Liza. I hope you're not upset or anything?"

Liza was so relieved to hear his apology, she didn't even wait for him to finish. "No, I'm sorry. I shouldn't have been so . . . pushy or something, asking you all those questions. It wasn't even polite. I guess, I just care about you and I want to know you better," she admitted. "But I'll never bug you about it again. You can tell me more when you feel like it—or never."

"I will tell you, sometime," he promised. "I'm just a very private person, and I don't like talking about the past. It's nothing personal," he assured her. "Can you have some patience with me?"

When he looked at her that way, it was hard for her to refuse him anything.

Of course she could have patience with him. Not a problem.

"I understand. . . . I mean, I'm trying to," she said finally.

"I'm trying, too." He cupped her cheek with his

hand and smiled into her eyes, then pulled her close for a sweet, tender kiss.

Liza closed her eyes and kissed him back. Sometimes words can take you just so far, she thought.

It felt so good to be close to him like this. Maybe he hadn't told her every last detail about his life, but she felt closer to him now than ever.

Chapter Four

THE next morning Liza woke up before her alarm went off. She lay in bed, thinking about her date with Daniel—how it had gone so well, then so badly, then much better again. Pretty much an emotional roller coaster. He might as well have taken her to an amusement park, she thought with a little smile.

But she loved being with him, even when they weren't on the same page. She hadn't dated in so long, she had forgotten about the ups and downs. They had managed to navigate that rough water, and that was a good sign, she thought.

The alarm clock finally rang, reminding her it was time to get up and prepare for the Bennets.

She jumped in the shower, wondering what to wear. Something professional looking, she thought, but not too somber or serious. This wasn't a boardroom presentation for a million-dollar client. It was about a wedding at a country inn.

She quickly found a long graceful skirt, a flowered pattern on a field of dark blue, and a matching blue top with a rounded neckline.

She put on a pair of small pearl earrings and decided to wear her hair swept up again. Along with the earrings, it did make her look more responsible, she thought. "When in doubt, wear pearls," her mother used to say.

When she went down to the kitchen, Claire was putting on some coffee. She turned as Liza walked in. "You look very nice, Liza. Very polished."

"Thanks, Claire. Would you let me plan your wedding?" Liza asked playfully.

"Absolutely. Though I'm sure you'll find plenty of customers who are more likely prospects for a wedding."

"Oh, you never know." Liza tried to catch Claire's eye, but the housekeeper wouldn't look at her.

Claire was another mysterious personality, come to think of it. A lot like Daniel. Maybe it was something in the water around here, Liza thought.

The only difference was that when Liza had asked Claire if she'd ever been married, Claire had answered directly and simply. "Yes, I was. For twenty-three years."

But beyond that, she had not offered any detail, and Liza had felt awkward asking for more. Liza wasn't sure if Claire was divorced or widowed, though for some reason, she tended to think it was the latter.

She did know that Claire was one of a handful of hardy, native islanders. Most of the full-time residents, like Daniel and Audrey, were not. Claire had once told her that her father had been a fisherman, and she'd been raised on the other side of the island, in a fishermen's colony, one of three children.

Marion Doyle had told Liza that Claire's family tree dated back to colonial times and the legend of the angels.

Claire did seem to have a protective, healing way about her—almost angelic, Liza would say. So the silly bit of gossip did make some sense.

"Are you nervous?" Claire asked, calling Liza back from her wandering thoughts. "You don't seem to be."

"I thought I would be nervous, but I'm not," Liza said honestly. "I have the event plan to show them and a good caterer to suggest and a ballpark figure of what it will cost." She shrugged and took a cup of coffee. "What will be, will be, I guess."

Claire stared at her a second, looking as if Liza had stolen her line. Then she gave a pleased smile. "Exactly," she said. "That's just what I was thinking."

• • •

JENNIFER Bennet and her mother, Sylvia, arrived exactly on time. Liza was ready and waiting for them. She'd taken extra care to clean up her little office area in the corner of the sitting room, hiding it from view with the wooden screen her aunt had hand painted. She also brought in a vase of flowers from the garden, forsythia mostly, which was suddenly in bloom.

Right after breakfast Liza had checked all the rooms on the first and second floors, knowing Mrs. Bennet would want a full tour. Claire was always cleaning, so Liza had no fear on that score. But there was some necessary pillow fluffing and curtain adjustments. She also had a pad and pencil handy, ready to jot down notes about special requests and emergency repairs. She had a feeling the list would be a long one.

As they worked through the usual greetings, Liza showed the Bennets into the sitting room. Jennifer sat beside her mother on a love seat, and Liza took an armchair.

Sylvia Bennet was the image of her daughter in looks. But Liza could tell, just by her expression as she gazed around the inn, she was the opposite in disposition.

"Well, here we are," Sylvia announced. She glanced at the slim gold watch at her wrist. "We know you must be very busy, Ms. Martin, and we don't want to take up too much of your time.

We also have appointments at a few other places in the area."

Jennifer turned her head and glared at her mother. Sylvia shrugged. "Well, we do. Ms. Martin must realize we have to make the rounds, see what's what—"

"Call me Liza. Please," Liza cut in while Jennifer gave her mother another embarrassed glare.

"My mother is making the rounds. I already know what's what."

Liza just smiled. Molly had already warned her that at this type of meeting, the bride and her parents might be going off in different directions. Liza chose to ignore the mixed signals and plowed ahead.

"Here are some ideas I've put together. I've made copies for both of you," Liza said, handing each of the women their own copy of the pages. "The more I thought about this celebration, the more excited I got," she said honestly. "With a small guest list, you have a lot of flexibility. Let's go over the highlights, and then you can take the folders home and look through them more carefully."

Jennifer leaned forward eagerly to see Liza's plan. Sylvia took a pair of reading glasses from her purse, then peered down at the pages with a skeptical expression.

"I've listed all the items we need to decide

upon. But let's just hit the high points." Liza felt more relaxed now. This meeting felt a lot like her former job, making presentations to potential— often skeptical—clients.

"Oh, I like this photo of the flowers. Those are pretty, aren't they, Mom?" Jennifer held up a photo of a flower arrangement of trumpet lilies and roses.

"Since your wedding is in the summer, you have a wide variety of flowers in season to choose from. That will really keep the cost down," Liza noted.

She'd read about all this and, luckily, she was a quick study and now sounded fairly knowledge-able.

"That's great," Jennifer said. "We don't want to spend a fortune on flowers but I would like something . . . special on the tables and in the ceremony area."

Liza flipped through the folder. "Oh, I found a really nice arrangement for that spot. I'm really excited about this. . . ."

Sylvia sat back and put her copy of the proposal on the table. "I can see you have a lot of creative ideas here, Ms. Martin."

"Call me Liza. Please," Liza insisted for what seemed the umpteenth time.

"What field of work were you in before you came here?" Sylvia asked curiously.

"Advertising. First in the art department and later, I was an account executive."

"Really? This is a jump. I would have thought your background would have to be in the hotel industry or food service to run an inn of this size . . . and plan big events, like weddings," she added.

Liza could see where this was going. She'd been conflicted about whether or not she really wanted to take on this wedding. But Sylvia had now thrown down the gauntlet, and Liza just couldn't resist the challenge.

She also felt a heart-melting sympathy for Jennifer, who sat huddled in the corner of the love seat, leafing through the photos at the back of the presentation folder, as if she were wishing she wasn't here for this part of the conversation. The girl clearly needed a champion, and Liza was willing to step up to the plate.

"I have years of management experience," Liza said smoothly. "And I spent just about every summer, until I went to college, at this inn, helping my aunt and uncle. I haven't found it a hard transition at all," she bluffed in a bright tone. "Maybe this business is just in my DNA. I know I would really enjoy putting on this wedding, and I think I'd do a great job for you."

"Well, good for you." Sylvia smiled back and glanced at her daughter. "This plan is very nice," she said carefully. "But before we get too carried away on the fine points—the flowers and music, et cetera—I'd really love to take a look around at the property. First things first, don't you think?" she asked, casting Liza a bland smile.

Liza knew what she really meant. If the building and grounds weren't up to her approval, it was pointless to talk about anything else.

Though Liza wasn't eager to give the grand tour, she put on her game face and quickly stood up. "I think that's a good idea. Would you like to start with the inn or go outside first?"

Sylvia finally looked at Jennifer. "Doesn't matter to me. What do you think, sweetie?"

Jennifer shrugged, avoiding her mother's gaze. "We're already here. Let's just look at the rooms on this floor."

"I love a logical bride." Liza knew she sounded like a seasoned professional—and it was almost scary.

Sylvia didn't say much as Liza talked about how the sitting room and dining room and even the porch could be utilized. She barely seemed to be listening, craning her head back to look up at the ceilings or inspect the crown moldings.

"These rooms have such beautiful detail, don't they, Mom?" Jennifer said at one point.

"Oh, they do," her mother agreed, and nodded. Then she turned to Liza and pointed at a tiny mark on the dining room ceiling. "Is that a water stain up there?"

Jennifer looked up, too. "Oh, Mom, who really cares? Is anybody going to be walking around at

104

the cocktail hour, staring up at the ceiling?" Jennifer marched around the room with her hand out, as if holding a drink, and her chin pointed at the ceiling.

"Very funny," her mother snapped. "I hope you don't hurt your neck like that."

Liza wanted to laugh but examined the spot with a serious expression. "I don't see anything from here, but I'll get a ladder out later and make sure," she promised.

The women headed out through the front door next, talking about how the porch and railings could be decorated and little bistro tables set out there as well.

Some real work had been done on the building—a paint job, new shutters, and windows—but the grounds were an easier target, Liza knew. As they walked around to the back of the property, Liza felt a bit more anxious. But she'd worked on her strategy with Molly and knew what she had to say.

Despite Sylvia's look of disdain as she gazed around the garden, Liza jumped right in.

"There's not much in bloom right now, and the beds have to be cleaned. But we'll be planting a lot of fresh perennials and a lot of colorful annuals, too. In fact, once you decide on your color scheme, I'll coordinate the planting to complement the party."

How much more accommodating could you get?

Liza could see Jennifer was pleased by the idea. "I was thinking of sort of vintage colors with the bridal party and flowers—lavender, yellow, cream. I'll only have one bridesmaid—she'll be the maid of honor, actually—my best friend, Megan."

"That sounds really lovely," Liza said sincerely.

"Yes, it does," Sylvia agreed. "But I don't see how you can get this property in shape in time. The garden is a disaster." She turned and looked at her daughter. "Do you have any idea how much work they need to do back here? It will never look nice enough in a few weeks, Jen. You might as well just get married out in some big weedy field."

Liza winced at the indictment, but it was hard to argue. The back of the property did look like a big weedy field—with a few rosebushes popping up here and there.

"Mom, just stop it already. You're making me crazy. We don't need to be married in the Public Garden with a reception to follow at the Ritz, okay? This is where Kyle and I want to say our vows and have our celebration. If Liza says she can make the garden look good in a month or so, I'll take her word for it. For goodness' sake, all you need to do is stick a few big pots of flowers around, and it will look fine. There are going to be chairs and tables all over anyway."

That was practically what Molly had told her, Liza thought.

And Molly knew where to get the plants wholesale.

Sylvia looked about to argue but pursed her lips and glanced at her watch. "Well, I think we're done here. We need to get over to town in a few minutes. Thanks for your time today and putting together this information," she said politely. "If we have any questions, we'll call you."

"Please do," Liza replied.

Jennifer stood with the big cream-colored folder that Liza had prepared tucked to her chest. As if her mother might take it from her—and toss it over the nearest cliff once they were out of sight, Liza thought.

"Thanks, Liza. I wish we could just settle everything now," Jennifer added, glancing at her mother.

"But Dad wants to see the information," Sylvia reminded her. "And he'll probably want to stop by to see the inn, too."

Liza wondered if Jennifer's father was anything like her mother. If that was the case, she might as well hang up her wedding-planner shoes right now.

"That would be fine," Liza replied graciously. "Anytime. And your fiancé, too, of course."

"I'll bring Kyle over very soon. He's excited to see the place again. Maybe this weekend," Jennifer replied.

If your mother doesn't book the Spoon Harbor Inn by then, Liza thought.

"I can't wait to meet him," Liza said agreeably.

The three women said good-bye, and Jennifer and her mother headed to Sylvia's car, a white Volvo sedan that was parked in the circle in front of the inn.

Liza went inside through the back door, trying not to worry over the garden. She found Claire in the kitchen, unpacking groceries from a string shopping bag. "Look what I found at the market today. Artichokes. Aren't they beautiful?"

Liza had never really thought of vegetables as beautiful—until she met Claire. But now, knowing how Claire could transform even a humble brussels sprout into a mouthwatering treat, she was beginning to see the hidden beauty in produce.

Claire glanced at her. "How was your meeting?"

"Jennifer was her usual sweet, agreeable little self. Her mother is sort of a witch. She didn't come right out and say it, but she obviously thinks the inn is run-down and seedy. Not nearly what she has in mind for her daughter's wedding. I doubt she'll even look through that plan I gave them. The amazing thing is," Liza added, "I started off totally opposed to the idea of doing this wedding, and now I know I'll feel totally disappointed if I don't get to do it. Isn't that crazy?"

"Not at all," Claire said evenly. "Life would be very dull if we never had a change of heart, if we never felt ourselves unexpectedly . . . inspired."

Unexpectedly inspired. That was a good way to describe how she felt, Liza thought. "Maybe I won't get to do Jennifer's wedding," Liza said, "but at least I know now that I want to try."

"Yes, now you know. But don't give up on the idea yet." Claire searched under the kitchen sink and came up with a pair of rubber gloves. "The mother of the bride is always the most difficult to please."

"Frankly, I think Sylvia is probably difficult, no matter what's going on in her life," Liza reflected.

"Well, there you are. Another reason you shouldn't take it personally," Claire noted.

She had pulled on the gloves and now set up a big bowl full of water and squeezed sliced lemons over it then tossed in the empty lemon skins.

"What's that for?" Liza asked, watching her.

"So the artichokes don't get brown. They stain your hands and nails something fierce. That's why I wear gloves. . . . How did you leave it with the Bennets?" Claire asked.

"Sylvia said they planned to visit some other places today. I'll probably get a call in a few days, saying they booked the wedding someplace else. I'm sure Jennifer is getting an earful in the car right now."

"I'm sure she is. But that girl is tough . . . like a little sand crab. She's sweet and tender inside, you can see. But she has a hard shell. Don't count her out. I think she'll get her way," Claire predicted.

She picked up an artichoke, yanked off the tough outer leaves decisively, and chopped the pointy tips to a blunt edge.

Then she pulled it open and started scooping out fuzzy bits with a grapefruit spoon.

"What are you doing now?" Liza asked, peering over her shoulder.

"You have to get the pointy leaves at the bottom out."

"It looks like hard work."

"It's time-consuming," Claire conceded, "but worth the effort. I only bought a few, just for you and me. No one's called for a room at the last minute, have they?"

Liza shook her head, reluctant to admit that the inn would be empty of guests this weekend. All the more reason to keep hoping the Bennet wedding would come through. But now that she had met Sylvia, she wondered if she ought to be more careful about what she wished for.

"NOW, this place had a very pretty pond in back with a gazebo where we could hold the ceremony. Or Jen and Kyle could just take photographs there."

Jennifer watched her mother hand her father a brochure from the Spoon Harbor Inn. They were all sitting around the kitchen table, discussing the wedding venues that Jennifer and her mother had visited after meeting with Liza at the inn the day before.

"And it's a much larger space," Sylvia continued. "I don't think the inn can really accommodate the number of guests we'll have."

"But Kyle and I really want a small party, Mom. We don't need a restaurant the size of Fenway Park," Jennifer countered. "That's not what we're thinking of."

"Please, Jennifer, let's be realistic. There are friends and relatives we have to invite. It would be rude to exclude them, even if they aren't on your list." Jennifer's mother glanced at her father, sending a distinct, "Help me out on this, would you?" kind of glance.

"Let's talk a little more about the location and then worry about the guest list," Frank suggested, spreading the brochures out on the table in front of him. They all showed smiling brides posed in gardens and gazebos.

"I spoke to the manager of the Spoon Harbor Inn this morning," Sylvia continued. "He has a cancellation in August. The groom got cold feet. Someone's misfortune, our good luck."

"How did you like the place, Jen?" her dad finally asked.

"It was okay, I guess. I think it's a little hokey. Kyle will, too," she said.

"And the Angel Island Inn isn't hokey? It's seedy and run-down," her mother said. "You'd rather be married in that empty lot she calls a garden than a lovely, picture-perfect setting?"

"Now, Sylvia, calm down. We need to try to figure this out," her father cut in.

"It's not that bad, Dad," Jennifer insisted. "You can go see it for yourself. I don't want to be married in some cookie-cutter, Barbie-bride factory."

"No chance of that if you get married at the inn. It looks like a hotel in a horror movie," Sylvia railed.

"Fine. Just . . . fine. This conversation is getting us nowhere." Jen jumped up from her chair and marched toward the doorway.

"Where are you going, Jen? Kyle's train won't be in for two hours yet," her mother reminded her. "You say you want to get married tomorrow, but you won't talk with us long enough to make plans."

"Let her go, Sylvia," Frank urged. "You're both upset now. We're not getting anywhere."

He picked up the folder with the inn logo on front and opened it, looking over Liza's proposal. "You didn't like this woman. Is that it?"

"She was very professional," Sylvia admitted. "Though I know she's never done a wedding before. That fact alone should make us steer clear—if we had any common sense about this situation."

"Well, what didn't you like? The information she put together seems reasonable," he said, putting the folder aside. "The prices look good, too. She's also offering a discount for guests who need to stay over. We do have a lot of out-of-town relatives," he reminded her.

"Well, believe me, you won't want your mother staying over at that place once you see it." Sylvia dropped down in an armchair across from her husband. "I guess some people would call it charming or quaint. Some of the rooms were presentable. But whenever I've imagined Jennifer's wedding, I pictured something much more elegant and . . . polished. She's dreamed about her wedding day ever since she was a little girl. Remember how she used to play bride all the time?"

"Yes, I do," Frank said with a soft smile. "I had to hum the music. '*Here comes the bride, all dressed in white . . .*' I never knew the lyrics after that," he added with a laugh.

"I know this place has sentimental memories for her and Kyle. I think that's sweet. But that's made her see it through rose-colored glasses. She doesn't realize what it really looks like. I mean, to someone who didn't fall in love there. Maybe she thinks it will be magically transformed on her wedding day—like an old shoe turning into a glass slipper?"

"Maybe," Frank said thoughtfully. He paused and looked down at the folder, at the etching of the inn on the cover. "Maybe it will be, for her. . . . Would that be so bad, Sylvia?"

Sylvia sat back, startled at her husband's question. "Don't tell me . . . not you, too? You have to see this place, Frank. I promise you, you won't like it any more than I do."

"I'll take a look tomorrow. But I think I've already seen it. Two views. One through your eyes and one through Jen's." He paused. "I don't want to force her to get married someplace she doesn't like, and see her unhappy on such an important day, Syl. This is the last thing we're really doing for her. Before she leaves our house forever."

Sylvia swallowed and looked down at her hands, twisting her wedding band around her finger the way she did when she was nervous. "Oh, you get so dramatic sometimes. She's going to live in Boston. We'll see her all we like. She might even rent a little weekend place out here."

"I get dramatic?" He laughed out loud. "Sylvia, just think about what I said, okay? This is Jen's day. I want her to have what she wants. Not what we want."

Sylvia seemed about to answer but her husband

stood up. "I need some air. I'm going out to walk the dog. When will dinner be ready?"

"Oh, not for an hour or so. I still have to put the potatoes in the oven."

Sylvia returned to her cooking. It had been a long day. At this rate, she would never make it through this wedding, no matter how simple Jennifer wanted it.

Jennifer and Frank just didn't get it. The real burden was on her shoulders. Jennifer might have her lovely daydreams, but she didn't understand the realities of a wedding. If she got her way, she wouldn't be happy with the results. Sylvia was almost sure of it.

She heard her husband call the dog, a golden retriever mix named Margo who'd been part of the family since Jennifer was in fifth grade. Margo was really Jen's dog; she slept in her room and followed her everywhere when she was around.

Sylvia wondered if Jen would take Margo to Boston but suspected that would be impractical. The city would be hard on the old dog. Margo would miss Jen. They all would.

For an old dog, she still had spirit and stumbled down the stairs when Frank called. Sylvia heard him click on the dog's leash, then call upstairs again. "Jen? Want to take a little walk? I'm bringing Margo out."

Sylvia stood very still, listening. "Okay. I guess I have time," Jen called back.

Sylvia's heart sank. She knew what that meant. They would talk things over, and Jennifer would convince her father she just couldn't have a happy wedding day if she didn't get married at the inn. It wouldn't take much. He already seemed more than halfway there.

Well, what can I do? I tried my best. Sylvia sighed and started in on the potatoes, resignation setting in.

They can't say I didn't warn them.

Chapter Five

ON Saturday morning, Liza decided to tackle the garden. Sylvia could have been more diplomatic, but her critique had struck a nerve. Liza knew the woman was right; the entire back of the property needed attention, especially now that the warm weather had come on so suddenly. It seemed as if the plants—and the weeds and clinging vines—had sprung up overnight.

Since there were no guests staying over, Claire was taking the weekend off. Liza didn't really know what the housekeeper and cook did with her time away from the inn. Maybe she visited friends or attended her church in town, where it seemed she was involved in a lot of committees and activities. She never mentioned any family, though.

Of course Claire had her own life, apart from the inn. But for some reason, it was hard for Liza to picture it. Claire seemed so much in her element under this roof.

Liza had made herself some coffee and now stood on the brick patio near the back door, surveying the daunting job. Getting rid of the weeds and the overgrowth was the first thing to do. Then she could figure out how to fix up the flower beds.

She didn't know much about gardening, though she had helped her aunt from time to time. Elizabeth used to say that the garden was like a canvas. It was a big blank space with infinite possibilities. It was up to the gardener to fill in the colors and shapes with flowers and make a masterpiece.

Liza headed into the shed and rolled out the red wheelbarrow that held garden tools and gloves. She pulled on the heavy gloves and knelt down at the nearest bed. Her aunt was an artist, and the garden had been a masterpiece when she lived here and had her health. Liza knew that with some work, it could look lovely again—well, with a lot of work and an outlay of funds for the new plants.

But it would be worth it. Not just for the wedding—that might not even happen now—or even for the guests who would visit this summer. But because the inn deserved to have a lush, bountiful garden, the way a beautiful woman looks even lovelier in a special dress.

Liza worked a few hours. The sun rose higher in the sky and brought the heat of the day. She grabbed a big water bottle and put on a baseball cap and some sunblock and she kept working. She got the Weed Wacker going and swiped it along the overgrown edges of the beds, careful not to mow down everything in her path. It made an awful sound but got fast results.

She was concentrating hard on steering the machine to avoid obliterating good plants along with the weeds when she heard a voice at the gate. Liza took her finger off the controls and looked up to find a large group of people, peering at her over the gate.

She quickly recognized Sylvia and Jennifer. There was also an older man, who stood with his hand on Sylvia's shoulder—obviously Jennifer's father. And a young handsome man about Jen's age, who stood right beside Jennifer, obviously Kyle, the groom.

"Hi, Liza. Sorry to bother you. We called but there wasn't any answer," Jen explained as they opened the gate and walked through.

"Oh, sorry. I started out here early. I must have missed the message when I went inside before."

"This is my dad, Frank," Jennifer said.

Frank shook her hand and smiled. "It's a warm day for gardening."

"Yes, it is, but I have to get started sometime."

"—and this is Kyle," Jennifer added, an unmistakable note of pride in her voice.

"Hi, Kyle." Liza stretched out her hand, then realized it was covered in dirt. "Sorry," she said. "But it's good to meet you."

"It's great to meet you, Liza," he said sincerely. "I was so sorry to hear that your aunt passed away," he added. "She was such a great lady."

"Yes, she was," Liza agreed. "Thank you."

"It's wonderful the way you've taken over this place. Preserved it, I mean," Kyle said.

"I'm sure you had some good offers from builders for the property," Jen's father added.

"Yes, we did, my brother and I. We own it together. He lives in Arizona," Liza explained. "But we decided that I would give a try at keeping up the family tradition."

"Lucky for us," Jen said, ignoring the look her mother was giving her.

"I was afraid that Jen was going to tell me that the inn had been knocked down and all she found was a big modern house or some condos," Kyle added. "The place looks terrific, just the way I remember it."

He looked over the building with a warm expression, as if seeing an old friend he'd lost touch with over time.

Kyle was very much the way Liza had pictured him. Tall and fair, his good looks a match for

Jennifer's natural beauty. He seemed smart and mature, if a bit more serious than Jennifer. "Could we look around a bit?" Jennifer asked. "We can find our way without your help, if that would be all right."

Liza didn't mind that idea at all. She felt dirty, sweaty, and self-conscious and figured that the family probably wanted to talk privately.

"Of course, go right in. Take your time. Go upstairs if you like," she added.

"Thanks. We won't be long," Frank said. The group let Jennifer lead the way. Liza could tell she was excited to show the inn to her father and Kyle. She wondered what they would think of it, particularly Frank Bennet.

Surprisingly, Sylvia remained outside. She hadn't really said hello, Liza realized, and now stood with her arms folded, looking over the lawn—the piles of clippings scattered everywhere—and the partially weeded flower beds.

She wore a turquoise blue linen shift and large sunglasses that hid most of her face. Liza couldn't really see her expression, but it didn't take a mind reader to guess her thoughts.

Liza glanced at her, not sure if she should start up the trimmer again. "Would you like a cold drink?"

"Thank you, I'm fine. You realize that you're not supposed to cut back a hydrangea this late in the spring, right? They won't bloom."

"Yes, I know that. I'm just going to take off the deadwood."

"With care," Sylvia suggested. "They probably brighten up the yard a lot when they're in flower. What color are they?"

"Blue and lavender."

Sylvia didn't answer. She gave the garden one more sweeping glance, then walked toward the house and let herself in the back door. Liza put on her gloves again and cleaned the gunk from the bottom of the trimmer. She didn't want to get her hopes up, but Sylvia's concern for the hydrangeas seemed a good sign.

Liza had made some real progress, reaching halfway around the yard with her edging, when Sylvia and Jennifer finally came out the back door.

Jennifer waved, looking happy. Liza felt her own heartbeat quicken. She turned off the machine and yanked off her gloves. Then she remembered the baseball cap and pulled that off, too. She wished she had time to clean up, but there was no help for it.

"We've decided," Jennifer said brightly. "We're going to have the wedding here, Sunday, June nineteenth. Do you think that would be possible?"

Liza was stunned. She hadn't expected them to show up today, and she hadn't expected a "yes" either.

"June nineteenth?" She did a rapid mental

121

calculation. That was just over five weeks away. It seemed ridiculously soon, but she wasn't about to back out now. "I guess I could do that. It also depends on your decisions, with the food and flowers and all that." She remembered the lines Molly had given her. "There are some requests I can't fulfill on such a tight time line."

"I understand," Jennifer said.

"I don't understand any of this, but go ahead. Don't worry about me," Sylvia cut in.

Liza wasn't sure what to say. "Where's Mr. Bennet and Kyle? Are they still inside?"

"We took two cars. My husband and Kyle have a tee time at a golf course in Ipswich. They left ten minutes ago," Sylvia explained. "Do you have a letter of agreement or some sort of contract we can sign? I'll give you a deposit." She sighed and glanced at Jennifer, her expression softening. "If this is what Jen and Kyle really want, well . . . what can I say? When I saw the way Kyle was swooning over the place, too, I knew I was beat," she said with an indulgent little laugh. "I'm happy if they're happy. So here we go. The countdown has begun."

"I do have a letter of agreement. Come inside," Liza said, feeling almost sorry for Sylvia. It was clear that she was baffled by the couple's choice, but for her daughter's sake was going along with their wishes. "I'll print out the form, and we can look it over."

Molly had e-mailed a form letter that she thought would come in handy. Liza was happy now that she had it on hand. She was eager to get this deal settled, too.

Liza led the Bennets into the sitting room, then printed out the letter of agreement and handed it to Sylvia. "Why don't you look this over for a minute and see if you have any questions? I'll be right back."

While Sylvia read the letter Liza took a moment to clean up in the powder room off the foyer. She could partly overhear a hushed conversation. The tone and the few words she was able to catch told Liza that Sylvia was making one last desperate pitch to Jennifer. But this time, Liza felt confident that Jennifer would hold fast. Claire had been right about her; she was as tenacious as a little sand crab.

Liza felt so confident that she took a few extra minutes to fix a tray with iced tea and a plate of Claire's homemade chocolate chip cookies.

When she returned to the sitting room, the mother and daughter were not talking anymore. In fact they weren't even looking at each other. Jennifer was paging through one of the many bridal magazines Liza had picked up to study. She looked quite calm and content. Sylvia, who was staring glumly out the window, sat up with a start when Liza set the tray on the table. "I brought you some iced tea and chocolate chip cookies."

"Thank you. Just the tea for me," Sylvia said as she watched Liza pour a glass. Liza handed it to her, noticing she didn't add any sugar, only lemon. Sylvia obviously watched her figure and was very trim and fit.

Jennifer took both a glass of tea and a cookie, biting in with relish. "Um . . . these are great. Can we work them into the cocktail hour somehow?"

"Jennifer, really?" Her mother looked helplessly horrified.

Jennifer laughed at her reaction. "That was a joke, Mom."

"Thank goodness. I can hardly tell the difference lately."

Liza glanced at both of them, deciding it was best to get on with business. "Any questions about the letter of agreement?"

"It seems fine to me," Sylvia replied, "though we may need to add a few more guests to this estimate," she added.

"A few more shouldn't be a problem," Liza said. She noticed Jen looked a bit distressed by that idea but didn't argue with her mother. She had won her big battle today and probably didn't want to push her luck.

Sylvia picked up a pen. "What do you want me to do here? Fill in our names and the date of the wedding, I assume?"

"That's right," Liza said. "I've marked an estimate for the cost of the wedding there," she added, pointing at the bottom of the page. "And this is what I'll need as a deposit. Then we'll have to meet to finalize all the details, and I'll give you a longer contract, with a precise cost."

"Yes, I understand." Sylvia's tone sounded bleak and resigned. But she signed the document, then took her check holder from a neat leather purse and wrote Liza a check for the deposit.

"Thanks. I'll just make a copy of this for you, and then I guess we're all done for today," Liza said happily.

She walked over to her desk and hit the Copy button.

"Thanks, Mom. I know it wasn't your first choice." Jennifer leaned over and gave her mother a big, impulsive hug.

Liza glanced up to see Sylvia's reaction. She seemed surprised, her reading glasses knocked sideways by Jennifer's embrace. But Liza could see her tension quickly melt away and her entire expression transformed with deep love and affection as she hugged her daughter back.

"No, not my first choice," she agreed in an amused tone. "But, what can I say? It's your wedding day."

Jennifer lifted her head and grinned. "Yes, it is. Or it will be." She stood up and practically spun around. "I'm so happy. I can't wait to tell Kyle it's all settled!"

"Except for the other ten thousand things we

have to figure out now," Sylvia muttered. But Jennifer's happiness was contagious, and her mother's mood seemed lighter now, too. Liza handed her the copy of the letter and the check, and Sylvia dropped it into her purse.

"Oh, I almost forgot." Sylvia reached back into her purse. "I made a little list for you, Liza. Some of the repair issues we talked about the first time we visited? We'd like all of this done by the wedding. You don't have to bother noting it now in this little letter. But I'd like that list in the final version, as part of our agreement."

Liza unfolded the sheet of paper and took a quick look.

The list was long, extremely long. She didn't remember discussing half this stuff. She was tempted to make an excuse to leave the room and consult with Molly on her cell phone. But she remembered her client-handling skills from her former life and reminded herself to stay calm.

"I really will do whatever I can to make the wedding absolutely perfect," Liza promised. "I'll go over this list with the carpenter who does most of the work here and see if it's possible to have these items completed by the middle of June."

Sylvia didn't seem entirely satisfied by that answer but, luckily, she didn't argue. "All right. Well, you can get back to us about it."

Jennifer seemed eager to leave, already

standing by the door, with her big handbag hooked over her shoulder.

"Good-bye, Liza. Thanks so much. We'll be back next week to talk about all the other stuff, okay?"

"The sooner, the better," Sylvia added in her sharp tone.

"Monday or Tuesday sound good?"

"Either day would be fine," Liza said brightly.

"We'll call you." Sylvia slipped on her sunglasses and headed out the door. "Have a nice weekend."

"Same to you."

Liza shut the front door, then sagged against it in relief. It was a good thing there were no guests staying over this weekend. She would need the time to rest up for her next meeting with the Bennets.

But the wedding was booked! She could hardly believe it.

She couldn't tell if she was happy or terrified. The June wedding date didn't leave much time, and Liza couldn't help but remember something Molly had said—if the party was a success, it would be great publicity for the inn. But if the wedding was a flop and word got around, well . . .

Liza didn't even want to think about it.

She wouldn't think about it either. Just positive thoughts, Liza reminded herself. It did feel like a victory of some kind just to secure the commitment, and she was bursting to share the news. A few names came to mind—Claire, Audrey, Molly.

Daniel.

Most of all, Daniel. He was always at the top of her list lately, and Sylvia's list provided the perfect excuse. The long, nitpicking document did have an upside.

Liza quickly dialed Daniel's cell. She was pretty sure he would be out on a job somewhere. The noise in the background when he picked up confirmed that.

"Hello, Liza. What's up?"

"Wedding news . . . The Bennets, complete with the father of the bride and the groom, made a surprise visit and decided to have the wedding here. I thought for sure when they left the last time, I didn't stand a chance."

"Wow, that's exciting! I knew you would reel them in. You'll do a great job for them, too, I have no doubt."

"Thanks. I'll do my best. The bride's mother is a tough customer. She handed me a laundry list of repairs she'd like done before the party. An 'or else' kind of list. I told her I had to speak to you about it. The wedding date is June nineteenth. There's not very much time."

"Don't worry. We'll figure it out. Listen, I'm in the middle of a roofing job and I have to get back to the crew."

"Sorry. I didn't mean to go on about it." Liza felt self-conscious now about calling him.

"Don't be silly. I'm glad you called. Why don't you come over tonight, and we'll go over this laundry list? I'll make you dinner."

"To your house?" Liza had never been to Daniel's house. She didn't even know where he lived.

"Yes, my house. That's where I usually cook dinner." He laughed and paused. "I know it's short notice. You must be busy," he backtracked.

"I'm not busy. I don't have any guests booked this weekend. What time should I be there?"

They quickly set a time and Daniel gave her directions. His house was on the other side of the island, which was largely unpopulated, except for a cluster of cottages that was once a fishermen's colony. She guessed that Daniel must live in one of them.

"I don't know that side of the island very well. I always wanted to go inside one of those cottages," she admitted.

Daniel laughed. "Don't get your hopes up. My place isn't much, and neither is my cooking."

She hung up, dazed by the unexpected invitation. Two *real* dates with Daniel in one week? That was a new record.

Feeling happy and energized, Liza headed outside again to pick up where she had left off in the garden. She worked her way around the yard with the edger, then weeded a few more beds. By the hottest part of the afternoon, Liza felt she'd done enough. She gathered up the clippings and watered everything, adding some plant food to give the flowering plants a boost.

Finally, she put the tools away and sat in the cool shade of the back porch with her bottle of iced water.

Not bad for a day's work, Liza thought. She felt encouraged and thought the garden did, too. The roses, hydrangeas, tiger lilies, and daylilies already looked refreshed, ready to spread and burst into flower now that the choking weeds had been cleared.

With some consistent attention, there was no reason why the garden would not look great by the time of Jennifer's wedding and provide a perfect backdrop for a beautiful ceremony. It might even pass Sylvia's meticulous inspection.

Liza didn't need to be at Daniel's house until seven, and had plenty of time to clean up. Even enough time to make dessert, she realized. She did want to contribute something to the dinner.

What to make was the question. She wandered into the kitchen and opened the fridge. She hadn't eaten a thing since breakfast and tore open a yogurt, spooning it up as she looked over the rest of the shelves.

She spotted a few containers of berries. Claire mentioned that she'd picked them up in the market just in case there were some last-minute check-ins. Before she left on Friday, she'd urged Liza to use them before they went bad.

Claire would have put them in muffins or maybe pancakes. But they would be perfect for a dessert. Something easy. Liza wasn't up for a complicated recipe or even capable of pulling one off. She considered calling Claire for advice but didn't want to bother her on her day off.

The next best thing was Claire's recipe collection—practically a sacred text, Liza thought with a smile. Claire sometimes consulted recipes from standard cookbooks, like *The Joy of Cooking*. But Liza knew that was just to refresh her memory, or strike off in a certain direction. Claire never followed a recipe to the letter, even when she had all the necessary ingredients on hand, and she rarely made the same dish twice the same way. The only constant was that the food she cooked was always delicious.

Liza found the big binder on the countertop, tucked next to the row of white canisters that held loose tea, sugar, flour, and other necessities.

Liza handled the thick, messy book carefully. The black cover was worn and tattered, the pages dotted with stains of sauces and soups and marked with notations in Claire's familiar hand—"extra Worcestershire and horseradish" or "buttermilk better." Next to the list of ingredients for her famous crab cakes—"one egg beaten is okay."

Liza felt as if she were reading something very private, like a diary. That was silly but, in a way, true. These were Claire's trade secrets at the very least.

There didn't seem to be an order in the book at first. Then Liza came to a thick wad of dessert recipes with a clip on top.

"Eureka," she said under her breath.

The first few were too hard. Liza wasn't about to tackle making a pie crust from scratch. She skipped a mousse recipe entirely—too many steps.

Finally, she found one that looked easy enough. All it said on top was, "Very Good Crumble." Reading it through, Liza recalled Claire making the dish in late winter when apples and pears were in season.

Some fruit was mixed with sugar, spices, and a little flour, then you made crumbs with butter and sugar that you spread on top, then baked it all together. She even had cream in the fridge to whip for a topping.

This could be good, Liza decided as she searched the cabinets for a suitable pan. She'd often heard that the way to a man's heart was through his stomach. She figured her chances were probably double, using one of Claire's recipes.

The dessert had to bake only half an hour, which left Liza time to shower, rest, and dress.

She searched her closets, looking for a casual but attractive outfit. Most of her wardrobe was left over from her office days and seemed too formal for the island. But among her summer clothes still at the back of the closet, she finally found a graceful skirt and a soft, sleeveless top with a draped neckline. She wore her long dark hair down and slipped on a necklace and silver bracelets. It was still warm out, but she took a thin Pashmina shawl along for later, knowing it would cool down at night.

The directions to Daniel's house were simple. The island had only two main roads, one that ran north and south and the other, that ran east and west. The east–west road connected to the land bridge that brought you to the mainland, west of the island. Daniel lived on the southwest coast, along a little peninsula that stuck out in the ocean called Thompson's Bend.

If viewed from above, the topography of the island did look a bit like a winged figure, especially if you used your imagination and were inclined to believe the island's legend.

Living at the inn, Liza didn't often think about the legend but now, approaching the remote corner of the island, the entire notion seemed more believable. The landscape was flat and empty. The sky seemed so vast, merging with the sea. Even the air seemed clearer and full of soft, radiant light.

The island was unique, she had no doubt, and she could easily believe it was a place touched by the powers above, a place that was closer to heaven somehow than the rest of the world. She did think there was something to the idea that the island was a place for healing. Liza knew she had come here with a battered spirit, full of doubt and even fear. But her months on the island had healed and restored her, even if she hadn't met any angels—at least none that she was aware of. Then again, her aunt and uncle had put a plaque near the entrance of the inn, with a saying from the Bible: *Be not forgetful to entertain strangers, for thereby some have entertained angels unaware. Hebrews: 13:2.*

So maybe she had come across some angels in disguise. Liza certainly felt as if she was doing what she was meant to do, living out her dream. The Bennet wedding was a sign, she thought as she glanced at the sun sinking low over the sea. A sign that she was on the right track.

And so was this unexpected invitation from Daniel, she hoped.

Chapter Six

A S Liza arrived at Thompson's Bend she drove up a narrow road flanked by tall beach grass and trees, and a mass of low cottages came into view. The main road branched off into narrow cobblestone lanes with quaint names, like Teapot and even Fish Bone.

Daniel lived on Hasty Lane, number seven. She made a right-hand turn at the corner and drove along, looking for the number on fence posts and mailboxes. She could already tell his cottage would be on the left side of the street, with a view of the ocean in back.

When she found it, she pulled into the narrow drive and parked behind his truck. The house was beautiful but in a decidedly masculine way. She couldn't really say what style it was—a cottage but not like the other white, rose-covered cottages on the lane. It was possibly built in the Craftsman style, but it wasn't a pedigree of that school either.

Like so many of the houses in coastal New England villages, its weathered shingles were dark brown, and the trim and shutters painted gray blue, colors that made the small house seem to blend perfectly with its surroundings, as if the little cottage had sprouted up, right on that shady spot.

The front yard was bordered by trees and the garden planted with lush green hostas and other plants that thrived in the deep shade. The windows and front door, which appeared to be part of a recent renovation, hinted at Mission style within, which Liza thought would suit Daniel perfectly.

As she took her shawl and the dessert from the backseat, Daniel appeared at the door. He was wearing khaki shorts and a white shirt with the sleeves rolled up. He had acquired a tan from working outdoors the last few days, and his smile flashed white and even against his lean, tanned face. He looked very at home and very handsome, she thought.

He met her halfway down the walk and gave her a quick, friendly kiss hello on her cheek. Liza kissed him back, and her heart skipped a beat.

"What's this?" he asked, looking at the pan. "You didn't need to bring anything."

"It's just some dessert."

"Actually, you did need to bring that," he admitted. "I forgot all about dessert, and we're pretty far from any stores."

"You're far from everything. It looks like the edge of the world out there," she teased him.

"It might be," he said with a laugh. "So, what's in the pan? It smells good." He lifted the corner of the foil and took a peek.

"A crumble with different kinds of berries, one of Claire's recipes. She just calls it 'Very Good Crumble.'"

"I'm sure it will be. Come on in, everything is ready."

He smiled at her again, and she could tell he was happy to see her. She felt happy, too, as she followed him into the house.

"Let's sit outside. It's much cooler. I'll get you something to drink."

Daniel disappeared into the kitchen, giving Liza a chance to look around. The main room was a spacious living room–dining room combination with a row of French doors that framed an ocean view.

The beamed ceiling was low, and the living room had a rustic hearth with a mantel made of smooth gray stones. Liza could imagine the cottage being very cozy and comfortable in the winter as storms raged outside.

The furnishings were dark and masculine-looking but stylish, she thought. A brown couch covered with kilim-patterned pillows and a big leather armchair sat near a standing brass reading lamp. There was also a rocking chair made of bent tree boughs, and covering the polished wood floor, an oval area rug with a traditional pattern.

She sensed Daniel's hand in the floor-to-ceiling bookcases that covered one wall, filled with titles on a wide range of nonfiction subjects, as well as novels. A few shelves held interesting extras— sparkling geodes and carved figures from Native American lore.

There weren't any photographs, Liza noticed. Then she saw one in a small frame and picked it up to get a closer look. It was taken on a beach, at the shoreline. A man and a woman stood on either side of a little boy and tugged on his arms, lifting him high in the air as he jumped over a frothy breaker. Everyone looked happy and carefree. The little boy, especially, looked ecstatic.

Liza took a closer look at the child's face. She couldn't say for sure, of course, but she had a good guess that it was Daniel. Something about the eyes and the smile. He'd certainly been a cute kid.

"Liza, would you like to sit outside?"

Liza turned at the sound of Daniel's voice. She wondered how long he'd been standing there, watching her. She quickly put the picture back where she'd found it. She wasn't sure why, but something in his expression made her decide not to ask if it was a family photograph.

"It gets a little warm in here. I don't have air-conditioning," he added.

"You don't need it with these great breezes," she said.

He stepped back and let her walk through the door first.

There was a table with an umbrella set up on a brick patio and a short distance away, a large outdoor grill that held a big stainless-steel stockpot. Liza could see that the fire underneath was hot, and whatever was cooking under the lid was letting out a steady stream of steam.

The backyard wasn't very deep; it ended abruptly on a cliff that looked out over a narrow strip of beach. Liza walked to the edge of the lawn and gazed down.

"Wow . . ." She looked back at him. "I bet you don't throw too many big parties back here."

"No, I don't. Too risky," he said with a laugh. "I don't have many guests at all. You're the first in a long time."

Liza didn't know what to say to that, though his admission did make her feel special.

"I've thought about putting a fence up. But I don't want to ruin the view. The sunsets are spectacular."

"I'll bet they are." She was looking forward to watching the sunset here tonight. With him.

She walked back and sat at the small table across from him.

Daniel had set out two glasses of white wine and a platter with cold shrimp and two kinds of sauce, one red and one white.

She tried one of the shrimp with red sauce. The sauce was pleasantly spicy, and the shrimp tasted fresh and sweet.

"What were you up to today? Besides booking weddings, I mean?" he asked her.

"Except for the Bennets stopping by—and shocking me clear out of my socks—I started to work on the back garden. I let it go too long. What a mess."

"That's a big job."

"And a dirty one," she finished for him. "But somebody has to do it. I put in a few good hours and it looks much better. At least the plants coming up have some room to grow now."

"I can't wait to see it." He smiled at her encouragingly. "Flowers are subtle touches. If they aren't there, many people wouldn't notice. But when you do step into a beautiful garden, it's like walking into a magical world or something."

"That's what it used to be like when my aunt and uncle were strong enough to keep up with the work. I'd like to make it look like that again, if I can. Once I get all the beds filled, I want to put in some interesting touches. Maybe a pond way in the back and a shade garden, where guests can read and relax. . . . All I need now is someone handy who could do that for me," she teased him. "Any recommendations?"

He smiled at her, his eyes crinkling at the corners. "I think I know a guy who would work out just fine."

I think I do, too, Liza nearly answered. But she caught herself just in time.

Daniel grabbed a pot holder off the table. "Excuse me a second, I think I'd better check the food."

He rose and headed over to the big outdoor stove. Liza watched as he lifted the lid and checked the contents.

"What's for dinner?" she asked curiously.

"A lot of stuff," he replied. "I hope you like it. I have a pretty simple approach to cooking. Just put it all in a pot and hope for the best."

"Sounds good to me. I'm pretty hungry."

"Just what I like to hear. Let me get the plates and we can start right in."

"Let me help you," Liza offered.

They went back into the house and gathered the plates and utensils on a tray. Daniel's kitchen was small but looked well used, despite his disclaimer about his cooking skills. A big rack of worn pots hung from the ceiling above the stove, and shelves held rows of seasonings and spices.

They quickly set the table outside, and Daniel headed over to the cooking pot. With mitts on both hands, he took the lid off and carefully tipped out some hot water. "Looks like we're in business. Why don't you bring over those big bowls?"

Liza brought the bowls, and Daniel began to empty the pot, sorting the contents into the bowls. "We have some clams and mussels. And some corn and potatoes and, last but not least, a few lovely lobsters. I know a guy down the street who's a fisherman. He caught all this stuff this morning."

"Daniel, what a feast!" Liza was in awe. "How are we ever going to eat all this?"

He laughed and grabbed two of the bowls, leaving her to carry the lobsters on the plates. "I'm bad with amounts," he admitted. "But I don't mind leftovers. It won't go to waste."

Liza laughed. "Looks like you'll be eating lobster rolls for a week."

They dug in with relish, neither talking much for a while. Daniel had to help her crack some of the tough shells. He did it easily in his large, strong hands.

"So, what's this about some list of repairs the bride's mother gave you?" Daniel asked her.

"It's pretty long," Liza reported. "I'm not sure you can manage it all by the wedding date."

"Which is?"

"June nineteenth."

Daniel's mouth was full but his eyebrows jumped up. "Wow, that is soon," he said. "Today is May fourteenth, so that's—a little more than a month away?"

"Thirty-six days, to be precise." Liza had already counted. "I'll get the list. You can tell me what you think."

Liza wiped her hands, then found her purse in the living room and quickly returned. She handed the sheet to Daniel and stood behind him as he read it aloud. She was tempted to rest her hands on his broad shoulders but somehow resisted the urge.

"Regrout or replace tile in powder room off foyer. Do something about water stain on dining room ceiling. Repair or replace brick patio; brick is uneven. Add trim colors to shed to match main building. Repair or replace bricks in walkway to garden . . ." Daniel glanced up at her, tilting his head back. "This is . . . substantial," he said.

"What happens if all of this isn't done in time?"

Liza shrugged and sat down at the table again. "I'm not sure. Sylvia Bennet said she wants the list included in the final contract. Not a good sign, right?"

"I don't know much about the wedding business, but I'd have to agree with that feeling." He thought a moment. "Don't worry, Liza. I'll just hire a few of my regular guys. If we could put the roof back on your house in a week, I'm sure we can take care of most of the things on this list."

Liza would never forget the night that a tree right next to the inn was struck by lightning and a huge branch crashed through the roof. The inn was up for sale at the time, and the necessary repairs held up everything. At the time, it seemed like a disaster to Liza and her brother, who were both hoping for a quick sale. But Liza soon came to see the bolt from the blue as a blessing in disguise. It had slowed down the situation long enough for her to decide that she really wanted to stay on the island and take over the inn. Daniel's help fixing it—and his help and encouragement when she was trying to make that decision—had been another blessing.

Liza sat back and glanced at him. "I'm sure you can handle it, too. But you're always running to my rescue, Daniel. I'm starting to feel like a damsel in distress."

He leaned over and took her hand. "Maybe I just like helping you. And you're anything but a damsel in distress. You are the most un-damsel sort of woman I've ever met."

"And you're the most dependable, helpful knight in a white pickup truck I ever met," she said lightly. "But I sometimes wonder whom you call when you need help. Everybody needs a hand from time to time."

"Oh, don't worry about me. I'm fine." He smiled as he spoke but sat back and withdrew his hand. "Why don't we clear this stuff away and get on to that dessert you brought?"

"Sure. I'm definitely done. It was delicious. Every bite."

Liza rose to help clear the dishes. She wondered if she had gone too far again. Well, she could only edit herself and her feelings so much, she reflected.

They quickly cleared away the remains of dinner, and Daniel brought out coffee and the berry crumble and whipped cream.

He took a taste, his face lighting up instantly. "Wow, this is good." He pointed down at the dish with his fork, clearly impressed. "You made this?"

"Yes, I did," she answered with a laugh. "I know you suspect that Claire had a hand in it, but she was off for the weekend. I did use one of her recipes, though."

"And did an excellent job with it," he said, taking another bite. "Her Banana Crunch Muffins are my favorite," he added.

Liza made a mental note of his preference. "Whatever the cooking equivalent of a green thumb is, Claire's got it. Everything she makes is completely delicious."

"No argument there. Claire could write a great cookbook."

"Yes, she could," Liza agreed, finally tasting the crumble herself. It *was* delicious. The fresh berries were both tart and sweet, and the crumbs were a buttery, cinnamon and sugar perfection.

"But please don't tell Claire that," she added after another bite. "Not until she decides to retire."

"I don't see that happening very soon . . . if ever."

"I hope not. I'm not sure I could survive without her," Liza admitted.

"You say that now, but sooner or later, you'll realize that she's pushed you out of the nest and you're flying solo."

"Yes, I guess so." Liza knew that was true. In just a few short months, she'd learned so much from Claire about running the inn. "Claire's a quiet kind of teacher," Liza said. "You never feel as if she's bossing you around or pushing her opinion. All the time that she helps keep things rolling along, you hardly even notice her there at all."

145

Daniel grinned. "She's like an invisible safety net."

"That's one way of describing her, a safety net I really need right now," Liza agreed. "But you may be right. Sooner or later, Claire just might push me out of the nest."

"Well, we all have to make our own way, sooner or later."

He sounded thoughtful and even a little sad. Liza looked across the table at him. The sun had set in a blaze of rose and violet clouds, disappearing under the sea. The table was lit by a small white lantern. A candle glowed within.

She wondered what he was thinking about. His own family? A past romantic relationship? She wished she could ask but was afraid to ruin the comfortable mood between them.

"It's a beautiful night," she said, turning her head to look at the night sky. "I feel like we're sitting up in the stars on this cliff."

"I don't know about you. But I am." He pushed her hair off her cheek with his hand, then leaned closer and kissed her.

Liza kissed him back, tasting traces of blueberries on his lips, savoring the moment. He pulled back slowly and stared into her eyes.

"Want to take a walk on the beach? The moon is out."

The moon was out, almost full, too, a silver orb shining over the blue-black water.

"That would be great. I think my shawl is out here somewhere." Liza stood up and looked around. It had grown much cooler since the sun went down and she needed the wrap, whether they went onto the beach or not.

Daniel found it for her on one of the extra chairs. He opened it and wrapped it around her shoulders with care, hugging her close for a second. Then he stepped back and took her hand.

Liza peered over the edge again. "Is there an elevator or something? It's a long way down to the beach from here."

"Haven't gotten to that improvement yet, sorry. There's a flight of stairs that I keep in good repair. And a flashlight." He led her across the lawn to the top of a railed staircase. It was partly concealed by the brush at the cliff's edge, and she hadn't noticed it before.

Daniel walked down first, holding out the light, and Liza followed. She was wary on the first few steps, then realized that the stairs really were very solid and descended in stages against the side of the cliff.

They were soon down on the beach. The sound of the waves crashing on the shore filled the night. The dark sky above seemed endless, a black, diamond-studded canopy arcing above them. The ribbon of beach stretched out in the distance, marked by only a few twinkling yellow lights of houses.

"We ought to leave our shoes here," Daniel said. "No one will touch them."

"I believe you. They could probably stay here untouched for years," she joked. The spot seemed that desolate.

"People do come here in the summer. But the access ways are private. This beach is one of the hidden treasures of the island."

A treasure—yes, that was a good way to describe this wild, beautiful spot. "The whole island is a bit of treasure, don't you think?" she asked.

"Absolutely. I know it should be shared, but I worry about it being ruined by these so-called improvements. The new beach and recreation center. The ferry service. There will be a lot more traffic coming over the land bridge, too," Daniel remarked. "I hate to think of how all these improvements are going to affect the wildlife."

Liza agreed with him, but she also knew that the ferry service and new beach would be a great boon to the inn. It was one of the reasons she was able to convince her brother that they should keep the inn and she should try to run it.

Daniel took her hand and they started to walk, soon reaching the damp, smooth shoreline where the waves were washing in.

"I know what you mean. I'm not against all the changes. But I'd hate to see the island change too much. Right now, it's pretty much the same as it was when I was a kid visiting my aunt and uncle."

"Yes, it is," he agreed.

Liza thought about his reply. "Did you come here, too, when you were younger? You never told me that."

He glanced at her. "I didn't? I must have mentioned it. Probably when we first met."

"Maybe," she conceded, though she was pretty sure he hadn't. "Did you come here with your family?"

He nodded. "My parents and my older sister, Rebecca."

"So where did you stay?"

"We used to come for a few weeks each summer and rent a cottage in this area. My folks liked it. It seems a little quiet, but there were always kids to play with and things to do. We'd be on the beach all day."

"That's what I remember, too. Though Peter and I had the inn. There were always interesting people coming and going. And Aunt Elizabeth and Uncle Clive were always enlisting us as helpers."

"Child labor?" Daniel joked.

"Exactly, but Elizabeth and Clive had a way of making all their projects seem like fun. Did you grow up near here?" she asked, still curious about him.

"No, I grew up in Northampton," he said,

naming a large town in western Massachusetts, near the village of Amherst. "Coming to the beach was a long trip, the thing we looked forward to all winter and spring. Maybe that's what made me love the ocean so much. It was such a treat. I was landlocked the rest of the year."

"Is the cottage where you stayed still here?"

"Sure is. You just had dinner there."

"I should have guessed," she said with a laugh.

"My parents liked it so much, when the place came up for sale they bought it."

"Do they ever come back?"

"Only once a year, if that. My mother passed away a few years ago. Breast cancer. My father is retired. He lives in North Carolina, near my sister and her family. I don't know how we all fit, but we manage."

"You can send a few of them down to me next time. I'll give your relatives a good discount." Of course, they both knew she would put them up for free.

"You're on. My sister has three wildcat boys. They wreck the place when they stay over."

Liza laughed. "As long you do the repairs when they leave, the offer still holds."

"Okay, that's a deal."

"So, let me just think about this a minute. We must have been on the island at the same time," she said, knowing Daniel was just a few years older. She stopped in her tracks and turned to him, her voice becoming more excited. "All those summers . . . we must have seen each other at some point—maybe lined up for ice cream at the General Store? Or went swimming at the same beach? Or walking down Main Street in Cape Light?"

The realization gave her a strange feeling, as if she and Daniel were meant to meet all along, that their paths had been invisibly intertwined, and it had been just a matter of time—the right time—when they would finally come together here, on Angel Island.

Daniel turned to face her. It was hard to read his expression in the shadowy light. He didn't say a word but she thought he might be smiling.

"It's definitely possible. But I would have remembered you, Liza. Even if we'd never exchanged a word."

Liza stared up at him. She felt the same. She would have remembered Daniel if their gazes had met for only one moment. She felt his strong grip on her shoulders as he drew her closer. As he bent to kiss her Liza twined her arms around his waist, caressing his strong back. The steady ocean surf roared in her head, and Liza knew she could easily drown in his embrace. This was what she had always longed for—this closeness, this physical, emotional, and even spiritual connection.

She had never felt like this with Jeff, her former husband. She had never felt like this with anyone. Even if she still had questions about Daniel, they had come a long way and she was content. More than content, she was floating among the stars that drifted overhead.

Finally, they walked back along the beach toward the wooden staircase. Daniel's arm was tight around her shoulders and Liza's arm wrapped around his waist. When they parted to slip on their shoes and start the climb, she felt the sudden absence of his warmth. The breeze off the water was strong and cool now, and Liza hugged her shawl close as she made the long climb back up the cliff.

It was late and her long, eventful day suddenly caught up with her. When they reached the top of the stairs, she smothered a yawn with her hand. "I'm sorry . . . it's been quite a day. And I did all that gardening."

"I understand. That roofing work is catching up with me right about now, too. I don't think either of us needed all those stairs tonight."

"Maybe not," she agreed with a laugh, "but the walk on the beach was certainly worth it. Thanks for making me dinner. It was delicious . . . and I loved seeing your house," she confessed.

He didn't say anything at first, and it was hard for her to read his expression.

"I'm glad you came, too. Very glad." He tilted

his head to one side, appraising her. "Are you too tired to drive? I can take you back to the inn, and you can pick up your car tomorrow."

"I'm all right. It's not a very long drive."

"Are you sure?" he asked, still not convinced. "If you don't want to leave the car, I can follow you in the truck. I don't mind."

"I'll be okay. But thank you." She picked up her purse and fastened the strap on her shoulder. Then Daniel led her around the side of the cottage to her car. He opened the driver's side door for her and she slipped inside.

"Call me when you get in, okay?"

"I will," she promised, touched by his concern.

She smiled at him briefly as she backed out of the drive. He looked so handsome standing there—his dark hair mussed from the breeze, his white shirt clinging to his tall, lean body. His eyes were shining as he smiled and waved good-bye.

Liza felt her heartbeat quicken and the breath catch in her throat. It suddenly seemed amazing to her that this man had come into her life in such an accidental way and now seemed to care for her almost as much as she cared for him.

It was simply amazing.

But maybe, it was just meant to be, she thought.

Chapter Seven

LIZA woke up late on Sunday morning. Warm sunlight glowed behind the lace curtains in her bedroom, mirroring the happy glow she felt inside.

She thought about Daniel and their time together. It seemed as though she were remembering a wonderful dream—especially their walk on the beach in the moonlight.

She felt as if she couldn't stop smiling. Maybe he did care for her more than she had thought. It seemed he was trying hard to please her. She knew that inviting her to his house had been a big step for him.

Did she really know that much more about him? Well, not exactly. All she knew was that when they were together, she felt wonderful, her real and best self, shining through. Being with Daniel felt so easy and right.

Despite her hours spent working out in the sun the day before, she felt energized and ready to tackle the garden again. With an early start today, she hoped to finish in back and make it out to the front.

There was a real deadline now, the wedding date. Liza felt the pressure and the race was on to get the inn in better shape, inside and out.

She pulled on some clothes suitable for the

dirty work ahead and went downstairs for coffee and a quick breakfast; coffee and a muffin would do for now.

It was so quiet at the inn without Claire. The inn wasn't any noisier with Claire in it, but her presence resonated somehow. It was always good to know that she was there, ready to listen or give advice or share a cup of coffee.

Liza grabbed her mug and headed out to the porch to survey the work that was needed in front.

It was a brilliant sunny day, growing warmer by the minute, as the sun rose over the broad, blue swath of ocean visible from the porch.

Liza walked around the front yard, making notes on a small pad. She had found some old photos of the inn that showed the garden very clearly, and she hoped to restore some of the beds just as her aunt had originally planted them.

At the front of the property, there was a pretty little flower bed around the post and wooden sign that bore the name of the inn. Her uncle Clive had cut that sign and sunk the post, and Elizabeth had painted the lettering and surrounding vines and flowers.

Liza examined the post and sign. She needed to refresh the paint and lettering—a delicate task for sure—but she would never change it.

The flower bed around the sign had always more or less matched the colors on the sign, tufts of sun-loving lavender, bright white Shasta daisies, and hot pink phlox. Now she saw mostly weeds, with just a few stems of brave, persistent lavender trying to peek through.

Liza knelt down with her tool basket and got to work. It was about half past noon when the sound of a car coming up the gravel drive caught her attention.

She didn't recognize the shiny black convertible, but was happy to see Jen and Kyle in the front seat. Kyle was behind the wheel and Jennifer waved happily with one hand, holding back her long hair with the other as the car came to a stop.

"We should have called first. I've interrupted your work again. I'm sorry," Jennifer apologized as she walked across the lawn to meet Liza.

"Don't be silly, I'm glad to see you." Liza quickly yanked off her gardening gloves, and wiped her hands on a small towel.

"We didn't have a chance to walk on the beach yesterday. Kyle ran off so quickly to the golf course with my father," she explained. "So we came back today."

"I never got to say good-bye or thank you yesterday," Kyle added. "I'm so glad everything worked out. This is the only place Jen and I ever imagined being married. If we couldn't get married at the inn, I think we would have just pitched a tent down on the beach and gone through with it anyway."

"I'm much happier that you're having it here," Liza said with a laugh.

"I am, too," Jen added. "I can't wait to be married here."

"Neither can I," Kyle agreed, putting an arm around his fiancée.

Jennifer leaned against him. They were so easy and comfortable together; they seemed to fit each other perfectly. "Well, we won't keep you from your garden. My mother said she would call to set up an appointment, to go over more details."

"Yes, we need to meet very soon. Early this week, I hope," Liza urged her.

"Yes, early this week," Jennifer promised. "I know there isn't much time, but everything will turn out great. How could it not?"

Liza smiled in answer. If only she could bottle some of Jennifer's sunny outlook. It would come in handy the next few weeks, she was sure.

"So what are you guys up to today?" she asked the young couple.

"Well, we just went to church and had a visit with Reverend Ben after the service. We've started our premarital counseling," Jennifer reported. "And we're going up to Newburyport later to shop for wedding bands. We have so much to do, but that's the only thing we felt like tackling when we checked the list." She glanced at Kyle, and he squeezed her shoulder. "We don't have much time together right now. Just the weekends—and not always even that."

"Don't worry. The time until your wedding will pass quickly," Liza promised. And even quicker for me, she realized.

Liza watched the happy couple head toward the beach, hand in hand. She suddenly felt a deep connection to her aunt who, she imagined, had felt much the same when she befriended them and coaxed the romance along.

It was amazing how she had come full circle from Monday morning when Jennifer had appeared at the door out of the blue. Her request had seemed impossible then. But maybe anything is possible, Liza reflected, when you ask heaven for your heart's desire and won't take no for an answer. The way Jennifer did.

And the way I did, Liza reflected, *when I chose to stay on Angel Island.*

JENNIFER and Kyle quickly headed across the road and down the steep path to the beach below. Jennifer kicked off her shoes and ran to the water. "I missed you, beach. I really did," she called out. She picked up the edge of her sundress and waded into the foam. When she finally looked up, Kyle was standing a short distance away, watching her.

"I'm marrying a total nut. But she's a beautiful one."

"Thanks, honey. I'll take that as a compliment." Jen walked over to him and kissed him on the cheek, then wound her arm around his waist. "So how do you like our beach? Does it look the same to you?"

"Exactly, only better. Because now that we're going to be married, this place seems even more important to me."

"I feel the same way," she said. They walked along the shoreline awhile, their arms entwined and their steps in matching rhythm. "I'm so relieved that my parents finally agreed on the inn. Every time I think of it, I'm just ecstatic," Jennifer said happily.

"I'm relieved, too," Kyle admitted. "Now if we can only persuade your mother to keep the guest list down. I'm starting to worry that we're going to end up with a three-ring circus, Jen. You know that's not what we wanted."

"Don't worry. It will be fine. I'll talk to her about it, I promise. You have to remember, she gave in on the big thing—the inn. So we may have to compromise a little."

Jennifer felt Kyle's body tense but he didn't say anything. Was this the way it was going to be the entire time she was planning the wedding? She hoped not. The last thing she wanted was to be caught in the middle like this, between what her parents wanted and what Kyle wanted.

"The weekend is passing so quickly," she said. "I feel as if we hardly had any time together. Maybe I should come into Boston next week and we can have dinner one night or work on the apartment. With the wedding so close, we'll never get to paint."

"I can hire some painters; that's not a problem," Kyle replied quickly. "Listen, I got an e-mail from Ted this morning. He wants me to go down to New York tomorrow to work on that big project I told you about. I'll be there a few days, maybe even over the weekend."

So they couldn't get together this week in Boston, Jennifer realized. "Do you have to stay there on the weekends, too? That doesn't seem fair."

Jennifer didn't mean to complain. But they had so much to do and only five weekends to do everything. You couldn't count the weekend of the wedding; even she wouldn't do that.

But she decided not to make a big deal out of this. Kyle was the only one working right now, and his job was important to their future.

"I'm the low man on the ladder right now, so I have to do what the boss says. And look happy about it," he added in a joking tone. "Besides, being asked to go to the main office is an honor. Even if I could turn it down, I wouldn't want to."

"I understand. You have to seem like a team

player and all that," Jennifer agreed. "You're so smart, I'm sure they need you there. Just make sure you solve all their problems in New York in time for our wedding, okay?"

Kyle laughed and stared into her eyes. "Don't worry, I'll absolutely do that, I promise."

Then he kissed her hard and swung her around in a circle, right off her feet, splashing with his bare feet in the foam.

Just like he'd done when they were teenagers.

And she knew what he was going to do next, too. "Kyle, put me down!" she called out as he slung her over his shoulder, fireman style.

"Feel like a swim, honey?" he teased over her screams.

"No, I don't! It's too cold and this dress can only be dry-cleaned and—"

"Okay, okay," he said, laughing. He carried her back to the dry sand and set her down. Then he collapsed on the sand with an exaggerated grunt. "You feel a little heavier than you did in high school, Jen. I'm not even sure I could still throw you into the water."

Jen made a face at him but she knew he was still teasing. She was, in fact, quite a bit thinner than she'd been as a teenager.

"Maybe you're just not as fit as you used to be. You really need to get back to the gym," she teased back. "I don't want a flabby hubby on our honeymoon."

He laughed at her comeback. "Good one. We're even. Now come over here and let's look at the water awhile."

Jennifer gladly joined him, sitting close and snuggling against his chest, his arm wrapped around her shoulders.

"We'll always come back to this beach," she said quietly. "And we'll always be together and be incredibly happy."

"Yes, we will. And we will . . . and we will. I promise you," he replied, answering each of her vows.

"I promise you, too," Jennifer said solemnly.

She sighed and stared out at the water, the sound of the waves merging with the beat of Kyle's heart.

Their love was just as limitless, she thought, stretching out in all directions, like the vast ocean and the blue sky above. Filling all the empty places inside her, like the rushing water. Warming her deep to her soul, like the brilliant sun. Lighting every day of her life.

She and Kyle would always be this happy, she promised herself. Always and forever.

CLAIRE and Liza had just finished breakfast Tuesday morning when Daniel tapped on the back door. Liza jumped up to open it. He had been tied up on another job and, though they'd had a few casual conversations on the phone, she hadn't seen him since their dinner at his house on Saturday night.

"Good morning, ladies. Do I smell pancakes?" He sniffed the air. "Or is that some amazing new perfume you have on, Liza?"

He leaned perilously close to her cheek, waited a moment, then finally kissed her.

She had to laugh. "I'm sure I smell like maple syrup. But that was totally unintentional."

Claire was standing at the stove, with her back turned. If she had seen the kiss, she didn't show it.

"Sit down and have a bite, Daniel," Claire urged him. "There's a stack left over, just for you."

"Claire, you talked me into it." He smiled and took a seat near Liza. "I had to leave the house very early. I only had time for coffee."

"That's not healthy, Daniel," Claire scolded in a motherly tone, "especially with the hard work you do all day." She set a plate of hot, airily light pancakes on the table in front of him. "No more coffee for you. You need some orange juice first," she added, bringing him a glassful.

"Wow, what service. Thanks, Claire. You always take care of me."

"I do what I can, when I can," Claire said. "You don't seem to take very good care of yourself. I'm starting to think you need someone on that job full-time," she hinted broadly. "But that's none of my business."

"No, it's not . . . but thanks for your interest." Daniel laughed, pretending to look shocked at her pronouncement.

Liza felt her cheeks warm. Daniel must think I tell Claire about my romantic dilemmas, she thought. That wasn't really the case, though Claire seemed to have a special radar about these things. So no doubt, she'd already guessed what was going on—or not going on—between them.

"I didn't expect you this morning," Liza finally managed to say. "You told me you weren't going to finish with the porch in Cape Light until Wednesday."

"I've got some guys on it. I thought I'd stop here first before I joined them—just to go over some of the items on this list."

"That's good," Liza said, feeling relieved. "Jennifer and her mother will be here this morning to go over wedding details."

He took a folded sheet of paper from his shirt pocket, and Liza could see he had made a lot of notations.

"She wants the grout and any broken bricks out back replaced?"

"That's what she says. She's afraid it's too bumpy and people will trip. Women in high heels, you know. I think if we can figure out how to make it look fresher and smoother, that would be okay," Liza suggested. "Is there some way to do that?"

"The bricks are probably about one hundred years old or more, so they're going to have a few lumps and bumps. Patching spots with new bricks will stand out like neon Band-Aids. Maybe we can find antique bricks that would match. Sometimes people save them after they renovate or tear down."

"That sounds expensive."

"Not so much, but it's not easy. You try to replace one and end up cracking two or three more in the process. It's cement. It's not like cleaning up the tile in a bathroom."

"Yes, I see." Not good news on that one. But Daniel's dark eyes were so distracting, it was hard to feel that concerned.

He had taken care shaving this morning, she noticed. She longed to touch the smooth line of his cheek and straight, firm jaw.

"Why don't we go out and look at it, see what we can figure out?" His suggestion broke into her wandering thoughts.

"Good idea," she said quickly.

Taking their coffee mugs, they went outside to the back of the inn. Liza blinked at the strong sun. It was going to be another warm day; she could feel it. She quickly raised the dark blue market umbrella over a wrought-iron table in order to give them shade.

Daniel set his mug on the table and gazed around the yard. "You did do a lot of work back

165

here. It looks much better, Liza. I didn't realize you had a green thumb."

"Neither did I," she admitted. She stretched out her hands, examining them. "I think I sort of developed it over the weekend, along with all these broken fingernails."

"A small price to pay," he told her. "It's coming along."

"Thanks, but I still have a way to go."

She turned from the flower beds to look down at the bricks. The patio was a bit of a mess. Bright green weeds and mossy stuff sprang up between the bricks and lines of cement. She hadn't had a chance yet to work on that.

"It doesn't look very good, does it?" she asked him.

"It's not so bad. You could get those weeds out for a start, then power wash it."

"That's a good idea." Liza sighed. "I never noticed that it was so uneven. But maybe Sylvia thinks people are going to be dancing out here. Molly says I can have a dance floor put down by the tent people."

"I guess you could. But I can see the charm in dancing here, under the arbor. You can put some little lights up in those vines." He tilted his head back to look over the wisteria that twined above them on the structure.

"Hey, nice touch. Forget the repairs, you should help me plan the wedding," she teased him. "I'm going to steal that one."

"It's all yours. But I think we ought to test out the theory first."

"The theory?" She wasn't sure what he was talking about but noticed an interesting light in his eye as he took a step or two closer.

"We don't want any of the guests to twist an ankle or fall down out here. Think of your liability. We have to test the bricks for danceability, don't you think?"

"Danceability?" She smiled at him and was about to answer when he took her hand and slipped his other arm around her waist, sweeping her onto the experimental dance floor.

He was humming a song that she couldn't identify, but she couldn't help but dance along. It felt wonderful to be in his embrace, even pretend dancing.

Daniel began another song, a standard wedding-type tune. It was familiar, but Liza couldn't be bothered to think of the name. She was wondering what it would be like to really dance with him. She was sure she'd just drift off on a cloud. She was nearly drifting off right now.

"Sorry for the humming. I can never remember lyrics," he confided.

"You're a pretty good hummer. I don't mind."

She lifted her head and looked into his eyes. He was still humming and suddenly stopped, though their bodies still swayed together to notes of music only they could hear. He gazed down at her, and she thought he was about to kiss her. She closed her eyes, her grip tightening on his shoulder.

"Mom, please. Let's just go back to the front door."

Liza heard a hushed whisper. Jennifer Bennet's voice.

Liza's eyes sprang open and she turned, practically spinning out of Daniel's embrace.

Sylvia and Jennifer were standing at the gate that opened to the drive. They were early, Liza thought, quickly checking her watch. But not that early.

She had lost track of time.

Chapter Eight

HI, Liza," Jennifer said as they came through the gate. "We rang the bell at the front door. But no one answered."

"Oh, sorry. Claire must be upstairs."

Liza exchanged greetings with Sylvia, while Sylvia stared curiously at Daniel.

"This is Daniel Merritt," Liza began the introductions. "He's doing the renovation on the inn. He's an expert in old houses and building techniques. Daniel, this is Sylvia and Jennifer Bennet."

Jennifer smiled and shook his outstretched hand. Sylvia shook his hand also but didn't smile.

"Really?" she drawled. "I thought you were the dance instructor."

Jennifer cast her mother an appalled look.

Liza didn't know what to say, but Daniel seemed amused. "Liza and I were just testing the brickwork as a dance floor," he explained calmly. "To make sure it's safe for your guests. I think it will be fine," he reported. He stepped toward Sylvia and opened his arms. "Would you like a turn? You can see for yourself."

"No. Thank you." Sylvia stared at him and shrank back.

Daniel glanced at Liza, looking awfully satisfied. *My work is done here,* his smile seemed to say.

"Well, I'll leave you to your wedding plans. I have this list to work on," he added, waving her list in the air as he grabbed his coffee. "See you later, Liza."

"Yes, see you." She gave Sylvia what she hoped was a reassuring smile. "So, shall we get to work?"

Sylvia glanced at her watch. "We don't have much time. We're heading into the city this afternoon with Jennifer's maid of honor, to shop for gowns."

"That's exciting." Liza turned to Jennifer. "Do you have any particular style in mind? There are so many choices. I don't know how brides can figure it out."

Before Jennifer could answer, her mother replied. "We'll have to do it somehow, and in record time. And it will have to be a dress that won't take too long to order or need too many alterations." She sat down heavily in a chair, as if she had already been shopping for hours and the quest had exhausted her.

"I have a few pictures from magazines to work with," Jennifer said mildly. "I just want something simple. Off the shoulder maybe. Not too much going on."

"She has a perfect figure, so that's going in our favor," her mother conceded. "She looks gorgeous in anything she tries on. A burlap sack would probably work out, with a headpiece of some kind."

Liza couldn't tell now if Sylvia was being sarcastic or just plain hysterical.

"Great idea, Mom. And my maid of honor could wear a potato sack and the flower girl could wear . . . a flour sack?" Jennifer added.

Sylvia was trying not to laugh, but Jennifer had at least made her smile. "Stop being so silly. We have a lot of work to do."

"Would you like to sit out here?" Liza suggested. "It's such a nice day. I can bring out all my notes and some iced tea."

"That sounds fine," Sylvia said. "This table looks large enough."

Liza went into the house to fetch her wedding

files, unsure of what Sylvia meant by that. Had she brought along a giant, ten-thousand-piece jigsaw puzzle? One with the picture of a royal wedding perhaps?

But when Liza returned with her files and wedding binder, the question was answered. Sylvia had made her own binder, already as thick as a phone book, and there was also a long yellow legal pad with several pages of lists.

Please, no more requests for building improvements, Liza silently prayed. Then she slipped on an invisible suit of armor and stepped out into the arena.

Liza had found a complete, thorough, and well-organized wedding checklist that she wanted to work from. "Shall we start with the number of guests?" Liza began.

"No, I want to start with table settings," Sylvia said. "Then we can discuss the music."

So it went. Sylvia's list had the same items as Liza's but in a different order, and Sylvia insisted they follow her list. She interrupted Liza and took over the conversation so many times that Liza finally gave up and they worked from Sylvia's list.

If that makes you happy, fine, Liza said silently, her face locked into an accommodating smile.

More than two hours later, they had worked their way down the items, discussing such essentials as budget, number of guests, the color scheme, and type of flowers. Then there was the type of tent they wanted Liza to rent, the chairs, tables and table settings, and even the type of tablecloths.

The one thing the Bennets agreed on was that Reverend Ben, from the old stone church in Cape Light, would perform the service. As for the rest of it, the possibilities went back and forth between mother and daughter, like a Ping-Pong match.

They each had a clear idea of what they wanted, with Jennifer arguing for simple and Sylvia insisting on elegant—and Sylvia somehow thinking that Liza was the problem.

"Will we get to see a sample tablecloth for approval?" Sylvia asked. "I mean, my idea of pale yellow, Liza, and your idea can be worlds apart."

Not to mention Jennifer's idea, Liza thought. Jennifer had already stated that she wanted ivory tablecloths with rose-colored napkins. But what she said was, "Of course, you can."

"We want real linen," Sylvia went on. "Not some polyester nightmare that just hangs there."

"I'll have samples of table linens for you very soon," Liza promised. "Now that I know the colors." Privately, she decided she would order a couple of pale yellows as well as a few varieties of cream. That way, hopefully, they could agree on something.

"What about chair covers?" Sylvia asked. "They won't add that much to the cost, and they make a nice decorative accent."

"I'll look into that for you and see what I can come up with." Liza didn't even realize there was such a thing as chair covers until recently. Now she sounded like a chair-cover consultant.

"I saw something that's much more fun and looks really pretty," Jen cut in. "You take some sort of gauzy fabric and wrap it around the back of the chair and put a fresh flower in the bow. Wait, I have a picture."

She whipped out a magazine page from her own folder and dropped it in the middle of the table.

Sylvia examined the photo, peering over the edge of her reading glasses. "I don't know. . . . Do you really like that? I can't imagine a room full of chairs that looked like this. People would be bumping into the flowers. I think it would be too gaudy. You don't want that sort of look, Jen, do you?"

Liza couldn't help but notice the sinking look on Jennifer's face. Her mother overrode nearly every suggestion she made.

"I've never seen this before," Liza cut in before Sylvia could go on. "I think I should get some of this fabric and experiment. It is hard to tell from the picture. Maybe you could use it on a few chairs at each table?" she suggested.

"That's a good idea," Jennifer said, brightening again. "Get some pink," she added quickly.

Sylvia cleared her throat. "Now, we've asked a few people we trust about caterers. We even went into the shop this weekend and sampled the food at Willoughby's—"

"Secretly," Jennifer added with a laugh.

"We've decided to go with your recommendation and use Molly Willoughby for the food. Frankly, we just don't have time to shop around."

"I don't think you'll be disappointed," Liza said. "Everyone loves Molly's food. I think I gave you a copy of the menus and the pricing?"

"Yes, you did. We haven't reviewed it yet. When do we need to work out the menu?"

"We have a little time on that," Liza told her.

"That's good." Sylvia cast Jen a thoughtful glance. "Jen and Kyle want to serve a lot of appetizers and finger foods passed around on trays. Frank and I really don't think that's a good idea. It's a bit awkward, juggling a plate and a drink all night, especially for the older people. We want the guests to be comfortable."

"But, Mom, there will be plenty of tables set up if people want to sit down. We just won't have a formal seating arrangement and all that. People can eat and mingle. Then move to another table if they like. It will be fun," Jennifer added in her best persuasive tone.

Liza could see that Sylvia wasn't swayed. "Oh, I don't know, Jennifer. That can work for some other sort of party, a backyard barbecue perhaps. But for a wedding, the guests expect something more substantial. Some of them are traveling a long way. They'll expect a real sit-down dinner. You don't want to be roaming around all night, finding an empty chair at some messed-up little table."

Liza could see that Jennifer was getting upset. "Well, how about a buffet?" she offered, the idea coming to her suddenly. "It's not as formal as a dinner with several courses, and it gives the guests more freedom to mingle."

Sylvia tilted her head, considering the idea. Jen looked a bit encouraged, too. "It isn't what Kyle and I pictured," she said. "But it's better than a long, fussy dinner."

Sylvia gave her daughter a long, appraising look, as if she were deciding on which battles would be worth fighting. "I suppose these menus list all the options?" she asked.

"Yes, they do. If you have any questions just call me, or you can get in touch with Molly directly," Liza replied.

"We need to consider the number of guests we'll be serving, too," Sylvia added, glancing at the menus again. "We need to add a few more guests to the list." She sighed heavily. "It's hard to keep the guest list under control. So many people we know would love to see Jen and Kyle get married."

Liza was sure that was true. Jennifer was such a charming girl. But Liza hoped her fan club wasn't too large. One of the big reasons she had agreed to take on this job was because Jennifer had promised the wedding would be small.

Jennifer looked uncomfortable again. "I don't even know half those people, Mom. They're all your friends and Dad's."

"But we've been to the weddings of their children. We have to reciprocate."

"Not really," Jennifer quietly insisted. "Kyle doesn't want a lot of guests either. We want to keep this close and intimate. We really don't want a circus."

"It's not going to be a circus. For goodness' sake, Jen." Sylvia sounded amused but also as if she was the one who definitely knew best about these things. "I'll explain it to Kyle. He'll understand. Your father and I want to give you a beautiful, memorable celebration, dear. Not some tiny, quiet little party, without any real food or— pizzazz. Is there anything wrong with that?"

Yes, if you don't want pizzazz, Liza expected Jennifer to answer. But Jennifer just sat back and glanced at her watch. "I have to call Megan. I should tell her that we're running late."

"Go ahead, dear. We won't talk about anything important until you come back." Sylvia cast a loving smile at Jennifer as she walked out into the yard, her cell phone pressed to one ear.

Sylvia was annoying . . . but fascinating, too, Liza thought. She could be totally oblivious to Jennifer's feelings and opinions one minute, then oozing with adoration the next. It was almost as if she didn't even realize how single-minded she was and how often she shut her daughter out of this process.

Liza sighed inwardly. She wasn't going to be the one to tell her either. Though she was tempted.

Sylvia cast a quick glance in Jennifer's direction. "She's going to make such a beautiful bride," she said quietly.

"Oh, that goes without saying," Liza agreed.

"I'm almost afraid to see her in a gown," Sylvia confessed. "I'm sure I'll be shedding a few tears today."

Liza nodded, finally understanding the reason that Sylvia seemed especially prickly and difficult today. She was nervous about shopping for Jennifer's wedding gown.

"I went shopping with a friend for her wedding dress a few months ago, and there were boxes of tissues everywhere. We needed them, too," Liza said, her voice gentle. "There's something about seeing someone put on that dress for the first time. It makes it all seem suddenly real."

"Yes, it does make it real. Like seeing your

child wait for the school bus the first time . . . or go off to sleepaway camp. Or even college." Sylvia's eyes looked glassy and her chin trembled. "In some ways, it's the final milestone, don't you think?"

"In some ways, perhaps it is," Liza said sympathetically. "I'm sure it's difficult, seeing your little girl all grown up. It's a happy time but a big transition."

"Yes, a big transition. That's what Frank keeps telling me. He's seems to be doing better with it. But you know men, they don't like to reveal much. They keep it all bottled up inside. Most of them, anyway."

"That's true," Liza agreed heartily. She knew one man in particular who fit that description.

"I know Frank's feeling it—or he will, once Jennifer moves out. Luckily, she's not going far, just to Boston. Though that's far enough for me," Sylvia admitted with a laugh. "I would love it if they could stay out here. Jennifer's best friend, Megan, was married recently and they settled down right in Cape Light, only a block or two from Megan's parents. I wish Jen and Kyle were doing something like that. Maybe she'll move back once they start a family. But when she's in Boston—I'm afraid I'll barely see her. I know it's not far, but young couples get so busy. We may not see her very much at all."

Sylvia's voice grew suddenly shaky, and Liza

thought she might start crying now for real. But Sylvia reached into her purse and took out some tissues, dabbing carefully under her eyes so she wouldn't smear her makeup.

"That's why the wedding is so important," she went on in a steadier voice. "It's the last thing we can really do for her before she leaves us. Jennifer has dreamed of a wedding like this all her life. I know she seems laid-back and unconcerned about the details. But believe me, she has a certain idea in mind, and I know she won't be happy if it isn't the way she's imagined it. If it doesn't live up to her fantasies. Jennifer just assumes it will all be perfect. She doesn't realize that some magical wedding fairy does not come and make it perfect for you. That's where I come in," Sylvia said wryly. Then she looked serious again. "We really want to give her this special day, her dream come true."

"Of course you do," Liza said. "Doesn't every mother?"

"Maybe. But I can only speak for one mother, me. I know I can easily drive a person crazy. Jennifer and my husband rarely hesitate to remind me. But my daughter is everything to me. I'd do anything for her. I just want to see her happy. I'm not sure you can understand if you don't have any children yet, Liza. But maybe you do."

"I do understand, and I promise you that I'll do everything I can to make the wedding perfect."

For Jennifer and *for you,* she wanted to add.

Sylvia's confession had made Liza feel a great rush of sympathy for her. But Liza could also see that Sylvia was the type of person who loved from her own perspective. She instinctually and fiercely believed that she knew what was best for her child, even if it wasn't what her daughter really wanted.

Claire appeared at the back door. "Are you ready for lunch? I can fix you a salad or some sandwiches," she offered.

"Is it lunchtime already?" Sylvia sat up and checked her watch, then looked around the property and finally saw her daughter standing under a tall tree, still talking on her cell phone. "Jennifer, we have to go."

"I guess Sylvia and Jen can't stay, Claire. But thank you," Liza finally replied. Claire answered with a small smile and disappeared into the house again.

Sylvia stood up and gathered all the clippings and her wedding notebook. "I think we got something accomplished this morning. But there's a lot more to talk about," she added.

"Yes, there is," Liza had to agree. "Maybe we should try to talk over the phone during the week?"

"That's a good idea. I'll call you," Sylvia said decidedly.

Jennifer returned and picked up her purse. "So

long, Liza. Wish me luck with the wedding-gown hunt."

"Good luck. I'm sure you'll find the perfect dress," Liza replied.

"We'll do our best," Sylvia said. "What else can you do with only four and a half weeks left to plan a wedding?"

"Come on, Mom." Jennifer took her by the arm and led her to the gate. She glanced back at Liza with an amused expression.

Poor Jennifer.

And poor Sylvia.

AFTER the Bennets left, Liza continued working on the wedding, sitting outside. She already had her laptop and a phone out there, as well as all the necessary folders and paperwork. And it was a beautiful day. This was definitely one of the perks of running your own business and working from home, she thought.

Sometime later when Daniel reappeared, she knew that was another perk. Surprise visits from a handsome man.

"Is the coast clear?" he asked in a mock whisper. He looked around, presumably for Sylvia and Jennifer.

"They've been gone awhile now." Liza was writing a list of florists to call and didn't pick her head up immediately to look at him. "Are you back to give more dancing lessons?"

"I will . . . if there are any willing customers."

She laughed and finally looked up at him. "You're not a bad dancer, Daniel," she said honestly. "But I don't have time today for another lesson. Sorry."

He shrugged. "I understand. I'm pretty booked myself. How about Friday night? Are you free then?"

Liza was surprised by his invitation but tried hard not to show it. Gee, this dating business was getting to be a regular thing. Her heart did a secret cartwheel across the green lawn.

"I am free on Friday night."

"Me, too. Okay then. I'll mark my dance card." He smiled into her eyes and she had a warm, happy feeling. "How's the wedding business going? Any sudden regrets that you took on this challenge?"

"Not really," Liza said. "Sylvia means well. She can be difficult, but no more than some of the clients I dealt with at my old job. She opened up to me a bit while Jennifer was on the phone," she added. "I think I understand her better now."

"That's good. It's always good to have some insight into your adversary," he teased her.

"She's not my adversary. Not exactly. Though she does act that way at times," Liza conceded. "I wish she would let Jennifer have more say over things. They disagree on just about everything, and then I can't get a straight answer. We still have to settle on the color scheme, the flowers, the cake, the photographer, and whether or not we're going to have gold-embossed place cards."

Liza could see Daniel's eyes glaze over. She didn't blame him. The list was endless.

"But it's coming along," she concluded. "I think it's going to be a really nice party. I promised Sylvia it would be perfect," she confessed.

He smiled at her, looking impressed. "I'm sure it will be."

"I hope so," she said sincerely. "Or something close enough."

She had promised Jennifer's mother she'd do everything in her power to give Jennifer a beautiful wedding, and that's what she was determined to do.

"HI, honey . . . What do you think of the gowns I tried on today?" Jennifer asked Kyle excitedly. "Did you see the photos? I sent them to your phone."

"Were they different from the photos you sent Tuesday night?" Kyle's tone was contrite. Jennifer could tell he hadn't noticed the e-mail, or if he had, he hadn't opened the photos yet.

"Yes, they were different. I've been dress shopping for two days straight. We've narrowed it down to three gowns, I think. I really need your opinion."

"I'm sorry, Jen. I didn't get a chance to look. I was really swamped today."

How long could it take to look at a few photographs? Jennifer wanted to ask, but he sounded so pressured that she didn't want to make things worse. "That's okay. I'm pretty sure about the one I really like. You'll just have to be surprised."

"Aren't I supposed to be? I thought it was bad luck or something for the groom to see the bride in her dress before the wedding."

"That's what Megan said when she took the pictures. But I don't think it counts if I didn't buy it yet."

"I wouldn't be a good judge, Jen. I'm sure you look gorgeous in all of them."

Kyle was so sweet. He always made her feel special and really loved. Jen knew how lucky she was to be marrying him.

"I don't know about that. But I do need to find something. I have a lot more to take care of. Do you know what tomorrow is?"

"It's . . . Thursday?" Kyle's worried tone almost made Jen laugh. "Did I forget something? Some anniversary or birthday . . . or something?"

"Not yet." She laughed. "Tomorrow is May nineteenth. In exactly thirty-one days we'll be married. Can you believe it? I still have so much to do."

"I'm sorry I'm not able to help you more. But

think of it this way, in exactly thirty-two days, we'll be on our honeymoon. Ted says the hotel we're staying at is the best."

While Jen worked on the wedding, Kyle was making all the arrangements for their getaway. Jennifer had told him that they didn't have to spend a fortune or go someplace totally exotic. She didn't even care if they rented a cottage on the Cape or up in Maine. Being married and alone on vacation for two weeks was more than enough to make her happy.

Kyle had his heart set on a trip someplace tropical. He'd talked to a lot of the guys in his office, and his boss had recommended a hotel on the island of St. Barts, in the Caribbean. So that's where they were headed.

"I hope it's not too expensive for us, Kyle. I'm not working yet," she reminded him.

"Don't worry, I've got it covered."

Kyle had been at the investment firm for two years. He was doing very well; Ted had hinted he was definitely on the way up. He had already gotten two generous raises plus bonuses. He was even talking about buying a house soon, once they knew where Jen would be teaching.

"Yes, I know, honey," she replied. "But I do really want to find a job. Any sort of job, if I can't find one teaching. Once we get back from our honeymoon, I'm going to focus on that."

"You don't have to rush into anything, Jen. Just

focus on the wedding. I'm glad that you haven't signed a contract to start at a school in September," Kyle added. "There's a lot going on in my office right now. Ted wasn't supposed to tell me, but we were working late last night and he gave me a few very broad hints."

"Hints? What kind of hints?" Jennifer got a funny feeling. She hoped it wasn't a merger or downsizing. The last ones hired were usually the first fired.

"It's not anything bad," Kyle assured her. "You know how they sent me down to New York this week to work on this project? It wasn't just a random thing. Ted hinted that there's going to be an opening here for a high-level analyst. It would be a major step up for me. But he says I'm in the running and people are watching me."

"Oh . . . that's great, honey." Jennifer wasn't sure how she really felt about it. But Kyle seemed so excited that he was being considered, she didn't want to sound discouraging or negative. "I'm not surprised," she said honestly. "You're so smart and you work so hard, I'm sure your boss would consider you for any good opening that comes along."

"Well, this one's a plum. I went out to lunch with some guys down here, analysts at my level, and they were all drooling over it. I didn't say anything. It's pretty competitive, a real shark tank."

"That sounds rough. You might not like that side of it."

"I'd get along okay. I know how to handle myself."

That was not the answer Jennifer was hoping for. But she didn't reply. A job at the New York office? Would they have to live down there? Of course they would. She couldn't get married and see her husband only on weekends. That would be ridiculous.

"So, how does this work? Do you go through interviews? Or do they just tap you on the shoulder one day and say, 'Tag, you're it'?"

Kyle laughed. "I wish. I don't really know, but I hear that it's not exactly a sudden decision. They ask quite a few people to apply, then there are interviews with the department heads and the partners. It takes a while before they decide."

Jennifer wanted to make sure she understood. "So even though Ted said they like you, it's not a done deal?"

"Not at all. A lot of guys are going for this job, especially from the New York office. I'm not really sure of my chances."

Jennifer breathed a sigh of relief, and they soon got on to other subjects. The wedding mostly.

"We have to meet with Reverend Ben again after the service on Sunday. I told you that the other night, right?"

"Yeah, you did. But thanks for reminding me. I'd better put that in my BlackBerry."

"With a little buzzer or something," Jen teased him. "I know New York is pretty dazzling and distracting, but this getting married stuff is important, too."

"Absolutely," Kyle agreed with a laugh.

They had met with Reverend Ben about the wedding twice so far. This next time they would mostly be talking about the ceremony. Jennifer had initially been a little nervous about the sessions, wondering what the reverend wanted to discuss with them. She and Kyle had both grown up in Reverend Ben's congregation and had known him since they were children. That helped to make these talks far more relaxed. It was almost like talking with a beloved, older relative or a friend of the family. Besides, the meetings had turned out to be very helpful.

She and Kyle agreed on their faith and they both wanted children, so that was two big questions covered. They also talked about expectations they each brought to their marriage. Big questions that could cause conflict down the road—whether Jennifer would work once they had children; how they would handle everyday matters, from joint bank accounts and financial decisions to figuring out who cooked dinner and who put out the trash. Jennifer came to realize that many of her expectations were based on the way she had watched her parents make a life together. But that wasn't necessarily the way it had to be.

More important, they talked about how they would continue to maintain a feeling of closeness, pulling together instead of pulling apart when the realities of life set in—like working long hours at their jobs, handling the household, paying bills, raising children. Communication was a big part of that, Jennifer knew. And not letting little things build up.

She was trying hard to follow this advice, even before the big day. Planning their wedding was giving her lots of opportunities to practice, that was for sure.

"So, what's new with the wedding? Any progress, besides gown shopping and seeing Reverend Ben again?" Kyle asked.

"Not too much." Jennifer hesitated but finally pushed herself to continue. She needed to be open with him. "There is one thing. Remember how we decided I would ask Carrie to be a bridesmaid?" Carrie had been Jennifer's roommate all through college, and she was almost as close a friend as Megan. "I asked her and she said yes."

"Oh, that's good. I always liked Carrie. If you want her in the wedding, I'm glad she can do it."

"You're not mad?" The other day when she'd told him that she wanted to have another bridesmaid, he had seemed upset. But he had been at work and it wasn't a good time. He must have been feeling distracted and stressed.

And then last night, she had told him that her parents really needed to invite more guests. That was another difficult discussion, but they eventually smoothed it over.

"It's fine with me if you want Carrie in the bridal party. But now I have to find another usher. Maybe I'll ask Max," he said, mentioning his old college roommate. "Or Ryan," he added, recalling a friend from high school he was still in touch with.

Kyle had already asked his brother, Tim, to be his best man. Jennifer was relieved that he was able to think of two choices. That gave her the courage to continue.

"Sounds like there are a few guys you can ask. The thing is, that once I invited Carrie to be in the wedding party, my mother thought I should really ask my cousin Elena. I was in her wedding party and we've always been close. We were thinking that if I don't ask her, I might hurt her feelings and my aunt Nan might be insulted, too."

She heard Kyle sigh and knew that was not a good sign.

"Do you really want Elena to be a bridesmaid? Or is this all your mother's idea? I mean, it's *our* wedding, Jen. I like Elena and your aunt Nan, but I thought we were going to keep the bridal party small and not have some big parade marching up to the altar. I really only wanted my brother to stand up with me," he reminded her.

"Yes, I know. I didn't think of Elena right away," Jennifer said honestly. "But once my mother mentioned her, I realized that she would feel hurt, seeing Carrie there. And my aunt will feel bad, too. I bet she's already asked my mother about it. It seems only fair to ask my cousin since she's family."

He was quiet a moment. "Okay, if you really feel that way, then we'll have a bigger wedding party. I'll ask Max and Ryan to be ushers."

"Thank you for understanding," she said sincerely.

"I understand, Jen," he said quietly. "But that's it, right?"

"That's it," Jennifer replied. She winced as she spoke. What she still hadn't told him was that her mother really wanted them to include Elena's two adorable daughters as flower girls. Sylvia just wouldn't let go of the idea. The girls were twins, four years old and absolutely precious. But Jen didn't dare mention it. She would have to convince her mother that they didn't want flower girls. Kyle had barely agreed to the extra bridesmaids.

When they finally said good night, Jennifer sent Kyle her love in between sleepy yawns. She shut out the light in her room and got into bed.

Even though she was bone tired, it was hard to

fall asleep. Wedding worries filled her head. And now this situation with Kyle's job, an opening in the New York office. Was he serious—or just flattered to be considered? She thought it was probably the latter. It was a plum position, he said, and there were a lot of other guys vying for the spot, many of them more experienced than he was.

She knew that everyone thought he was very sharp. What had Ted called him at their office Christmas party? A rising star. Still, even if his boss believed that Kyle had a chance, it hardly guaranteed he would get the promotion. It sounded as if Ted didn't have that much say in the final decision.

Which was fine with Jennifer. She couldn't believe that Kyle could seriously think they would move to New York City, right after they were married. That was just . . . impossible.

She could never live so far from her parents. They would have a fit. Her mother was already upset that they were going to live in Boston, which was not even two full hours away. Kyle's parents would be upset, too, she thought. He knew that. Didn't he?

All their family was up here, and their friends. They had plans. They were already fixing up the apartment and had bought all that furniture.

No, he didn't mean it. It was all just talk. Sort of a guy fantasy—being tapped by the boss for the big promotion. But to actually change all their plans and move down to New York City?

She loved Kyle and thought he was terrifically smart and deserved every bit of recognition at his job. But she really didn't want to move to New York. Jennifer had only been a few times and didn't like it. She couldn't imagine living there. Boston was a much more friendly, livable city.

Why can't we just enjoy the wedding and have a moment for ourselves before we have to get so worked up and focused on our careers? she wondered. Sometimes Kyle seemed more focused on his job than getting married, Jen worried. *He's so worried about us sticking to our plan for getting married. . . . What about the life we planned?* It didn't include New York, she recalled.

But what was the point of getting into some long drawn-out discussion about that tonight? The chance of Kyle winning this position was small. He said so himself. It was definitely not worth starting some big messy argument over.

Jennifer hated to argue with anyone. Especially Kyle.

It wasn't worth it. Not about something so unlikely.

Chapter Nine

WHEN Claire arrived at work on Thursday morning, Liza was in the kitchen, eager to greet her with some good news.

"The leader of a cycling club called late last night and asked if we had any vacancies for the weekend. 'How about a completely empty inn. Is that vacant enough for you?' Of course, I didn't say that," she quickly added.

"Of course not." Claire slipped off her light cotton jacket, exchanging it for an apron that hung on a hook by the kitchen door.

"It turns out there are fifteen people in the club. They're based in New Jersey somewhere, and they're coming up to New England to ride around Essex County. They booked a bed-and-breakfast in Ipswich, but something got confused with their reservation and now that place is filled up. So they looked on the Internet and found us."

"We're on the Internet?" Claire asked with surprise.

"I took a listing on the Chamber of Commerce website, and there's another group of local innkeepers who have a site. It wasn't very complicated and doesn't cost us much."

"Seems it's paid off already. How many will be coming?"

"Fifteen," Liza said happily. Claire didn't say

anything, but Liza could tell from the look on her face that she was wondering where all these guests would sleep.

"I know it's more than we can accommodate in the renovated rooms. But they agreed to take a few of the rooms that haven't been renovated yet, on the third floor, and I might move out of my room for a night or two," Liza added.

"Anything for the cause," Claire offered with a smile.

"It's not a big deal. But I gave them a good deal—an off-season group rate and an additional discount for the old rooms. The person I talked to sounded very happy. They don't plan on being in their rooms very much. They'll be out biking all day and will just drop into bed at night, exhausted. They won't even notice the old wallpaper. I hope," she added.

"I don't think those biking groups are hard to please, as long as we serve a good breakfast and put out a lot of bananas," Claire added decidedly.

Liza gave her a curious look.

"Oh, cyclists love bananas," Claire said as she poured herself a mug of coffee. "Gives them lots of energy and keeps them from getting leg cramps."

"Oh, right. The potassium or something," Liza recalled. "Well, let's put that at the top of the shopping list. We need to start getting the place ready. They'll be arriving separately, some as early as noon tomorrow. They asked to have a group dinner on Friday. Can we do that?" Liza realized suddenly she should have asked Claire before agreeing to the request.

"No problem. I enjoy cooking for a good-sized group."

"That's what I was hoping you'd say. I already told them it was fine," Liza admitted.

The two women laughed and began to make their plans, sitting at the big oak kitchen table. Liza felt suddenly as if she were flowing along in a gentle current, a force of nature, nothing to fight against, just enough to carry her along. She felt in the flow of being an innkeeper, working hard, but truly enjoying herself.

After they had strategized preparing the rooms and meals and other touches, Claire sat back and laughed. "I think that working on the wedding has changed your perspective, Liza. Now you don't bat an eye at fifteen guests for the weekend, even though the most we've had so far is six."

"I didn't think of that but you might be right," Liza admitted as she rose from the table. "I'm just excited to hang out the No Vacancy sign on Friday night. If I can find it."

"If you can remember to do it. You'll have your hands full with that many guests hanging about. Some will go off to town, I'm sure, but the others will be asking for this and that until they turn in. I'll stay over if you like," Claire offered. "I have to be here very early Saturday and Sunday morning anyway."

Though Claire lived in a cottage on the other side of the island, she also had her own room at the inn, on the third floor, and had practically been living there full-time when Liza's aunt was sick. She had not stayed over much since Liza had taken over the inn, but once they got busy in the summer season, Liza expected that she would need to stay often.

"I'd really appreciate that," Liza said. "I think we ought to start on the worst rooms first, and see how we can make them look better."

"Good idea," Claire agreed.

Claire grabbed a bucket of cleaning supplies from the mudroom, and Liza found the vacuum cleaner in the closet on the second floor. Liza practically ran up the steps, vacuum in hand. The idea of the inn filled with guests was amazingly energizing and completely lifted her spirits. She felt as if she could clean the place from top to bottom in an hour.

When had she last seen the place that busy? When she was a child probably and her aunt and uncle were at the helm. Now it was her turn, and she was ready.

But as Liza reached the second landing she suddenly remembered that she had made a date with Daniel for Friday night to go out dancing. All week long she had been imagining their romantic evening, wondering what to wear and where he might take her. Now she would have to explain she had to work the whole weekend. She sighed, turning on the landing to the third floor, hefting the vacuum up the narrow staircase. She hoped that he would understand and keep the invitation open.

She could practically hear his deep voice, humming in her hair again. Having to give up this chance to be with him just when things were going so well seemed terribly unfair. But Liza knew she really had no other choice.

After cleaning and preparing the rooms all morning, Claire headed into town with a big shopping list and sent Liza to the Gilroy Farm next door for other necessary ingredients for her recipes—fresh herbs and goat cheese, mainly, and Liza wanted some of the beautiful lavender bouquets Audrey sold to decorate the bedrooms.

She pedaled her bike to the farm and down the dirt road flanked by white fencing. A few of the goats grazed in the meadow beside the road, and Liza waved to them. Audrey and her husband had nearly three dozen goats in their herd now. The herd grew quickly, and the Gilroys had sold a number of the kids in the spring, but Liza still knew many of the goats by sight and even by name. She thought they were very sweet, especially the kids. She had even considered having a few at the inn but wasn't sure how that would go over with the guests.

Liza parked her bike near the small shop where the Gilroys now sold their products. Audrey had originally sold her goods in the big room used for cheese-making, but just last month she had converted an old toolshed into a tiny but charming shop. Liza could see Audrey inside, through the small window. The shed was painted yellow, inside and out, with dark blue trim. The old wooden door held a big wreath of fresh lavender that smelled wonderful when you walked in.

Audrey, who was stocking the refrigerator with logs of fresh cheese, turned to greet Liza. "Hey, stranger, what a nice surprise."

"Hi, Audrey. Sorry I haven't called you lately. I really meant to, but I've been super busy."

"With the wedding? Are they using the inn?" she asked eagerly.

"Yes. The wedding is set for June nineteenth." Liza quickly filled Audrey in on the wedding plans and the adventures she'd had so far working on it—including how Daniel had asked her to his house for dinner and then how she and Daniel had been dancing on the brick patio at ten in the morning and Sylvia Bennet had snuck up on them.

"Sylvia sounds like a handful," Audrey said.

"She's not so bad," Liza admitted. "I'm starting

to think she's just very stressed about the idea of letting go of her daughter."

"Wait . . . let's rewind a bit. Did you just say that Daniel asked you to his house for dinner?"

Liza nodded happily. "Sylvia handed me this long list of repairs she wants done for the wedding, and Daniel invited me over to his house to discuss it."

"And did you talk about the repairs?"

"Among other things. We talked a bit about growing up. It turns out he spent summers on the island when he was a kid, just like I did. We figured out that we might have even seen each other at times. Isn't that amazing?"

"Quite a coincidence," Audrey agreed. "What's more amazing is that he told you that much about himself—and made you dinner."

"I thought so, too." Liza felt almost starry-eyed, thinking back to that night. "He asked me out for tomorrow night," she added, "but I just booked a huge group for the weekend, and I have to cancel. I hope we don't move back to square one."

Audrey listened with concern while she straightened out a display of scented soaps, all made from goat's milk. "Don't worry, Liza. He'll understand."

"I hope so. But I still wonder why it's so hard for him to talk about his past. You've known him longer than I have, Audrey. Why is he so secretive?"

Audrey sighed and shrugged. "I may have

known him longer, but I probably don't know him any better than you do, Liza."

Liza felt an old doubt niggling at her. "He's not involved with someone else, is he?" She hated to ask the question, but she couldn't help it. Her ex-husband, Jeff, had been unfaithful to her and she'd never seen it coming. She had trusted Jeff completely. And now she worried about her own judgment with men. She couldn't let herself be betrayed like that again.

Audrey shook her head. "I don't think it's anything like that. In all the time we've known Daniel, he's never mentioned anyone. He's never even seemed that interested in anyone, certainly not as interested as he is in you."

"That's good to know." Liza sighed. "But there must be something," she reasoned.

"I've thought so, too, at times," Audrey admitted. "But anything I do know . . . or I've guessed . . . well, you need to hear it from Daniel. We've worked together at the clinic for over two years now, and all I can tell you is he's a complicated person—and a first-rate EMT."

Liza instantly felt contrite. "I'm sorry, Audrey. I shouldn't have asked you. I didn't mean to put you in an awkward spot. It's just that at times I feel like I've hit a wall."

"I understand," Audrey sympathized. "He's a good man, really. Maybe he's made some mistakes, but who hasn't?"

Liza nodded in agreement, but Audrey's words made her wary. Had Daniel had a run-in with the law of some kind? Was that why he ended up on the island?

"So, tell me about this huge group of guests who are showing up for the weekend," Audrey said. "Do they like goat cheese?"

"I hope so. Claire sent me over to buy out your store."

While Audrey filled Liza's shopping list, Liza told her about her lucky break with the cycling group.

"Seems like good things are coming your way, Liza," Audrey said, totaling up her bill. "First a wedding, now a sold-out weekend, and it isn't even Memorial Day."

"I can't complain," Liza replied. As usual, she noticed that not only had Audrey given her a generous neighbor discount, she had also thrown in several bars of soap, lavender bunches and sachets, and a big box of goat's milk fudge.

"Audrey, I have to give you more money for all this," Liza insisted, barely able to lift her canvas tote bag.

"Don't be silly. It's free advertising for me. I'm sure they'll all want to go home with some goat cheese when they taste Claire's omelets and quiche."

"Good point. I'll make sure everyone knows where to come." Liza took a few flyers about the farm from the counter and stashed them in her bag as well.

She strapped the big bag into the basket at the front of her bike and slowly made her way back to the inn. She did believe that Audrey didn't know much more about Daniel than she was telling. Was he really, as he claimed, just a very private person? Or was he hiding something, some unfortunate episode in his past?

Liza was actually glad now that Audrey had not divulged any deep, dark secrets. If there was some secret, she wanted to hear it from Daniel when he trusted her enough. If he ever did.

Why did it matter so much, she wondered, pushing the bike the last few yards up the road to the inn. Was she falling in love with him? She felt as though she was. It was scary—and wonderful.

So, of course, she wanted to know everything about him. But she resolved not to bug him anymore. There are issues in every relationship, even the good ones, Liza reminded herself. Nobody is perfect, though he seemed just about perfect to her. She had to just focus on the present and be happy with what he was willing to give. And see what happened from there.

When Liza reached the inn, she saw Daniel's truck in the drive. He had just arrived and now he jumped down from the cab to meet her. She parked the bike and took the big bag out of the basket, carrying it pressed to her chest with both arms.

"Did you just make a goat-cheese run?"

"I did." Liza nodded and smiled.

"Looks like you bought out the shop."

"We're having a big group in for the weekend, a cycling club based in New Jersey. They just called last night. There will be fifteen of them."

Daniel gave a low whistle. "Sounds like a full house."

"You're not kidding," Liza said. "I'm even giving up my room and sleeping in the attic. They agreed to use some of the older rooms. I'm giving them a discount rate on those."

"What the rooms lack in decor you'll make up for with fresh cheese, I'm sure," he said, looking at the bulging bag again.

Liza laughed. "It's not all cheese. Audrey gave me soap and other stuff." She suddenly looked up at him. "But this means I can't go out with you on Friday night. I have to stay and watch over things. I'm really sorry about that."

"Don't worry. I understand. What if someone needs an emergency cup of herbal tea in the middle of the night?"

Now he was kidding and making her laugh again. "Exactly. I don't expect to sleep a wink."

"How about next weekend?" he asked hopefully.

Liza was about to happily agree, then realized

that next weekend was a holiday, the unofficial start of the summer season, and she had more guests coming in.

"I'd love to but that won't work either. It's Memorial Day, and I have more guests coming."

"That's a good thing, Liza. Don't look so glum. We'll figure it out." He leaned close for a moment and dropped a quick kiss on her cheek. "You won't get rid of me that easily," he added in a softer tone.

"I hope not," she said sincerely.

BY the time the cyclists were due to arrive on Friday, Liza and Claire were ready and waiting. The upside of expecting so many guests at once, Liza realized, was that it had momentarily distracted her from the wedding plans.

The group's leader, Josh Cabot, was the first to arrive. He drove up in a hybrid hatchback with a huge bike rack on the back, and came to the door wearing a T-shirt and cargo shorts with a big blue pack over his shoulder. He was about Liza's height and very fit looking.

"What a beautiful place," he greeted Liza. "I'm beginning to think it's a good thing the reservation in Ipswich didn't work out. The club will love it here."

"I hope so. We're all ready for you, but maybe there are a few special requests I should know about?"

"Actually, there are," Josh replied. He took a folder out of his pack and flipped it open. "We have three members who have requested vegetarian meals and one who's a vegan." Liza nodded. She thought she knew the difference but was going to look it up, just to make sure.

"No problem," she said. "Just let me know their names, and I'll make a note in the kitchen."

"Then there are a few requests for nonallergenic pillows . . . and nonwool blankets."

"All the pillows are new and made of hypoallergenic materials," she promised him, "and we have plenty of cotton quilts." She should have known this group would have at least a few health nuts.

"And a question I should have asked you on the phone the other day," Josh went on. "Do you serve yogurt at breakfast and if so, is it organic?"

"Yes, and yes. Claire, our cook, has even put smoothies on the menu this weekend," Liza replied quickly. It wasn't entirely true, but it would be in a few minutes. "And we have a lot of fresh organic goat cheese products on hand. Not to mention, lots of organic bananas."

Josh looked happy to hear that. Her shopping spree had not been in vain. "How about granola, trail mix, fresh fruit—that sort of thing?"

They didn't exactly have trail mix on hand, but Liza knew there were enough varied ingredients in Claire's cupboards to whip up a quick batch of mix before Josh had emptied his pack.

"I think we're covered on all of that, and I can always run into the village center or down to Cape Light if there's anything the group needs."

Josh took his room key and grinned. "How about the weather? Can you arrange that for us, too?"

Of course she couldn't. But maybe Claire had some pull, she thought with a smile. "I'll put in a good word," Liza promised. "Welcome, and I hope you enjoy your stay and your time on the island."

"I know I will, Liza. When the group sees this place they're going to think I'm a genius."

Josh's prediction was accurate. The cycling group loved the inn but kept Liza hopping throughout Friday afternoon and well into the evening. They were an early-to-bed, early-to-rise bunch and didn't wake her in the middle of the night. But there were plenty of requests, from organic shampoo to ice packs to yes, chamomile tea.

JEN was still in bed on Saturday morning when her cell phone rang. She picked it up from the nightstand and quickly saw that it was Kyle. "Hi, honey, did I wake you?" he asked gently.

"Not really . . . I was sort of awake. What time is it?" She hadn't checked when she picked up the phone.

"Seven o'clock. I was going to call you last night, but I was stuck in the office and it got too late."

Kyle was supposed to come back to Cape Light on Friday night, but he'd been asked to stay and work so was going to fly in that morning. It seemed a long way to go just for one night, Jen knew. But they did miss each other and any time together was important. They also had an appointment with Reverend Ben on Sunday morning. At least Kyle would be able to make that.

"What happened? Did you change your flight?" she asked.

Kyle's brother was going to pick him up at Logan Airport around nine and drive him back to Cape Light. "Do you need me to pick you up? I can drive in to Boston, it's no big deal."

"I'm sorry, honey. I can't make it back this weekend at all. I thought I could manage a day, but something's come up. I've been asked to meet with some guys on the executive committee about that job opening. They want to take me and some other guys out to dinner. They just asked me last night. It was really short notice," he added quickly.

"Yeah, that was short notice. Don't they realize you have a life?" Jennifer didn't mean to sound so crabby, but she was barely awake and he was wrecking their entire weekend.

"I know, just flexing their muscles, I guess. But it's really important that I go. Otherwise they'll just scratch me off the list."

And that would be a bad thing? Jennifer wanted to say. But she knew that wasn't the right response. Kyle obviously felt honored by this invitation, and she should try to understand and feel happy for him. Besides, she reminded herself, it was unlikely that he'd get this job if there was so much tough competition. There were other, far more experienced analysts being interviewed. She had to let him feel his moment of glory, didn't she?

"Jen, are you still there?" he asked quietly.

"I'm still here," she said with a forced, bright note. "So I guess it's a real honor to be invited to this dinner. You must be proud."

"I am, I guess. I just hope I don't freeze up when the conversation gets rolling and all the other guys start preening."

"You'll do fine, Kyle. You'll probably stand out because you don't preen. Besides, all you can do is be yourself."

"Ain't that the truth," he said with a laugh.

"You know what I mean. You work so hard and you're always well prepared. I think all you have to do is be you, and they'll see how smart and amazing you are."

"It's good to have you in my corner, Jen," he said, his voice sincere now. "If their opinion of me is even half of what yours is, I'll be fine. You're the best."

She could tell her encouragement had helped him. That was the important thing, she reminded herself.

"So I guess you won't be back tomorrow. I'll call Reverend Ben and change our appointment to next weekend. They won't keep you there over Memorial Day, will they?"

"Reverend Ben . . . Oh, Jen, I'm sorry. I completely forgot."

"Don't worry. I'll explain the situation to him. He'll understand."

"Thanks, Jen. I'll try to call him during the week, too," Kyle said. "And I'm glad you understand. You know I want to be with you this weekend, but this is something I'm doing for our future. It could be very important for us."

"I know. Really, I understand," she assured him.

Do you really think you can get this job? she nearly blurted out. But Jennifer held her tongue. He had already told her that it was unlikely. Highly unlikely. She didn't want to sound negative and critical. It would seem as if she didn't believe in him and wasn't on his side.

"Don't worry, honey. I have plenty to do. I won't even miss you," she added in a teasing tone.

"You won't? I'll miss you," he said with longing. "I'll call you tonight if I don't get in too late."

"You can call late, that's okay. I want to hear how it goes."

They talked a few more minutes before Kyle had to go. He had to be at his desk by the usual time, even though it was Saturday. He was working so hard, but he seemed to thrive on it.

Was this what she had to look forward to once they were married—Kyle being swept up and preoccupied with his job all the time, and asking her to understand?

She quickly put the thought out of her mind. Everyone was tense before a wedding. Maybe this new interview situation was just Kyle's way of distracting himself from his own anxiety. She knew he had no doubts about walking down the aisle, but he had to be a little nervous. That was only normal.

She decided to let him talk about this possible promotion as much as he wanted. She wouldn't worry about it. If he ever got the offer—and there was such a small chance of that happening—Jennifer was sure Kyle would still want the same things she did. He would never want to leave Boston and their hometown behind. Not when he really thought about it.

ABOUT half of the cyclists left on Sunday afternoon; the other half checked out on Monday morning. Liza and Claire began working on the rooms to get the inn in shape for the next wave of guests who were coming for Memorial Day weekend.

While Liza was grateful for the sudden spurt of occupancy, it was still a demanding schedule and left little time to keep up with the Bennet wedding. Though Sylvia had been discouraged from stopping by on Saturday, she still managed to call and e-mail every day, and usually more than once. Would the tent hold another two tables? Could Liza enter all of the wedding info on a website for out-of-town guests? Could Liza find napkin rings that coordinated with the silverware? Could she get a crystal vase for the flowers on the altar? (Cut glass was fine but Sylvia was not a fan of pressed glass.)

Some of these requests were so trivial that Liza wondered if Sylvia was really just trying to share her own anxiety. She knew that Sylvia was having trouble finding a mother-of-the bride dress. Which was in a way a blessing for Liza, since it kept the mother of the bride out shopping and not underfoot at the inn.

Liza only had a few more reservations scattered in the book for the weeks prior to the wedding. After Memorial Day she planned to focus totally on the wedding—unless some other huge group called at the last minute.

Meanwhile, Daniel was steadily working his way through Sylvia's list. Due to the other jobs he had going, he wasn't able to stop by every day, but Liza always managed to spend a few minutes with him when he did show up at the inn.

Sometimes they had coffee or lunch together in the backyard. Some days, there wasn't even time enough for that. The brief moments in his company always left her feeling happy and hopeful. But their time together also left her longing for more.

Daniel didn't reschedule their date to go out dancing, and Liza wasn't sure what to make of that. Had he changed his mind or simply forgotten? Liza decided that once Memorial Day weekend was over, she would figure out some diplomatic way to remind him. A night out with Daniel would be the perfect way to celebrate the inn's sudden spurt of popularity.

Chapter Ten

THERE weren't that many people in church on the Sunday of Memorial Day weekend, Jennifer noticed. She guessed that many families were away for the holiday. She still enjoyed the service, especially with Kyle sitting beside her. He had returned on Friday night, just as he'd promised, and would be in Cape Light until Monday afternoon when he was going back to New York. The sanctuary was dark and cool while outside the morning was bright with sunshine. Jennifer had grown up attending this church and had always found it a peaceful, restful place. She enjoyed Reverend Ben's sermons, which managed to mix insights about the Scripture with lessons from everyday life and even a bit of humor.

Kyle looked as if he was listening closely to the sermon, but Jen could tell he was a bit tense and tired. He needed a break from work. She hoped this long weekend would feel like a mini-vacation, with time to play golf and tennis, to visit the beach and go out on his parents' sailboat. They had a short meeting with Reverend Ben scheduled for after the service, then they planned to spend the day on the beach, taking a break from the wedding mania.

How could New York, with its traffic and crowds and not a green sprig in sight for miles, compare with a place like this? Cape Light felt like a resort town in the summer. There was no contest, as far as Jen was concerned.

Reverend Ben gave the final blessing, and the sanctuary quickly emptied out. Jennifer and Kyle waited in the back row while the reverend spoke to the members of the congregation as they filed out.

"What are we talking about today? I think we covered all the big topics," Kyle said quietly.

"I think we're up to planning the ceremony. The reading we want, the music and all that," Jennifer said. "But maybe he still needs to check if we're ready to get married."

"Then this will be a very short meeting. I couldn't be any more certain of that." Kyle picked up her hand and wound their fingers together.

A short time later, they were sitting with Reverend Ben in his office. They sat side by side on a couch and he took a seat in an armchair.

"Jennifer, Kyle. How nice to see you both," he greeted them. "So, the big day is getting close. You'll be married in—what is it?—about three weeks from now?"

"Three weeks exactly," Jen said. "June nineteenth."

"Don't worry, I have it marked on my calendar, I won't forget," the reverend promised with a smile. "You know, in all the times we've met, I've been meaning to ask you, any reason for the brief engagement?"

"It doesn't feel brief to us, Reverend," Kyle answered. "We've been dating since high school. We knew we wanted to be together forever, pretty much from the start. We were just waiting for Jennifer to finish college, or we would have gotten married even sooner."

"I suspected that was the reason, Kyle. I just wanted to hear what you would say. I've known you both since you were children," he reminded them. "And I know that you've been in a relationship a long time. In fact, I commend you both for getting the hoopla out of the way quickly. Not that a marriage shouldn't be celebrated," he quickly added. "It's one of the most important days of your life. But I find that there's often great thought given to the food, the music, and flowers—and not as much to the awesome task of opening your hearts to each other and truly merging your lives. What about preparing your heart and spirit for such a sacred, momentous step? Do you think that you're prepared in that way?" he asked solemnly.

Jen felt a bit awed by the question. "I do," she said quickly. Then had to laugh at her own answer. "I'm sorry . . . that sounds as if I'm up on the altar already, doesn't it?"

Kyle smiled at her and squeezed her hand. "Practice makes perfect."

"But I really do," she insisted. "I feel as if Kyle knows me completely and loves me, no matter what. I feel as if I can tell him anything and share the deepest secrets of my soul. I trust him totally and I couldn't imagine making a life, or having a family, with anyone else in the entire world."

Kyle was quietly smiling at her. He looked proud and even a little overwhelmed by her speech. "I feel the same as Jennifer does. I feel totally loved by her, even though I'm not perfect," he added with a grin. "I know she knows me and accepts me for how I am, and she sees qualities that I sometimes don't even see myself. I know I can be honest with her. Even if we disagree. I know we'll have disagreements, but I trust that we can figure things out. I believe that we'll be happy together and our love for each other will only grow as the years go by. I have to marry Jennifer. I can't imagine sharing my life with anyone else."

Reverend Ben nodded thoughtfully. "I hope you can remember those words when it's time to write your vows," he said with a smile. "It sounds as if you two have a close relationship based on respect, honesty, acceptance, and trust in one another. Marriage is not easy. I know you've heard me say that before. I'm sorry for repeating myself, but it's one of those truisms that you can only understand by firsthand experience. Too often young couples enter into marriage with expectations that can only disappoint them."

"What kind of expectations?" Kyle asked.

"Expectations that they love each other so much, they'll never disagree or argue. Expectations that the other person is perfect. Well, that's not possible. Or that their lives will follow a certain, predetermined plan. It's only natural to make plans. I'm sure you have plans for your future married life—where you're going to live and work. When you might start a family," he added. "But God might have other plans for you.

In fact, I can almost guarantee it. That's when the going can get tough," Reverend Ben warned.

Jennifer considered Reverend Ben's words. They did have plans, and she hoped that their plans worked out. Was it wrong to think that way?

Kyle had been talking a lot the last two days about this position in New York. Would this be her first challenge in their marriage? Was this God making His own plans for them—or was this a challenge for Kyle, to learn to put their married life above his career and personal ambitions?

"Jennifer, did you want to say something?" Reverend Ben's voice broke into her rambling thoughts.

Jennifer felt flustered. She looked up at the minister, his kind, encouraging expression and clear blue eyes. Part of her wanted to talk about Kyle's interviews for the job in New York, but another part of her didn't want to. She hadn't told Kyle she wanted them to talk to Reverend Ben about it. Maybe he would feel ambushed, and it would make things even worse.

Now Kyle was looking at her, too. "What is it, Jen? Is something the matter?"

"Um . . . no. I'm fine. I was just distracted for a moment," she said. "I'm sorry, please go on with what you were saying, Reverend."

"I was about to say that, just like any relationship, marriage is a journey that you take step by step, day by day. It isn't a static, stationary place that you just arrive at on your wedding day. As if you were stepping down off a train with your family and friends on the platform to meet you. It's more like you're getting on the train together and leaving for an amazing journey. One that is partly uncharted," he added.

Kyle turned to her and picked up her hand. "We're going on a journey together, Jen. Just you and me. And we don't know where we'll end up, but we'll be together."

Jen felt Reverend Ben watching her reaction. She forced a smile but was finding the entire conversation unsettling. She had the sinking feeling that she knew what Kyle was thinking. A feeling that was confirmed by his very next sentence.

"We might end up in New York," Kyle told the reverend. He glanced at Jen with an excited smile. But she couldn't smile back. She knew she looked nervous and quickly looked away. "I'm up for a position in my firm's New York office. I've had a lot of interviews, but I won't know for a week or two if I'm even a finalist."

"It's sort of an honor to even be asked to apply," Jen added. "But Kyle says it's pretty unlikely he'll get it."

Kyle glanced at her, looking a little hurt, she thought. But that was what he'd told her, hadn't he?

Reverend Ben glanced at Kyle, then looked back at Jennifer.

"That will be a big change. For both of you. How do you feel about moving to New York?" he asked Jennifer.

Jennifer's heartbeat quickened. She didn't know what to say. She wanted to tell Reverend Ben how she really felt about the idea—she didn't like it. Not at all. She wanted to tell both of them. But she finally decided that it was best to bring this up with Kyle first. When they had some time alone.

If she brought it up in here, it might seem as if she was blowing everything out of proportion. Kyle would say, "Why didn't you just tell me?"

And on top of all that, he hadn't even been offered the job, Jennifer reminded herself. So she would seem very silly and maybe even petty, complaining about something that hadn't even happened.

"We haven't really discussed it. We haven't had time," Jennifer replied finally. She knew she wasn't answering Reverend Ben's question.

"I see." Reverend Ben nodded and leaned back in his chair. "You know, sometimes when a couple is planning a wedding there's a certain pressure to act as if everything is perfect, like a picture in a magazine—or a fairy tale come true. But we all know that's rarely the case. Nothing is perfect. And that's okay." He paused. "I'm sure you remember what we were talking about last time—about couples communicating. And how denying or brushing aside troubling matters can cause even bigger problems later. So if anything is bothering you, Jen, it's fine to talk about it. That's what we're here for," he reminded her with a kind smile.

"Is something bothering you, Jen?" Kyle turned and looked into her eyes.

Jen paused. Then decided she didn't want to be the one to bring this up.

"I'm just a little distracted today, with all this wedding stuff going on," she said. Kyle seemed satisfied with that answer.

But Reverend Ben didn't seem to believe her, she thought. Not entirely. "Well, if there is something on your mind, or if something comes up that you'd like to talk about, please give me a call. We can meet anytime."

Jennifer met his glance and nodded. Should she do that? No, Jennifer decided. There was no use telling Reverend Ben what was bothering her. She had to talk to Kyle.

"I really am a long shot for the job. But it is fun to think about," Kyle admitted. "I guess we'll just figure it out as we go along."

"Yes, you will. It might not be easy to work it out. But try to remember, it's the big decisions that challenge a couple, that help the relationship strengthen and grow. And my door is open if you ever need any help sorting things out."

"Thank you, Reverend. That's good to know," Kyle replied. Jennifer finally smiled again. She had been incredibly relieved to hear Kyle admit his chances of getting the job were unlikely. It was just fun for him to think about. So why look for even more conflict and tension? There was really no reason to panic. Not yet. For goodness' sake, they were just about to get married. She just wanted to get over that hurdle first.

"So, now that I've told you all you need to know about marriage," Reverend Ben said in a humorous tone, "let's talk about the ceremony a bit. . . ."

Jennifer was glad for the change of topic. The ceremony was something she could talk about easily.

The meeting went on for another fifteen minutes. Then they left Reverend Ben's office with a booklet to help them plan their service.

"So, what do you think now?" Jennifer asked as they walked across the village green to Kyle's car. "Still want to get married?"

Kyle pretended to consider the question a moment. "I think we should give it a try. I'm not afraid of a few bumps in the road. Are you, Jen?"

She shook her head. "Not at all. What would life be without a few bumps? Very boring." She thought again about the New York job. That was not a bump in the road, she thought. It was more like a cavernous pothole. One that might swallow them whole if they tried to cross it.

They sat side by side in Kyle's convertible as he started the engine. She glanced at him. He'd told the reverend they hadn't really talked about what they would do if he did get the job. Was this a good time to have that conversation? Or did Kyle really believe he had so little chance, it wasn't worth talking about?

She glanced at him, wondering if she should be the first to say something now that they were alone.

"Jennifer?"

She turned to him. "Yes?"

"Do you want to go right to the beach, or should we stop someplace for lunch first?"

"I've packed up some lunch in the cooler with the cold drinks. I think we have everything."

Kyle smiled and started the engine. "Okay then, we'll stick with our plan."

"Fine with me," Jennifer said. She sat back and slipped on her sunglasses.

There would be a good time to talk to Kyle about this moving to New York problem, Jennifer reminded herself. She didn't need to feel guilty about not bringing it up in the counseling session. Maybe she could talk to him out on the beach today. Or even tomorrow, before he went back to the city.

The last thing she wanted to do on such a

beautiful day was cause some huge fight over something that might not even happen. They'd had enough little arguments lately about all this wedding business—more guests, more bridesmaids. And they still hadn't even decided on the food yet.

She just didn't want to start haggling about this, too. Not when they had so little time together.

Kyle could find out this week or next if he was a finalist. He might even be eliminated, Jennifer realized. Which meant they could get into a big heavy talk about this today, or a fight even, and it could all be pointless.

She glanced at Kyle, driving toward the beach and looking as if he didn't have a care in the world. The wind ruffled his thick fair hair, and the blue sky seemed a perfect backdrop for his handsome profile.

She decided to wait and see what happened. This could all blow away, Jennifer thought hopefully. Like the high white clouds in the summer sky overhead.

AFTER handling the big group of cyclists, Liza and Claire fairly breezed through hosting seven guests over Memorial Day weekend. This was a much different group, two older couples, traveling together, and a thirtysomething couple, with their four-year-old daughter.

Avery was the little girl's name, and she carried

around a stuffed cat named Wally all weekend and even placed it in a chair at the table while she ate. Claire made Wally a plate of miniature fish-shaped pancakes, served on a tiny china saucer, which delighted both Avery and her parents. And everyone else in the dining room, Liza noticed.

"That's why we like to stay at lovely inns like this one. It's the personal touches that make a trip so pleasant and memorable," the little girl's mother said when they checked out.

"Thank you. We try," Liza said sincerely.

She did try and was learning this golden rule better every day. Luckily, Claire was already a natural at it. She was so empathetic, considerate, and observant. She almost knew what a guest wanted before the guest did.

Both the cycling group and the Memorial Day weekend guests had been blessed with beautiful weather. It seemed as if the rain was on a timer, Liza thought, like a sprinkler system. The last visitor had barely turned onto the main road when the rain started falling on Tuesday morning and continued for the rest of the week.

"The rain has to fall sometime," Claire said. "Or we won't have any flowers in June."

Liza knew she meant for the wedding,

Liza didn't mind the rain either. She had a lot of catching up to do in her office and with the wedding plans. It was better not to be tempted outside by a sunny day.

The only downside to the rain was that Daniel didn't come.

Most of the work he needed to do at the inn was outdoors and a rainy day like this was a good time for him to do inside work at other jobs, he explained to her over the phone.

"I'll be back in a day or so. I'm sure I'll be done with that list before the wedding, so don't worry," he added.

"I'm not worried," Liza replied. *I just miss you,* she wanted to add.

They talked for a few more minutes. Liza felt distracted, wishing Daniel would ask her out again. She dropped what she thought was a broad hint, telling him that she didn't have any guests booked at the inn for the coming weekend, or the weekend after that. "It's so nice to suddenly have all this free time," she even said at one point.

But Daniel didn't get the message. Or he did get it but chose to ignore it.

After Daniel hung up, Liza quickly checked the weather forecast on her computer. Showers off and on until the weekend, maybe even through the weekend. At this rate, she'd never see him again.

Unless she took the initiative, she realized. After all, it was the twenty-first century. She could call Daniel back and ask him out on a date. He might even like that, she thought.

Then again, knowing Daniel, he might not.

Liza felt a bit stuck on the question and wandered into the kitchen to fix a cup of tea.

Claire was working at the table, measuring out a cup of brown sugar that she then added to a big metal bowl.

"What are you making?" Liza asked as she put the kettle on.

"Banana Crunch Muffins. I thought I would make a batch and put them in the freezer, in case we get another invasion of bicycle enthusiasts."

The cyclists not only liked bananas but any food that included the fruit. They had practically inhaled Claire's banana pancakes, bread, and muffins.

"Good idea. Everybody loves them."

Everybody . . . including Daniel, she suddenly remembered. In fact, he'd said those were his favorite among Claire's list of delicious confections.

"Can I help?" Liza asked. "I'd like to see how you make them."

"I'd be happy to show you." Claire smiled at her. "Put on an apron and you can take charge of this bowl."

Liza didn't often ask to help Claire with the cooking. The kitchen was Claire's domain, and she rarely seemed to need any help. Besides, Liza wasn't much of a cook. But since coming to the inn—and being around Claire—she'd become more interested in what went on in the kitchen.

She was particularly interested in this recipe, because the confection would give her the perfect excuse to see Daniel; she could even say that she had a hand in the baking.

The two women worked together, mixing ingredients and preparing a double recipe of batter. The pans came out of the oven and cooled on racks at one end of the long table. The sugary, buttery, nutty scent was nearly overpowering.

Claire sat at the table, waiting for the last trays to finish while Liza washed up the bowls and utensils. "We ought to taste test at least one before we put them in the freezer," Claire suggested.

Liza turned from the sink and smiled at her partner.

"Absolutely. We want to make sure they meet our high standards."

"All in a day's work," Claire agreed. She rose and put the kettle back on for more tea, then set out two china plates and cloth napkins, placing a small vase of rosebuds in between, making the table look as pleasing as if she were setting it for guests.

It didn't really take much to make life a little more pleasant and even luxurious, Liza thought as she sat down with Claire to enjoy the product of their labors. It was small moments like this one that made her so happy she had stayed here and so glad she had Claire to share the work—and fun—of running the inn.

Claire cut her muffin in half and took a bite. "I was a little heavy-handed with the cinnamon, but they're not bad," she said after a moment.

Liza tasted hers. "It's perfect. I love the extra cinnamon—gives it some kick."

"Kick? What does that mean exactly?" Claire asked curiously. "I hear it on the cooking shows. But is that really something you want food to do—kick you back when you bite into it?"

Her interpretation of the term made Liza laugh. "You know what it means. You're just pretending you don't."

Claire's eyes twinkled over the edge of her teacup. "I have no idea what you're talking about."

After their enjoyable break was done, they packed up the cooled muffins for the freezer. "I'm going to save a few of these for Daniel," Claire said, as if reading Liza's mind. "He does love them. Will he be coming back to work soon?"

"He can't work on the repairs with the rain. He'll be back when it clears," Liza told her. "Maybe I'll just drop them off at his house. So they don't get stale over the weekend." Liza said this as casually as she could while she wiped off the table.

If Claire guessed Liza's secret agenda, she gave no hint. "Good idea. I'll put the package right over here, next to the coffeemaker."

Liza just gazed at the package of muffins, her

ticket to a much-longed-for visit with Daniel.

You are obviously head over heels with the man, she told herself, *if you were willing to spend a few hours in a hot kitchen just to create an excuse to see him.*

Was there still any question about that?

CLAIRE left early that afternoon, soon after the kitchen was set back in order. Liza had a quick nap, a bite of dinner, then showered and changed. She didn't want to look as if she had spent hours in front of the mirror. That would be too obvious. But she did want to look attractive. It was a fine line.

She finally settled on a pair of good jeans and a peasant-style cotton top. She put on very little makeup, but she did blow out her hair and wore it loose.

That will have to do, she decided. He'll be so interested in the muffins, he won't even notice the outfit.

She headed for the far side of the island. The drive to Thompson's Bend seemed shorter this time. Liza turned down Hasty Lane and soon arrived at Daniel's cottage.

His truck was parked in front, and the windows glowed with golden light. He was definitely in there, she decided, even though it was a Friday night.

She suddenly lost her nerve and sat behind the

wheel, undecided about actually turning the engine off. The paper bag of baked goods on the passenger seat beside her suddenly seemed a dangerous, even terrifying, sight.

Was it too pushy to just drop over like this? Was she assuming too much?

Liza took a deep breath, recalling how warm and even sweet Daniel had been acting toward her lately. There was no reason to think he wouldn't be pleased to see her.

After a few deep breaths, Liza gathered her courage again, shut off the engine, and got out of her car, taking the bag of muffins with her.

She forced herself to walk up the path. It wasn't raining any longer but the air was so heavy with mist, it might as well have been. Liza could actually feel her thick hair curling up around her face and brushed it back with her hand. She stood at the door, straightened out her blouse, then rang the doorbell and waited, practically unable to breathe.

When Daniel didn't come to the door immediately, she nearly dropped the bag by the door and ran back to her car.

But then she heard the sound of his footsteps, and the door swung open. He stared at her, looking totally surprised.

"Liza? Hey . . . what's up? Is something wrong?" he asked with concern.

"I'm fine. Everything's okay," she said quickly.

Her voice came out a little squeaky, she realized. Like Minnie Mouse. Ouch. This was more awkward than she had imagined.

He didn't say anything for a long moment. His expression was unreadable. "Would you like to come in?" he asked, as if suddenly remembering his manners.

"Um . . . okay. But I can only stay a minute."

Why did you say that? Even if he wants you to stay longer, he won't ask you to now.

She stepped into the foyer but stood near the door. "Claire and I spent the afternoon baking for the freezer. We made some muffins. She put them aside for you, and I thought I'd drop them off— so they wouldn't get stale."

Now you've made it sound as if the muffins were from Claire.

Does Claire want to date him, too? a chiding little voice asked her.

Daniel took the bag and looked inside. "Banana Crunch, my favorite. Thanks. Thanks a lot. They look delicious."

He seemed pleased, yet something was a little off in his reaction. He seemed to be trying hard to say what he knew he should say, the things she wanted to hear. But she could tell he was really thinking and feeling something else altogether. He was honestly not that pleased to see her here and felt uncomfortable, even with his favorite dessert in hand.

"Would you like to try these with me?" he asked politely, holding out the bag. "I'll make some coffee or tea?"

"Um . . . no. No, thanks. I think I've had enough for one day," Liza said honestly. She quickly glanced at her watch. "I've got to get going anyway," she insisted, though she really had no other plans.

"You do? Are you sure?" He didn't believe her, she could tell. He knew very well that she had come all this way just to see him.

But Liza stuck to her story. "I'd love to hang out, but I really have to go," she insisted, feeling more embarrassed by the second. "Some other time maybe."

"Sure, some other time." He met her gaze, his expression serious. "Thanks for the dessert. I appreciate it."

"That's all right." Liza tried hard for an offhand tone. "See you when the rain stops, I guess," she said, heading for the door.

"The forecast says it should stop tonight. So I'll be by sometime tomorrow." He followed her to the door and opened it for her.

"Whenever you can make it is fine. I'm sure you have a lot going on besides my place," she said, unable to look him in the eye. "Good night, Daniel."

"Good night." Daniel stood on his porch, watching her walk to her car.

Liza focused on starting up the vehicle and pulling away. She tried not to look back at him but couldn't resist one swift glance. He stood on the top step in the porch light, his hands dug in his pockets. He looked thoughtful and sad. She had no idea why, but there was no other way to describe the expression on his handsome face.

"What a dumb move that was," she scolded herself out loud as she drove away. "You should have known that."

Maybe he was in the middle of something and was irritated by the interruption. Or maybe he just hated when people dropped by unexpectedly. Some people were like that. She should have guessed he would be that type.

Whatever the reason, she had clearly overstepped his boundaries. When she thought again about his serious, sad expression it made her feel sad, too. And she didn't even understand why.

JUST as Daniel had predicted, on Saturday the sky was clear and the world bathed in hot sunshine once again. The change in the weather made no difference to Liza. It was still cloudy and dismal in her heart. She dragged herself out of bed, feeling tired and low.

Claire was down in the kitchen and had already made coffee. Even though it was Saturday and there were no guests staying over, she had told Liza she would be by in the morning to work in her vegetable garden. Despite her own desolate mood, Liza was grateful for the company.

She took a cup and sat at the table. Claire had set out a plate of muffins and Liza pushed it away, as if the innocuous baked goods were now the enemy and the source of all her disappointment.

Claire, who was finishing her own cup of coffee, seemed not to notice the gesture. "I guess Daniel will start working again now that the rain has passed," she said.

"I saw him last night, and he said he would be back if there was clear weather."

"Oh, that's good."

Claire was very adept at avoiding questions that might be too personal. But Liza found that she wanted Claire's opinion on the previous night's disaster. The housekeeper had known Daniel a long time. Maybe she would understand why he reacted that way.

"I brought Daniel the muffins last night. But he seemed annoyed or something. Not annoyed exactly," Liza corrected herself. "He was perfectly polite. But it was awkward. I was sorry I went over there without calling him first."

"Perhaps you caught him in a bad mood."

"It seemed more than that. And Daniel doesn't really have too many bad moods, at least not that I've noticed."

"I think Daniel is a very private person," Claire said. "He's not the type who enjoys unexpected company."

"Yes, I know. I should have realized that. I don't know why I didn't. Wishful thinking, I guess." Liza sighed. "I thought we were past that. I must have been fooling myself."

Claire was quiet for a moment. She sipped her coffee.

"Not necessarily. These situations are seldom a straight march forward. Usually, they're more like a dance—one step forward, two steps back."

"Maybe, but it seemed more like Daniel was taking several steps back last night . . . clear out of reach," Liza admitted. "You know him, Claire. What is it, really? Is he hiding something in his past that I should know about? I'm starting to worry."

"I think just about everyone on Angel Island has a story to tell, a reason that brought them here. Even you, Liza," Claire reminded her. "As for Daniel, it's up to him to tell you."

"Audrey said the same thing, more or less."

"You asked Audrey about him?"

Liza nodded. "I was telling her about our date, and it just came out. All she would say was—"

Liza suddenly felt her breath catch.

Daniel stood in the kitchen doorway. She had no idea how long he'd been there. Claire must have left the front door unlocked, as she always did in the morning. Daniel was so accustomed to coming here, he rarely knocked.

Liza felt sick to her stomach. What had she done now?

"Daniel, good morning. I didn't even hear you come in," she said quickly.

Claire glanced over her shoulder. "Hello, Daniel. Would you like some coffee? Help yourself."

"Thanks. I will." He walked over to the coffeepot and filled a mug. Liza thought he sounded angry, but she couldn't really tell for sure.

He turned with his coffee in hand and gave her a look.

He had heard the entire conversation; she was sure of it.

"I just wanted to drop off a receipt for supplies." He reached into his shirt pocket and left a receipt on the table. "I have some extra help today so we can catch up. I'd better get out there and get them started. See you later, ladies."

Then he walked out the back door without even glancing at her.

Liza felt perfectly awful. She wanted to run up to her room, pull the covers over her head, and start the day over again, as if none of this had happened. In fact, she wanted to start from yesterday morning when she got the brilliant idea of surprising Daniel at his house—she desperately wanted someone to tell her what a stupid move that would be.

If last night's surprise visit hadn't ruined everything, then this situation put the last nail in, she thought.

Liza turned to face Claire. She had to ask. "Do you think he heard us talking about him?"

"Perhaps," Claire said honestly. "But Daniel's a reasonable man. He might be mad, but he'll get over it. Sometimes a situation like this can be a good thing," she added. "It can get people talking to each other more honestly."

"Oh, Claire, you can find the bright side to anything," Liza said.

"That's because the good Lord always provides one, if you look hard enough."

Liza didn't answer. She wanted to believe that, but it was hard sometimes to be so positive. Like right now, for instance.

IT wasn't hard to avoid Daniel for the rest of the day. She had a lot of phone calls to make about the wedding, and she also had to make a trip up to Newburyport to pick up sample tablecloths for the Bennets' approval.

The bride and her mother had finally decided on the wedding colors. Jennifer had prevailed with her choice of creamy white, pale pink, and lavender. Liza quickly got to work on the decorations, flower arrangements, and table settings.

As Liza drove back from Newburyport late that afternoon, she wondered if Daniel would still be at the inn. She hoped that he had left and she wouldn't have to face him again so soon.

But as she came up the drive, she saw him packing up his truck. There was no avoiding him.

She grabbed the box of tablecloths from the backseat and headed toward the house. Daniel stood at the back of his truck, waiting for her to pass. She couldn't tell from his expression if he was still angry.

"How did it go today?" she asked, trying hard not to sound overly chipper.

"Just fine. We made some good progress." He glanced at her a moment, meeting her eye, then peered into the back of his truck and moved a ladder to one side. "How's it going with you? What's in the box?"

"Tablecloths. A complete collection of samples for the Bennets to choose from."

"That sounds like fun."

"Oh, it will be," she replied in an equally dry tone.

She waited, wondering if he was going to say anything more. He seemed so distant, it was painful to her.

She wished she knew what to say. Her conscience suggested telling the truth. But she couldn't get her nerve up to ask him point-blank if he'd overheard her conversation with Claire and was mad at her for talking about him, complaining about him, actually. She just couldn't.

"Daniel . . ." she began. She paused and took a deep breath. "Are you okay? Is anything wrong?"

"Nothing's wrong," he said simply. "I'm just tired. I'm spreading myself too thin. I've taken on too many jobs, and the rain last week set me back."

She looked up at him. He did look tired but she knew in her heart, that wasn't it.

He knew it, too.

"I need a good night's sleep," he said finally, his tone of voice still flat and distant.

"Yes, maybe you do." She didn't know what to say after that. They seemed to be stuck in emotional gridlock. "Well, have a good evening," she said after another awkward pause. "I'll see you on Monday, I guess," she added, realizing it was Saturday, and he could have asked if she was free to get together that night if he really wanted to.

She turned quickly and headed for the house.

"Good night, Liza," he called after her. But she didn't turn around again.

Liza entered the inn and dumped the box of linens on the love seat in the sitting room. She had a sinking feeling in the pit of her stomach. Claire had left for the day, and there was no one to talk to. Liza considered calling Audrey, but she didn't want to bother her and, in a way, she didn't really want to talk to anyone right now.

She just wanted to be alone and get a good night's sleep.

But Liza did not get a good night's sleep. She didn't get much sleep at all, wondering and worrying. She decided that when Daniel returned on Monday, she would take the initiative and confront him with an honest, air-clearing conversation.

For better or worse. It had to be done.

She had messed things up so badly between them already, it couldn't get any worse. Could it?

Chapter Eleven

LIZA was up and dressed very early on Monday morning. She watched and waited for Daniel's truck, unable to start any of her usual work at the inn until she settled this situation.

Claire kept giving her curious glances, but Liza didn't want to confide in her about this plan. Maybe when it was all over she would tell Claire that she had taken her advice.

"Are the Bennets coming by this morning?" Claire asked.

"Sylvia is coming this afternoon, to look at the tablecloths," Liza replied. She picked up her cereal bowl and placed it in the dishwasher.

"Let me know if you'd like me to serve lunch,

or tea," Claire said. "It would be no trouble at all."

"Thanks. I'll let you know."

Just as Claire took out some cleaning supplies and headed upstairs, Liza heard a truck coming up the drive. She walked into the sitting room and glanced out the front window. Her pulse was pounding, as if she had just finished a series of sprints. But when she saw the truck, she breathed a bit easier. It wasn't Daniel; it was his crew. They must be starting work earlier than he was today, she realized.

She went to her desk in the little office area of the sitting room and got started on her own work while part of her remained tuned to the sounds outside. Over an hour later, when Daniel still had not arrived, Liza decided to go outside and ask his crew when the boss was coming.

"Daniel won't be here today," one of his men reported. "He had to deal with some problem at another job, in town. Need to ask him something? I can call his cell phone."

"That's okay. I was just wondering. I have his number if I need to call." Liza forced a smile and returned to the house.

This could be a coincidence. I shouldn't panic, she told herself. *Daniel told me he has a lot of work going on right now. Just because he misses one morning working here, it doesn't mean he's fallen off the face of the earth.*

She was dying to call him but stopped herself. That would be exactly the wrong thing to do right now. *Just more of the same anxious behavior that's gotten you into this mess to begin with.*

Liza wondered how she could distract herself from this latest distressing turn of events. She picked up the phone and called Sylvia Bennet.

"Hi, Sylvia, it's Liza. I have some free time this morning if you'd like to get together a little earlier than we planned."

"Good idea. There's still so much to do, and it's already June sixth, less than two weeks to the wedding, Liza. Can you believe it?"

Sylvia was in fine mother-of-the-bride form today, Liza thought. Her voice rose higher with every word.

"There are still loose ends to tie up, but I'm sure we can get a lot done today," Liza replied, trying to sound as calm and organized as possible.

"Yes. I'll plan to stay a few hours and we can just plow through."

"Good idea," Liza said, "I'll see you soon." She hung up the phone and prepared for the meeting. No sense sitting around sulking all day over Daniel. It might be difficult to be with Sylvia for hours on end, but at least she would be doing something productive.

Jennifer was clothes shopping with her best friend, Megan, for her honeymoon trip, so Liza was alone with Sylvia for most of the day. Which was exhausting. But Sylvia approved the cut-glass crystal vase that Liza had found for the altar, and they settled on the table settings and favors and agreed that Liza, who had studied calligraphy in college, would hand-letter the seating cards.

After Claire left that evening, Liza had a light dinner and decided to head upstairs to her room to read a little while in bed and go to sleep early. She hoped she was tired enough so that she wouldn't toss and turn again, thinking about Daniel.

As she started up the steps, she heard her cell phone ringing and realized she had left it in the sitting room. She went back down again but missed the call by the time she located the phone. She saw Daniel's number on the call list and went to her voice mail to retrieve the message.

"Hi, Liza. It's Daniel," he began. "I'm sorry I didn't get over there today or call to check in. There's a problem with a big job I have going in town, a porch on one of the old historic houses. You know, there are a million regulations about what you can and can't do to restore them. Anyway, it's complicated, and my guys made a big mistake the other day. I have to be there to watch things, and I guess I won't be back at the inn full-time until this is done. But my crew will handle everything for you and keep going with the list. You don't have to worry."

He paused. She thought that was all he was going to say. Then she heard his voice again. "I'll try to get back to check up on the work," he added. "If you have any problems or questions, just call me. I'm really sorry it worked out like this. I'll see you soon."

Liza had a sinking feeling in her chest. She felt he was apologizing for more than sending his crew to finish her work and not coming himself. He was apologizing for disappointing her and just about breaking her heart. He had to realize that was what he was doing.

She felt totally and irrevocably brushed off. A giant lump welled up in her throat and turned into tears as she slowly climbed upstairs, heading for her bedroom again.

She had been hoping all day that her fears were groundless, but she knew an Arctic blast when she felt one. Daniel just broke up with her. Even though they were never actually a real couple.

Funny how that can happen sometimes, she reflected. All this time, she had been fooling herself. She had felt a lot more for Daniel than he ever felt for her. And now he was running away. That was unmistakably clear.

Liza felt so bleak, she dropped down on her bed in the darkness and closed her eyes. Tears slipped down her cheeks, and she didn't even bother to wipe them away.

. . .

LIZA felt as if she hadn't slept a wink all night. She finally gave up around daybreak, pulled on some running shorts and a T-shirt, and headed down to the beach for a walk.

She had always been an early riser as a child. Her parents used to call her the human alarm clock. Peter had not been that way at all but Liza soon realized one person in her family did share the trait, her aunt Elizabeth. When Liza was visiting in the summertime, she and her aunt would often walk the beach early in the morning, sneaking out of the inn very quietly, careful not to wake the guests. They would walk across the road and down the steep path and set out for a sunrise adventure.

Sometimes they wouldn't talk at all, merely pointing out interesting sights to each other—a horseshoe crab or a jellyfish, unusual shells or a giant piece of driftwood washed up on the shoreline.

Sometimes her aunt would be in a talkative mood, inspired by the crashing ocean waves. Aunt Elizabeth used to say that the ocean could heal just about anything that ailed you.

"Why, your body is over ninety percent salt water, Liza," she would point out in her pseudoscientific way. "It's only natural that we feel better by the sea, that we feel energized and refreshed. And calmer and happier. Just looking at the ocean, so constant and limitless, makes you feel connected to something much greater, don't you think? The beauty and power of the natural world, its intricate design, is practically proof that God exists. And you realize that you are part of a much bigger picture, and you can trust in the essential goodness of things to carry you along. Just the way the ocean will support you if you just relax and let your body float."

Liza recalled those words now as she looked out over the sea and tried to capture the feelings her aunt had spoken of so often. Doing your best and letting God do the rest, Claire might say. There *was* something comforting and healing about the sea. Liza did feel a bit better walking here in a rhythm with the waves. The rushing water couldn't wash all her troubles away, but the beach walk did help her get some perspective on her romantic woes and ready herself to face the day.

Liza had been walking for quite a while and was just about to turn around when she noticed a lone figure a short distance down the shoreline, a fishing pole and gear in one hand. He turned and waved to her, and she recognized Reverend Ben. She waved back and walked up to meet him.

Reverend Ben often came out to the island to fish, fly casting off the shoreline, though in the many times Liza had met him on the beach, she had never once seen him catch anything. But he told her he enjoyed fly casting for its own sake, and it helped him relax and take some time for himself.

"Hello, Reverend. You're an early bird today," Liza greeted him.

"So are you," he returned with a smile. "How are things at the inn? How are the improvements coming along?"

"Slowly but surely," Liza reported. "As you know, we're going to have a wedding there soon."

"Yes, of course. Kyle and Jennifer. Not much time left now. I'll be there. As you already know," he added with a smile.

"Jennifer told me that you've known them both all their lives. It must be amazing to have blessed them both as babies and now, officiate at their marriage."

"It is amazing," he agreed. "It reminds me how quickly time passes, and how thankful I am to be a minister, privileged to have a role in the lives of my congregation at these important moments."

"They're a sweet couple, too," Liza added as they walked along. "I've enjoyed getting to know them. All that energy and optimism . . . and romance," she added with a smile.

Jennifer and Kyle were the very picture of a young couple in love. At least Liza thought so. She felt a wave of nostalgia, recalling how, before her divorce, she, too, had been euphoric and optimistic about relationships.

And then she had let herself feel that way again with Daniel—until she crashed from that lovely cloud.

Reverend Ben seemed to sense a change in her mood and glanced at her. "Young love is a wonderful thing," he agreed. "But there are many kinds of love, Liza. As many as there are stars in the sky. But all love comes from God. Love is an expression of God's spirit and His love for us, His creation. We must cherish and honor it, wherever and whenever we find it."

They walked along for a few minutes more, and Liza parted with him to walk up the path to the inn. It was still very early, and the entire island seemed shrouded in soft, early morning light like a gauzy veil. The world was eerily silent, except for the sounds of birds calling to one another in the treetops and the occasional braying of goats in the Gilroy meadow.

Liza thought of Jennifer and Kyle again. And about her relationship with Daniel.

She did hope the young couple's love would stand the test of time. They were such a sweet pair and seemed so well suited to each other. They had certainly known each other a long time and had a deep commitment and a strong bond.

Had she found love again with Daniel? She had really started to think so. Now it seemed those feelings would never be realized. But maybe Reverend Ben had been saying that there were many ways to love someone and keep them a part of your life.

Liza hoped that was so. The idea of not having Daniel in her life at all was devastating. It made her feel so bleak and empty, she could hardly bear to think of it.

LIZA had been working outside most of the day with her laptop, cell phone, files from the wedding, and a stack of papers and bills spread out on the wrought-iron table behind the inn. Late in the afternoon, Jennifer Bennet appeared at the back gate. Liza hadn't expected the bride today but was happy to see her and grateful for the distraction. Jen had brought along another young woman whom she introduced as "Megan Riley, my very best friend in the entire world and my maid of honor."

"Technically, I'm a matron of honor," Megan said, waving her left hand so Liza could see her wedding ring.

Liza remembered now that Sylvia had mentioned Megan. The two young women had met in grade school and were living mirror lives. Both had studied to be teachers, and Megan had just married her high school boyfriend and was living in Cape Light.

Jen didn't even need to tell Liza that she and Megan were close friends. It was evident from the way they talked and exchanged glances. The young women even looked similar, though Megan was not as tall as Jen and had chin-length dark hair.

"I never realized that there were so many types of tablecloths," Jennifer said. She dropped the paper carton on one of the wrought-iron chairs. "The one we liked best is on top with a sticky note. I'm sorry we took so long to figure it out."

"That's all right," Liza said. "I never realized there were that many kinds either."

"My mom asked if you could also order another table. She's asked eight more people to come." Jennifer made a face. "Kyle was not very happy to hear about the last wave of invitations, not to mention the fact that we're going to have two flower girls preceding us down the aisle. I'm not looking forward to telling him the head count is even higher now."

Liza knew that the couple's original idea of a small, intimate wedding had long since disappeared. The guest count was now nearly one hundred and fifty. Sylvia had definitely gotten her way on that front.

"I hope I can fit another table under the tent," Liza said honestly. "A few of the guests may need to eat in the kitchen."

Jen laughed. "I'm going to tell my mother that. I'm going to act really serious, too."

"Just don't tell her I said it first." Liza smiled up at the bride-to-be. For some reason, she looked a little older today, more mature. How could that be? She met Jennifer a little over a month ago. But it was true. Liza knew she wasn't imagining the subtle transformation.

Was it her dress? A simple linen shift with a tie belt, bright blue with white sandals. It was a little more stylish than her usual outfits.

She had also changed her hairstyle, Liza noticed. Her long, flowing, college-student hair had been cut and blown out in long smooth layers that just brushed her shoulders. She was wearing a touch of well-applied makeup, too—eyeliner and a pale lipstick.

Sylvia had said that they'd spent the afternoon at a salon last week, trying out hairstyles and makeup for the wedding. Jennifer must have gotten a cut for her wedding day.

"Your mother told me that you finally found a beautiful dress," Liza said. "Getting a little close to the wire, weren't you?"

Megan rolled her eyes. "I'll say. She finally found it on Saturday, with the wedding just over two weeks away."

"I did cut it close," Jennifer admitted. "But nothing really looked right. Luckily, this dress hardly needed any alteration. As soon as I tried it on I knew it was the one."

"The same way she felt about Kyle," Megan added.

"Meg found a great dress, too. When you're in

a bridal party, everyone always says, 'Oh you can wear that after the wedding.' But you know you never will—"

"But I can definitely wear this dress," her friend said, finishing Jen's thought for her.

"It's a beautiful shade of rose pink. I brought you a little snip of the material, in case you want to match it to anything. Like the flowers or the napkins or something?" Jennifer began fishing around in her big purse and dug out an envelope.

"Thanks." Liza took the envelope and placed it with her other wedding files. She had a huge collection of swatches of fabric and snips of ribbon and bits of things that were supposed to be matched to other things. She sincerely hoped the Bennets weren't keeping close track of all these snips and swatches.

"Oh . . . and here's the final menu. We met with Molly again last night and figured it all out."

Jen handed Liza a folded sheet of paper. Liza already knew about the meeting and was glad the food order was finally settled. Molly had e-mailed her a few times, reporting that the Bennets were very nice but mother and daughter disagreed about nearly everything. Liza was actually relieved to see that even a seasoned pro like Molly was having a hard time handling them.

She scanned the selections and glanced up at Jennifer. "Very nice menu. This all sounds delicious."

"I think it will be great, even though I didn't start off wanting a lot of food and a big sit-down dinner. My parents like that sort of thing. They think it's not a real wedding if the guests don't leave at least five pounds heavier than when they arrived."

"That's what the dance floor is for," Megan said, "to work off the calories."

Jennifer and Kyle had already figured out the music. A jazz combo would play standards and popular tunes during the cocktail hour and while the dinner was served. Then a DJ would take over to play dance music for the twentysomething guests. It was another compromise with Jen's parents, who seemed to be sparing no expense on the event.

"All we have left to take care of foodwise is a cake tasting at Molly's shop," Jen said. "Poor Kyle, he didn't get to have much input in all these plans. I want him to at least have a chance to pick out our wedding cake."

"Is Kyle coming home this weekend for the taste test?" Megan asked Jennifer.

"He'll be home on June fourteenth, the Tuesday before the wedding." Jen shook her head in mock amazement. "He's actually taking off a few days before we get married to relax and get ready for our honeymoon. He didn't want to take the extra time, but I talked him into it."

"Knowing Kyle, he would have come right

from the train station to walk up the aisle," Meg said. "I'm glad he'll be home early. He must be nervous about the wedding, too, even if he won't admit it. He needs a few days off to decompress."

"I thought so," Jennifer agreed. "This way, he can really just relax until Friday night when we have the rehearsal and dinner."

The wedding party, along with Reverend Ben, was coming to the inn on Friday, June 17, to rehearse the entire program—the order of the procession down the aisle and everyone's readings. Then they were all going back to the mainland for the dinner in a restaurant.

Liza wished that everything could be in place by then, but the tent wouldn't be delivered and set up until Saturday. She hoped Sylvia understood and wouldn't get too nervous.

She would have the landscaping and the list of repairs done by then. That list of repairs . . . she hated to think of it now, mostly because it reminded her of Daniel.

"I'm trying to get every single thing done before Kyle comes back so we can spend a lot of time together," Jen went on. "We'll be going to the beach, of course. Our beach," Jen added, nodding toward the beach by the inn. "But we won't bother you, Liza. I promise."

"Don't be silly. I want you and Kyle to come and see me." Jennifer was always so cheerful and upbeat, Liza always felt good after talking to her.

"You can come up for cold drinks on the porch anytime."

Jennifer smiled. Liza knew that they were both thinking now of Jennifer's visits with her aunt.

"We'll take you up on that," Jennifer promised. "Oh, I almost forgot. I brought the piece of tulle, see?"

Liza wasn't sure what she was talking about until Jennifer reached into her purse and pulled out a long piece of gauzy pink material, a soft, sheer netting.

"Oh . . . the material to decorate the chairs. This is very pretty. Let's see how it looks."

Liza found the photo of the chair effect Jennifer wanted, and the three women worked together to copy it. It wasn't very hard. The strip of tulle was wrapped around the back of a chair and tied in a big bow, and then a fresh flower was slipped into the knot.

Liza found a rose in the garden and used it as the finishing touch. Then they all stood back and looked at the chair.

"What do you think?" Jen asked her.

Liza liked it, but she didn't want to influence Jennifer one way or the other. "It's up to you, Jennifer. It doesn't really matter what I think. You have to like it."

"I do like it," Jennifer said decidedly. "I think we should put a different kind of flower in the bow, something larger with more contrast."

"A white daisy or a spider mum would be pretty," Megan said. "It would contrast nicely with the pink bow."

"Yes, it would," Liza agreed. "Do you want this on all the chairs, or just here and there?"

Please say here and there, she thought. *I can't imagine tying these bows on one hundred and fifty chairs . . . not counting that extra table that may need to be in the kitchen.*

Jennifer considered the question, her chin in her hand. "I think . . . here and there. All the chairs would be too much. And I'll buy all the material, Liza," she offered, "if you get the flowers."

That was a relief. Liza thought she'd seen this material on a website, but it would have to be ordered and who knew how long that would take. And when it arrived, it might not even be the color Jennifer really wanted.

"Thanks. I'll order the flowers, no problem. Is that going to be the daisies or the spider mums?"

"I like the daisy idea," Jennifer replied, making this decision much faster. "I'm more of a daisy person."

"Yes, you are," Liza agreed with a smile. "We won't have the chairs here until Saturday afternoon. If you bring the fabric on Friday to the rehearsal, we'll be fine."

"Wow . . . I can't believe we're almost ready. There must be something I'm forgetting," Jennifer said.

Liza felt the same way. But she wasn't going to admit it to the bride.

She had even woken up in the middle of the night, suddenly sitting up, wide-eyed, thinking there was something she'd forgotten to order or plan for the wedding. But all of her lists were practically checked off.

"Just twelve more days until the wedding. The time will go quickly now," Liza said.

"Yes, I know. I'm happy about that and feeling a little scared, too," Jennifer admitted. "But happy scared, if you know what I mean?"

"I do," Liza replied, smiling.

Jennifer glanced at her watch. "I guess we'd better go. Do you mind if we walk through the inn on our way out? Megan's never been inside. She wants a sneak preview."

"That's just fine. Go right in," Liza told them.

The two young women entered the inn through the back door, and Liza picked up the phone to call the florist and order seventy-five—no, make that eighty—daisies for the chairs.

"LIZA is really nice. I pictured her older for some reason," Megan said. "Oh . . . this hallway is really neat. I love the stained-glass window."

"Liza's been great. I'd definitely recommend her. If she hadn't agreed to do the wedding here, I'm not sure what we would have done," Jen said. "Here, this is the sitting room. We're going to

258

have the cocktail hour inside and out. There will be little tables on the porch, too."

Jennifer went out to the porch, and she and Megan looked out over the cliff to the beach and ocean below. "What a beautiful view," Megan said. "I hope you have good weather."

"If it rains, we'll have the ceremony inside. Liza has that all figured out with the caterer. And the tent is waterproof." Jen stared out at the ocean. "I can't believe I'm really getting married."

"Me either." Megan reached over and squeezed her arm. "It's really weird. But I guess you felt the same way when I got married."

"Yeah, I did." Jen turned and grinned at her. "One minute we were getting in trouble together in Mrs. Franklin's class, and the next minute, I was helping you squeeze into your wedding gown, and buttons were flying—"

"Thanks for reminding me of that adventure." Megan stuck out her tongue at her friend. "It's just my metabolism. If we were cavewomen—"

"Yes, I know, you'd be genetically superior and would survive harsh winters. I'd never even get asked on dates."

Jen had heard this explanation before. About a zillion times. She thought her best pal had a great figure and even envied her curves, but never got tired of teasing her about the buttons that had come off her wedding dress at the very last moment. Luckily, Megan's mom was cool, calm, and handy with a needle and thread.

"Don't you feel like we're still in middle school sometimes?" Megan asked her. "Even getting married didn't really change that. I mean, you don't feel all that different afterward. I don't know. You'll see." Megan sighed and gave Jen a hug. "I'm so happy for you. And I'm so glad you'll be in Boston, and we can see each other anytime. Maybe you'll even move back to Cape Light when you get tired of living in the city."

"I hope so," Jen said. She knew her friend meant when she and Kyle started a family. Jen couldn't think of a nicer place to raise children than Cape Light. Megan and her husband, Ed, were already talking about having a baby. Jennifer wasn't quite ready for that step yet. She wanted to teach a few years and enjoy her career.

But Megan's words did push other buttons. Jennifer hadn't told anyone yet about Kyle's interest in that New York job. Not her parents, not even her best friend.

"We're so lucky to live in such a beautiful place, Meg. I've been thinking about that a lot these last few weeks, coming home after graduation. I don't think I'd ever want to live anyplace else. I mean, not really any farther than Boston."

"Me either," Megan said.

"Something's come up at Kyle's job. It's got me a little worried," Jen admitted.

"What's the matter? Is the firm having layoffs?" Megan asked with concern.

"Nothing like that. Just the opposite. Everybody thinks Kyle is terrific. You know that he's working in the New York office on a big project, right?" Megan nodded. "Well, his boss told him to apply for a job opening there. It would be a big promotion for Kyle, a real jump in his title and salary."

"Wow. That sounds . . . well, great in a way."

Before her friend could say more, Jen quickly continued. "But a lot of other analysts at his level applied for it, too. So, at first at least, there didn't seem to be much chance he would get it. But now the search committee is narrowing down the list." Jen took a breath. "And Kyle is one of the finalists."

"He is?" Megan looked upset. She didn't bother to hide it. She looked as upset as Jen felt telling her about it. "Oh, Jen. Does he really want a job in New York? Would you have to live there, or would he come back home on weekends, like he does now?"

"I'd have to go with him, Meg. We'll be married. That was the whole point of rushing the wedding. We're tired of dating after all these years, seeing each other just on weekends. He'd be my husband. We'd have to go together."

"Yes, I know. I'd do the same thing. But Ed would never want to live in New York. He doesn't even like Boston much."

"Lucky for you," Jen said. "I just wish Kyle didn't want the job so badly. I think living in Boston would be perfect. I don't see why he would ever want to leave this area, where we've got family and all our friends."

"When will they tell him?"

"He's not sure. He hopes they'll make a decision next week, before he comes home for the wedding. But some big executive is in California right now, so they need to wait for him to come back before they announce their final choice."

Megan sighed and patted Jen's hand. "Maybe he won't get it. I mean, there must be guys who are more experienced than Kyle. It's not that I don't think he's real smart, Jen," she added quickly.

"I know what you mean, Meg. Don't worry. I've been hoping the same thing."

"How long have you known this was going on?" her friend asked.

"A few weeks. I think he told me after that first time we went out shopping for bridal gowns," Jen said, thinking back. She turned to Meg. "I'm sorry I didn't tell you. I haven't told anyone. It feels good to talk to you about it. I should have told you sooner."

"That's okay. I understand. But you haven't mentioned this to your folks yet?"

"No. I've been too scared to bring it up. They're so wrapped up in the wedding plans, especially my mom. You know how she gets. If I tell her about this job thing, I'm afraid she'll just wig out on me, totally."

Meg closed her eyes for a moment, commiserating. "Sylvia will have a double stroke. I don't even want to think about it."

"Exactly," Jen agreed. "And what if Kyle doesn't get the job? He might not, you know," she added hopefully. "I would just be driving her crazy for no reason."

"I guess." Megan shook her head. "It's really tough that this all came up in the middle of getting ready for the wedding. I don't know what I would do if I were you right now."

"You would smile, put your shoulders back, chin up, and walk very . . . very . . . slo-o-wl-y. . . . And *don't* deliver your lines to the floorboards, Megan—they can't applaud, you know. They can't even hear you."

The two young women collapsed with laughter, as if they were thirteen again and still in rehearsals for the ridiculous school play that was coached by the dreadful Mrs. Shrimpton. Jen and Meg still cracked up whenever they mimicked the drama teacher's endless advice.

"I'm glad you're making a joke out of this, Jen," Megan said finally. "Does that mean it won't really happen?"

"I hope so, Meggy. I really hope so."

Jennifer's cell phone rang. She took it out of her purse and checked the number. "It's my mom. She's probably wondering what happened to us. We'd better get back."

"Ed will be home in a little while. I have to make dinner," Megan said. "Gosh, I sound just like my mother now, don't I?"

As they walked to the car Megan looked back at the inn and then out at the beautiful view again. "You definitely picked a gorgeous spot for your wedding, Jen. Whatever else happens, at least you're getting married on what has to be one of the prettiest places on earth."

"I think it is. I would really hate to move too far away from here. I don't understand why anyone would," Jen said honestly.

Chapter Twelve

THE clock was ticking down. Liza knew that every hour of every day counted now. Fortunately, whenever she got too stressed, Claire would calm her down. "It's going to be lovely. Not perfect," Claire would caution. "Nothing is perfect this side of heaven. But lovely nonetheless."

Liza wanted to believe that. But when the florist called on Saturday morning, the weekend before the wedding, and said they couldn't find the pale pink rose petals the flower girls were supposed to toss as they walked up the aisle, Liza got upset all over again.

"What color can you find? Can I pick up a sample today? I have to show the bride and her mother a sample before I can change the order. This wedding is next Sunday, June nineteenth, eight days from now," she said to the woman on the other end of the phone. "Did you notice that?"

When she finally hung up she saw Claire standing nearby, looking at her. "I have to drive up to Newburyport for rose-petal samples. It won't take long," she said glumly.

"Oh, bother," Claire replied softly. "When the bride walks down the aisle ready to give her hand and her heart to her true love, she won't notice if the rose petals are pale pink, mauve, fuchsia, or any shade in between. If she does, she's definitely focused on the wrong thing. You just do your best, Liza. Let God take care of the rest. Including the rose petals."

Liza nodded and found herself smiling. She sat back in her desk chair, feeling far less urgency about the situation. She made a mental note to remember Claire's gentle but knowing advice when the next crisis erupted.

All in all, though, Liza was actually grateful for the busyness and distraction of the wedding. It kept her from dwelling on painful thoughts about Daniel.

She hadn't realized what a big part of her life he had become, how their friendship and his presence around the inn brightened her days. She had taken all that for granted, and now she missed him terribly. She had often, secretly daydreamed about some far-off day when she and Daniel might run the inn together, working side by side. She would take care of the guests and creative touches, and he would take care of the building. They would make a good team, she thought, just like her aunt Elizabeth and uncle Clive.

She and Daniel had made a good team, without her even realizing it. She knew that much now. If only their relationship could somehow go back to where it had been—easy and affectionate, with no pressure on either side.

But Liza knew now that it could never stay that way forever. She would always end up wanting more, and Daniel would end up pushing her away again.

Almost a week had passed since Daniel had assigned his crew to Liza's list. They had only talked once. He had called from a noisy job site. They could hardly hear each other, and their brief, fractured conversation had been confined to a cracked windowpane in a third-floor bedroom.

He had dropped by once to check the work his crew was doing, but Liza had been out, driving around on wedding errands. At first she wasn't sure if that had been a good or a bad thing, but finally, she was relieved that she hadn't seen him. She still felt hurt and even angry at the abrupt way he had cut her off.

She told herself that eventually she would get over her anger. Eventually, she would be able to conceal her true feelings and have a casual, normal conversation with him. In the meantime, she missed him like crazy—his smile and his voice, the way they always laughed together, the way he listened and gave her good advice, and his funny, gentle teasing. Her heart ached remembering. So she tried not to.

She was trying not to think about Daniel on Tuesday night, just six days before the wedding. There were only a few more finishing touches and small tasks to take care of. Like writing out the seating cards for each table. Liza sat on the porch of the inn and carefully copied the name of each of the guests.

Calligraphy required both focus and relaxation; some people even considered the practice a form of meditation. Liza enjoyed losing herself in any kind of creative work; it came naturally to her. But as she worked her way through the seating chart, she felt distracted by the starry night sky and the distant sound of the ocean waves. She couldn't help but recall the night she'd visited Daniel's cottage and they'd eaten dinner at the edge of a cliff, up in the stars.

When she looked up from her work and saw Daniel's truck pull into the drive, she blinked, thinking she might be imagining it. Was it a coincidence that Daniel had come here tonight? Or had her heart simply summoned him? She'd been thinking about him so much, it certainly seemed possible.

She took a deep, steadying breath but continued with her work—or at least pretended to. He looked nervous as he climbed out of his truck and walked toward her.

Liza tried to stay calm, though her heart was thumping wildly. She met his glance for a moment as he climbed up the porch steps. "Hello, Liza," he said, giving the cards a curious look. "Are you doing some artwork?"

"Not really. Not my own work. Just writing out the place cards for the wedding."

He leaned over and took a closer look. "Very nice. How do you do that sort of writing?"

"Very slowly," she said, half joking but half serious, too.

It almost hurt to hear his soft, deep laughter.

He turned and sat down on the top step of the porch. She could only see his profile as he looked out at the water. He had been carrying a paper bag and now he placed it on a small table near her.

"Here, I brought back your pan, from that berry dessert. I thought you might need it."

The baking pan? Some excuse to come here,

she thought. But not quite as lame as Banana Crunch Muffins.

"Thanks," she said. "I forgot I left it."

"I was thinking about the night you came to my house for dinner," he confessed. "That was a wonderful night. I enjoyed it."

She was surprised by his sudden, frank admission. "Me, too," she said. But she felt a little overwhelmed and couldn't say anything more. Not without giving herself away.

"I know you must be angry with me, Liza. Disappointed at least, after that wonderful time we had together. I don't blame you," he added. "I want to explain why I've been so . . . so scarce this week."

Liza didn't trust herself to reply. She longed to play it cool and tell him he didn't owe her an explanation, but that would have been an act.

When Liza didn't answer, he looked back at the water and continued. "I've been doing a lot of thinking. About you, mainly."

Liza could hardly breathe. That could be a good sign—or a bad one. "I'm listening," she said.

"Well . . . I think you're amazing. You're the most interesting, clever, artistic—not to mention, beautiful—woman I've met in a long time. Quite frankly, you just blow me away. From the first time I met you. And every time since."

Liza felt overwhelmed by his compliments. She knew Daniel liked her and was attracted to her, but she never realized he felt quite this way. But he hadn't finished talking, and she sensed that he was about to tell her some things that would be much harder to hear.

"The thing is, even though I feel this way about you, I can't have the kind of relationship you seem to want. That I want, too, to be totally honest. Things seem to be going in a certain direction between us, and part of me wants to find out where that could lead. But it wouldn't be fair to you, because I'm not free to do that. Not right now," he said, turning to look at her again. "Maybe never."

Liza put down her work, her hands visibly shaking. She took a deep breath and tried to calm herself. She didn't want to react with hysterics or recriminations.

"Do you have a commitment to someone else?" she asked quietly. "Is that the reason?"

Daniel shook his head. "No, it's nothing like that. I'm just not able to be there for you in all the ways you want and deserve. I'm not even sure how long I'll stay here, and you seem totally committed to the place. I sort of landed here three years ago and never meant to stay even this long."

"I see." Liza was too stunned to say more. She knew there might be a conversation like this. She just never expected his words would sound so final.

Her heart was just about breaking all over again, but she forced herself to hold it together until he was gone. She stood up and walked to the porch railing. He got up, too, and stood near her, his arms folded over his chest.

"Well, thanks for being honest with me. Finally," she added, thinking he could have told her this a few months ago, before she fell so hard for him. "I guess when I didn't see you all last week, I expected it was something like this," she added. "I'm sorry if you felt pressured in some way. I'm just getting over my divorce. I'm really not looking for any sort of serious relationship right now, honestly," she added, trying to save face.

He took a step toward her but didn't try to touch her. "I don't feel like you pressured me, Liza. That's not what I'm saying at all. We have a strong connection. A real connection. I care for you, very much. If I was going to get involved with anyone right now, it would be you. I wish it could be different, I really do. But I'm not the person you think I am. Please believe me."

Liza felt only slightly gratified by his confessions of affection. In a way, it made her feel even more puzzled and confused.

She turned and faced him. "But why, Daniel? Why aren't you the person I think you are? What is it that you won't tell me?"

He stared at her, and she thought he might finally take her into his confidence.

"You can trust me," she practically whispered. "You really can."

"I know I can. It's not that, honestly. . . ." He shook his head and took a step back from her. "Please believe me. It's difficult for me, too. But this is the right thing to do—the only thing I can do. I'm sorry," he said again. Then he turned and walked down the steps and out to his truck.

Liza watched him for a moment before she realized she didn't want to watch him drive away. It all felt too final, too wrenching. She ran inside the inn and up to her room. She sat on the edge of her bed, crying. "It's just as well," she told herself through her sobs. "You've only known him for a few months and you hardly even dated."

But that was beside the point, wasn't it? Their relationship had felt important to her almost from the start. There was something real between them, something genuine and rare. And Daniel was walking away from it, cutting it out of his life as if it—as if *she*—didn't matter at all.

ON Wednesday morning, Liza and Claire got to work early, readying the nicest rooms at the inn for the Bennets' out-of-town wedding guests. Some would arrive on Friday and the rest on Saturday. Liza wanted everything to be perfect, but she felt so depleted and battered from Daniel's visit, she was hardly up to the task.

"Are you feeling all right, Liza?" Claire finally

asked. "I think you've been working too hard lately. Why don't you take a rest this morning? I can handle this."

"I'm not tired, not really," Liza said, "I'm sorry if I'm so slow, but I need to be working right now. Doing something productive," she added.

"Wedding stress getting to you again? Everything seems in order. I think we have it under control."

"It's not that. For once," Liza said quietly. She turned from dusting a window frame. "Daniel came by last night. We had what you'd call 'a big talk.'"

Claire met her glance. "Did you have an argument?"

"No, not exactly. But maybe that would have been better," Liza replied. "People are sorry after arguments. They make up and get back together. This was different. It's really . . . over," she said bleakly.

Liza told Claire more of their conversation, how she asked Daniel point-blank to trust her and tell her what was really keeping them apart. But he couldn't—and that made a relationship impossible. "I'm probably lucky he cut it off," she said bitterly. "Because I can't be with a man who won't trust me. It would never work."

"At least he came back to talk it out. I think that shows that he cares for you, Liza, and respects you."

Liza tried to take some comfort from her words. But it was cold comfort now. "I know he cares. But that makes it even harder. It's just over, Claire, completely. He was very clear. He doesn't want that kind of relationship with me—with anyone right now."

Claire didn't answer for a moment. "I'm sorry," she said sincerely. "But if a thing is meant to be, it's meant to be. Even if it's not the right timing, or there are too many obstacles. All things are possible for God, you know."

Liza recognized one of the housekeeper's favorite Bible quotes. It had been one of her aunt's, too. But Liza still had no hope of things changing with Daniel. She was getting just the opposite message from heaven right now—that her relationship with Daniel was not meant to be.

THE inn was ready, inside and out, when the first of the wedding guests arrived early Friday afternoon. Liza had dressed with care to greet the guests of the Bennet wedding, choosing a navy blue dress with white trim and pearl drop earrings.

Kyle and Jennifer had picked up the couple at the train station and driven them over to the island. Liza soon learned that they were Jennifer's aunt and uncle, who lived in North Carolina.

After the relatives checked in, Claire showed them up to their rooms. They wanted to unpack and change before lunch, then maybe take a bike ride, Liza heard them tell the housekeeper.

Even the bikes had been cleaned and serviced. Liza was determined to give Sylvia very little, if anything, to complain about.

Liza stayed downstairs with Kyle and Jennifer. She was glad to have a chance to visit with the bride and groom for a few minutes.

"I brought you the netting for the backs of the chairs." Jennifer handed Liza a shopping bag that held several rolls of dark pink tulle. "I couldn't find the light pink color. It won't match the roses in the table arrangements now."

"Don't worry, we couldn't get the very pale pink roses. I think the ones the florist found are just about this color," Liza reported with a smile. "And this shade of netting will be perfect with the daisies."

Luckily, Jennifer laughed. She wasn't a Bridezilla; she just wanted a pretty wedding day.

"I think whatever flowers you found will be fine, Liza," Kyle cut in. "It's just one day. No one's going to notice."

Liza knew he was trying to let her off the hook but his tone was definitely tense and abrupt. Wedding nerves, she thought.

"Would you like me to help you cut the strips for the chairs?" Jen offered. "Or tie the bows? Then you could just slip them on the chair backs on Sunday."

The offer was tempting, but Kyle gave out a

great sigh at the suggestion. Liza didn't want to keep them stuck at the inn on such a gorgeous afternoon. They looked like they needed some time alone, to get away from the wedding awhile and relax.

"Thanks, but I can handle it. Claire will help me," Liza added. "Why don't you guys shut off your cell phones and run off somewhere? As long as you come back for the rehearsal tonight, I don't think anyone will notice."

"Thanks, Liza. That's the best idea I've heard all day." Kyle turned to Jennifer. "Let's take a walk on the beach, Jen. We've been talking about it all week and never got over here."

For just a moment Jen looked hesitant, but her sunny smile soon reappeared and she quickly took his hand.

"Good idea. Let's go. This could be the last time we walk down there before we're married," she said. "Isn't it strange to realize that?"

Kyle nodded, but didn't answer. He waved briefly to Liza and they left the inn, hand in hand, headed for the beach below the cliff.

"*Their* beach," Liza said to herself, looking on at the romantic vision.

JENNIFER led the way down the winding, steep path, with Kyle close behind. "Watch out for the rocks," she heard him say. "You should have kept your sandals on."

"I'm all right," she called back. "I'm going for a pedicure right after this. I don't care if my feet get a little sandy."

They quickly reached the bottom. The warm sand felt good under her feet, and the hot sun beat down on her shoulders.

There was something about the beach—any beach—that instantly restored her. But this place especially.

They dropped their shoes at the bottom of the path, and Kyle grabbed her hand. "Let's walk down by the water."

They were soon walking along the shoreline, where the foamy edges of the waves slipped between their feet. The waves were warm and gentle today, rolling in and out smoothly, the seabirds dipping down to snatch morsels in the tide pools.

"It's so beautiful here. I'm sorry we've been so busy this week. We should have come here, right away." Jennifer turned to Kyle. "As soon as you got home."

Kyle nodded but didn't meet her glance. His thick hair was ruffled by the breeze. She never got tired of looking at him; he was so handsome and such a wonder to her. She could hardly believe that in two short days, they were going to be married.

"It's not your fault, Jen. I thought about it, too, but all this wedding build-up is a little crazy. Like walking into the middle of a tornado."

Jen laughed. "I know. It's been that way for weeks. I'm so glad now we decided to get married quickly. I don't know how anyone stands a long engagement. I can't wait to get back to real life," she said honestly. "Our new real life, I mean."

"Me, too." He turned to her, slowing his step. "There's something I have to talk to you about. I've been waiting for a good time. I guess this is it," he added quietly.

Jen took a breath. She had a feeling she already knew what was coming. "Is something wrong?" she asked. "Is it something about the wedding?"

She hoped that's what it was. A problem with the wedding would be easy to fix.

"Everything about the wedding is fine. It's not what we originally planned," he reminded her. "But if it's what you want and it makes you happy, then that's fine with me."

Jennifer had hoped he would say that he liked it unequivocally, but she knew he'd been overruled on more than a few matters. She'd been overruled, too, come to think of it.

"It's something else, about my job." He paused a second and stopped walking. "They've offered me the promotion in New York. The one I've been telling you about. Ted told me before I left the office Tuesday afternoon."

"Oh . . . really?" Jennifer didn't know what to say. She wanted to be happy for Kyle. He'd gone through hours of interviews and had been put through the wringer competing for this spot. But she honestly didn't feel all that happy. This was the news she had been dreading.

She stared down at her feet, unable to look at him. "I don't know what to say. Do you really want this job? Or does it just feel really good to have beaten out all those other guys?"

"I do want it, Jen. Okay, at first I think there was some macho guy thing going on. I'll admit that," he said. "But the longer I was in the hunt, the more I knew this was a great opportunity and an area where I can really excel. Ted saw that before I did, I guess. Which is why he put me forward." He let out a long breath and stared out at the ocean. "I know it feels as if I'm asking a lot of you, Jennifer. But we have to think of our future. What you just said, our *new* real life together. I know it will be a big change, but I think we should take it, Jen."

Jen felt as if she couldn't breathe for a moment. All the times they skirted around this issue, never talking about it directly. Always hoping her secret thoughts—that he wouldn't get the job—would prove true. Now there was no avoiding it. No putting it aside to think about some other day. Kyle was telling her he'd gotten the job and he wanted them to move away.

He stared at her. "Are you okay?"

"I'm fine . . . I'm just thinking," she said.

"Well . . . what do you think?" he pressed her.

"Honestly?"

"Of course. What do you honestly think?"

She swallowed hard. "I know it's a great opportunity for you, Kyle. But the timing is terrible. I think we should wait before taking on a big change like totally uprooting ourselves and moving to New York. We need to get settled first and get used to being married, not change everything about our lives all at once. It might be bad for our relationship, starting out with so much stress," she pointed out. "Have you thought of that?"

"I did. But . . . it doesn't have to be that way if you could get your mind around the fact that this is a really good thing for us, both of us."

"It's a good thing for you," she allowed. "But what about me? How is it a good thing for me?"

Kyle seemed perplexed by her response. "I know you'll have your own career, Jen. But I'll be the main money earner in the family. If I can get a leg up and do well, why . . . we can buy a house and start a family. You can take time off from teaching to stay home with our children. . . ." His voice trailed off. "Our lives are intertwined now. What's good for me is good for you. . . . Isn't that how it's supposed to be?"

She sighed. "Yes, of course. I understand all that. But . . . oh, it's just coming at me. Out of the blue, Kyle. Right before our wedding day. I don't think this is very fair."

"Out of the blue? I've been talking about it for weeks."

"Yes, but always saying you didn't have much chance to get it," she reminded him.

"Well, I guess I was wrong. They did pick me. Out of, like, a hundred other guys. And it is coming out of the blue because it's a real stroke of luck, Jennifer," he insisted. "I may not have a chance like this for a long time. Maybe never. And not at this firm," he pointed out. "Once you turn down a job like this, they don't forget. I might as well start looking for another job."

"You're exaggerating," Jennifer insisted, though she suspected there probably was some truth to what he said. "Aren't you?"

Kyle shook his head. "No. That's the way it works in big investment firms."

"Kyle, please, try to think of it from my side. Getting married is a big enough change, don't you think? I don't even like New York. We've already started redecorating the apartment, buying all the furniture. All our family and friends are here."

"I know it will feel very different at first, but you'll get used to it, Jen, and you'll meet people. I know you. You make friends on the supermarket checkout line," he reminded her.

Jennifer couldn't argue with that. She did have a knack for striking up conversations with total strangers. But that wasn't the real issue here.

"The thing is," she said, "I feel as if you've already decided what we should do, and you're not even trying to understand how I feel about this."

He stared back at her and didn't answer.

Jennifer felt backed into a corner and like she was about to burst out crying. But she held back the tears.

Why was he doing this to her? Why did this have to happen now, during the time that should be one of the happiest in her life? She loved Kyle with all her heart, but he was ruining everything with this job problem. Didn't he see that?

"Kyle, please . . . I know this is important to you. I really know that. But, can't we just enjoy our wedding and figure this out after?"

"No, Jen. I'm sorry. I wish we could. Ted really wanted me to call him with an answer by today, but I told him we didn't know yet. I have to call on Monday though, before we leave for our honeymoon. I can't keep them waiting longer. If I say I don't want it, they need to ask someone else."

She could tell the idea of that happening pained him. She hated to see him feeling bad about anything, she loved him so much. But this . . . of all things to ask her to do.

"Oh, Kyle, I don't know." Jennifer twisted away from him. "How can I leave here? What about my parents? They'll be hysterical. They won't understand. My mother doesn't even like the idea of us living in Boston. What would I even say to them?"

Kyle's expression had been understanding at first, even sympathetic, but now he suddenly looked angry, as if he had reached the limit of his patience.

"I think that's the whole problem, Jennifer. Right there. You don't want to leave your parents. You're afraid of them, afraid of what they'll think and what they'll say. They've run this whole wedding, changing everything that we wanted. And now you want them to run our life."

"That's not true, Kyle," Jennifer argued back. "But they will be shocked. If we decide to move away, your parents will be shocked, too."

"Sure they will. But we'll just tell them that it's our life. It's as simple as that, Jennifer. We make the decisions now. Not them." He moved closer and stared down at her. "I don't know . . . Are you really ready to get married? Do you even understand what it means? It's not about rose petals on the runner and all the other trimmings," he said, waving toward the inn. "It's about you and me making a life together, the one that's right for us. Not for your parents or anyone else."

Jennifer knew he was right. But she still felt totally torn.

Why couldn't the life they wanted be one that

wouldn't upset her family? It seemed as if that had been their plan . . . now this.

"Okay, I know what you're saying. But you can't just spring this on me two days before our wedding. 'Hey, Jen, we're moving to New York, like it or not.' It's not fair. Don't I get a vote here? And is this what I have to expect from now on? I have to drop any plans I ever make and just jump if something comes up with your career? I'm sorry, Kyle, but there are more important things in life than a big promotion and being asked to work in the main office."

Kyle stared at her, his face red with anger. "Is that what you really think of me? That I'm on some ego trip and I'm just walking all over you? I'm trying to make a good life for us, Jen, and all you can do is whine and complain about it. A lot of women would be thrilled to live someplace new, someplace exciting like New York. They wouldn't want to be stuck in the same old place where they grew up."

"Well, maybe you should marry one of those women. If you don't want to marry me, well . . . that's just fine."

She burst into tears and ran down the beach away from him.

"Jennifer? What are you doing? Come on, come back." Kyle ran after her for a few moments, then stopped. "I'm not going to chase you, if that's what you think."

Jennifer wasn't sure what she wanted. If she stopped and turned and went back to him, they would only talk more about this problem. But she just couldn't deal with it anymore. She just didn't want to.

She slowed her steps to a brisk pace, walking along the water's edge. The hem of her long cotton skirt was wet and dragged in the water, but she didn't care. She glanced over her shoulder and saw Kyle down the shoreline, staring after her.

She stopped and looked back. He seemed about to come toward her, then suddenly turned and headed toward the path to the inn.

Jennifer felt tears well up in her eyes again, blurring her vision. She turned sharply, walking faster along the shoreline.

Her head spun. She felt as if she were stuck in a bad dream. How could this be happening? Tonight was the rehearsal dinner. What would happen then? Would they rehearse for the ceremony, still so mad at each other? Could they greet their family and friends, pretending that everything was all right—when it was all so wrong? How could she face her parents and Reverend Ben?

A weight in her chest stole her breath away, but Jennifer pushed herself to keep going. Walking on the ocean's edge was the only thing that made sense now, the only thing that made her feel any better at all.

• • •

LIZA was on the porch, making the gauzy bows for the chairs that Jennifer wanted when she saw Kyle cross the road from the beach path. He looked tired and windblown. He walked up the drive to the inn and stood at the bottom of the steps.

"Mind if I wait here for Jennifer?" he asked quickly.

Liza put down her scissors and the roll of tulle. "Not at all. . . . Is something wrong?"

How could they go on a romantic walk on the beach and get separated? And he looked so glum, no hiding that.

Kyle sighed. He walked heavily up the porch steps and dropped into one of the wicker chairs. "Yeah, everything's wrong," he said. He pulled out his cell phone and checked the screen. "I've called her a million times and texted twice. I know she has her phone. She won't pick up and won't call me back."

"The service on the beach is bad," Liza reminded him. "The cliffs and the water and all."

"I know. But she has to know I'm calling."

"Did you have an argument?" Liza asked gently, though the answer seemed obvious.

"Yeah we did. A real . . . deal-breaker argument. She ran off, and I thought maybe she came up at a different spot on the road."

Liza felt a little knot clench in her stomach. It was just the way he'd said it.

"A lot of couples argue right before the wedding," she said in her most reassuring voice. "It's very common. Everyone is so keyed up," she told him. "I don't mean to make light of whatever you were talking about," she quickly added.

He glanced at her. "I know. But this is serious. Something important has come up with my job and I know it's not a great time, but Jen and I need to make a big decision. Even if it is right in the middle of our wedding. That's life. You don't always get perfect timing, know what I mean?"

"I think so, yes."

"I can't make life perfect for Jennifer. I think she's been a little sheltered. It's time she grew up," he added, sounding frustrated. "I've been offered a big promotion. It's a great job. I had to beat out a mob of other guys to get it, too. But it's in the New York office and we would have to live there."

"That is a big decision," Liza said. "Did Jennifer know this was coming, or was it a total surprise?"

"She knew I applied and had all the interviews. But she does have a way of ignoring things that she doesn't want to deal with. And I was afraid to sound too optimistic about my chances," he added. "So in a way, I guess it was a shock to hear I got the job. I know she's intimidated by New

York. But she's mainly afraid to tell her parents. She's mainly afraid to just live her own life. That's what's got me so frustrated."

Liza nodded. "Maybe Jennifer just needs to think about this, work it out in her own mind."

"That's what I thought at first. But I don't know now. I didn't want a big fancy wedding. That wasn't really our plan. But somehow, it just kept getting bigger and bigger. I went along at every single stage, giving in to all of Jennifer's requests. But I can't give in this time. Is this what I have to look forward to for the rest of my life? Jennifer and her parents, telling me where to live, where to work, what to do every minute?"

"Have some patience with Jennifer," Liza urged him. "Go find her, talk it out."

Kyle glanced at her, then sat stoically, looking out at the ocean. "I thought of that. But that's what I always do. She's probably expecting me to chase after her and give in to her tears and say, 'Okay. You win. We won't move to New York if you don't want to.' But I'm not going to do that. And I've waited here for her long enough, too," he said, suddenly rising from his seat.

He walked off the porch and headed for his car. Liza took a few steps after him.

"What should I tell Jen when she comes back?" she called out.

He shrugged and called back over his shoulder,

"Tell her she's not the only one who has some thinking to do before Sunday."

Liza didn't like the sound of that. Or the way Kyle revved the engine of his car and flew out of the drive.

Liza returned to making the bows for the backs of the chairs. It was hard to concentrate on bows, though, as she watched and waited for Jennifer to come up from the beach. But she never appeared.

After a while, Liza guessed that Jennifer had walked a long stretch and come up at some other point on the road. But the couple had driven out to the island in Kyle's car, and Jennifer didn't have any transportation back to Cape Light. It was certainly too far to walk.

Finally, Liza couldn't stand the suspense. She found her cell phone and dialed Jennifer's number. Liza could instantly tell from her voice that the girl had been crying.

"Jennifer? It's Liza. I just wanted to make sure you were all right. Kyle told me that you had an argument."

"I'm all right," Jennifer replied, though she didn't sound all right. "I walked for a while and then I called Megan to pick me up. I'm over at her house. . . . You saw Kyle?" she added. "Is he still at the inn?"

Liza's heart fell. Jennifer didn't know where Kyle was. That was a bad sign.

"He waited for you awhile then said he had to

go. I thought he might have gone to look for you."

"If he looked, he didn't try very hard," Jen replied. "We had a big fight and now everything's such an awful mess. . . ."

Her voice melted into tears, and Liza felt terrible for her.

"Yes, Kyle told me all about it. It is a big decision and a hard one to work out, especially now. But I'm sure you can. You just need to get together and talk."

"We tried to talk about it, but it just got worse and worse. This isn't a little thing. It's major. I don't want to move to New York and Kyle thinks we have to. He's acting like I'm so immature or something. But I think he's being selfish and unfair. You just spring that on a person two days before your wedding? I don't think so."

Liza sighed. She didn't want to take sides, and she honestly didn't know whose side she would take anyway.

"All I know is that you and Kyle love each other very much, and you've waited a long time to be married and start a life together. Whether it's in Boston or New York . . . or Timbuktu. You just have to figure that part out."

Jennifer was silent for a moment. Finally, she said, "I know you're right. I hope we can. I don't know what to say about the rehearsal tonight," she added bleakly. "I guess we should call it off. I haven't even told my parents yet what's happened."

The rehearsal . . . oh, goodness. Liza had gotten so caught up in the couple's emotional drama, she had forgotten to ask about that. She glanced at her watch. It was after three, and the wedding rehearsal at the inn was due to start at five thirty. Then the wedding party and family were gathering for dinner at a restaurant in Newburyport afterward.

"I think you should postpone the rehearsal until tomorrow," Liza suggested gently. "You and Kyle will figure it out by then," she assured Jennifer. "Do you want me to call anyone?"

"No, that's all right. Meg will help me," Jennifer replied. "I'll call you after I see Kyle. Thanks, Liza. Thanks for listening."

"No need to thank me. Just talk to Kyle," she urged her. "The sooner, the better."

As Liza ended the call, Claire walked out onto the porch, carrying the box of printed programs for the ceremony. She looked over Liza's handiwork with an approving smile.

"The bows for the chairs are coming out well," she said. "Very festive."

"They do look nice. Let's hope the effort hasn't been wasted."

"Doesn't Jennifer like the way they look?" Claire set down the box, looking surprised.

"She hasn't seen them yet. Jen and Kyle just had a big fight."

Liza explained the disagreement to Claire and related what both the bride and groom had told her.

"He thinks Jennifer is afraid to be independent of her family, and she thinks he's being selfish and unfair. Right now it seems as if they're in some sort of emotional gridlock," Liza added. "Jennifer sounds devastated."

Claire gazed out at the water a moment, then said, "I know it sounds bleak, Liza. But let's try to be optimistic. I was just paging through the wedding program. Here, have a look at this." Claire handed Liza one of the folded sheets.

Liza opened it and saw the Bible verses the couple had chosen to be read aloud at the ceremony. Silently, she began to read. "Love is patient, love is kind . . . it . . . bears all things, believes all things, hopes all things, endures all things. Love never fails."

"Love bears all things and believes all things. Love never fails," Claire said.

"Oh, Claire . . . let's hope so," Liza said, trying to share Claire's faith. "They have until Sunday to make up, that's almost two whole days from now." Liza paused and looked at all the material waiting to be cut and made into bows. "Do you think I should bother finishing these bows?"

"Of course we should finish," Claire replied. "Our job is to get ready for the wedding. The rest is up to the bride and groom . . . and heaven," she added.

She picked up a pair of scissors and a spool of tulle and got to work.

Liza thought about it just a moment. Then she did, too.

Chapter Thirteen

ON Saturday afternoon, at exactly five o'clock, the wedding rehearsal was officially called off for the second time. Not a good sign. Not a good sign at all, Liza thought.

Frank Bennet made the call to the inn. His tone was flat and drained of emotion, as if preparing himself for worse calls to come.

"We can't have a rehearsal without Kyle," he said simply. "Even if we could, it wouldn't make much sense."

"No one's heard from him yet?" Liza asked.

"Not a word. He hasn't called or sent a text—to Jennifer or to his parents. Even to his brother, who's his best man," Frank added. "Second thoughts about getting married are not uncommon, especially for young men. But running away doesn't solve anything. What he's doing to Jennifer is not fair or kind. Not kind at all," he added, his voice suddenly showing emotion.

Liza could hardly imagine the way Frank and

Sylvia were feeling right now, how upset and disappointed they must be. How hard it must be to see your daughter so full of joy, then reduced to heartbreak and confusion.

"How is Sylvia taking this?" Liza asked quietly.

"Hanging in there," Frank reported gruffly. "Jennifer told us a bit about why they fought—Kyle wanting to take that job in New York. And Sylvia didn't look happy about it, but we have to stay calm for Jennifer's sake right now. We both know that."

"How is Jennifer?" Liza added, almost afraid to ask.

"Jennifer is . . . confused. At first she was angry at Kyle for disappearing. But she's gotten over that. I know she's trying to work it out in her own mind, but she's not talking about it and we're doing our best not to pry. We just wish we could help."

Liza believed him. She understood why Jennifer was not confiding more. She probably wanted the space and privacy to deal with the issue in her own way, without the pressure of her parents' opinions and reactions. Liza hoped so, anyway.

"Jennifer believes that Kyle will come to his senses by tomorrow, and they'll be married as planned," Frank continued. "In fact," he added in a quieter voice, "she refuses to consider any other possibility."

Liza wasn't surprised. She already knew how single-minded Jennifer could be in her sweet, lovely way.

"She knows Kyle best. Let's hope she's right," Liza said.

"I hope so. I pray that she's right," Frank admitted. He sighed heavily. "If we hear anything at all, we'll call you first thing. I'm sure it's tough for you, too."

"Thanks, I appreciate that. But please don't worry about me," Liza said. "The main thing is Jennifer and Kyle."

"Yes, that's the main thing. By noon tomorrow, one way or the other, we'll have an answer."

That was true, Liza realized as she ended the call. The twelve o'clock ceremony was less than twenty-four hours away. Jennifer and her parents had made the decision to go through with all their plans. Even if they tried to cancel things like the flowers, the cars, or the caterer, it was such short notice that there would be very little money refunded to them.

But Mr. Bennet hadn't sounded concerned about the money. Clearly, what was most important to him was his daughter's happiness. Liza admired that. She even admired Jennifer's attitude, though she wondered if it was inspired by true love or complete denial of what was really happening. True love, she hoped. "Love bears all, believes all."

This was a test of those words, all right.

There were a few guests at the inn, members of Jennifer's family, but Liza hardly felt anyone was there. All the guests had left the inn right after breakfast to visit with the Bennets for the day, offering their support as everyone waited for news about Kyle. Liza didn't expect them back until very late.

Liza found herself with very little left to do for the wedding. She had imagined reaching the end of her endless to-do lists as a moment filled with relief, even jubilation. But the uncertainty of the situation had robbed her of a sense of accomplishment and any personal satisfaction. She couldn't feel relieved until she knew that all was well between the bride and groom.

She stayed up until eleven that night, helping Claire make a wedding punch, following a handwritten recipe on a scrap of yellowed paper.

"This is your aunt's recipe, written in her own hand," Claire explained. "She said that every couple who has been toasted with this punch had a long and happy marriage."

"Is that so? Does it count if you toast to them before they're married? We could mix it up and give it a try tonight." Liza sliced an orange and gave it a good squeeze over a large stainless steel bowl.

"I don't believe a toast in advance counts for much," Claire replied. "All we can do tonight is pray for the best. I know it's hard on everyone. But I pray that all goes according to God's plan for the young people, never mind our own. We don't always understand what He wants for us. But ultimately, His plan is infinitely better than anything we can come up with."

Liza nodded and reached for another orange from the large pile. She knew that was probably true. She just didn't want to imagine Jennifer's shock and disappointment if she had to accept a plan that didn't include becoming Mrs. Kyle McGuire.

LIZA had set several alarms but woke on Sunday morning before any of them went off. She had only managed to get a few hours of restless sleep. She got out of bed, reaching for her cell phone to check the messages. No calls at all. Liza's heart fell. It was too early to call the Bennets again, but she knew she would have to at some point, later in the morning.

It was dark out, owing to the early hour. But the sun was not likely to shine at all today, Liza realized. The sky was low, a layer of thick gray clouds hanging over the shoreline and sea. Just like the wedding, the weather for today had been hard to predict. Forecasters had all said showers would come, but they weren't sure when. It looked like sooner rather than later, Liza thought. *Just what we needed.* She pulled on jeans and sneakers, ready to serve her guests breakfast, receive the many deliveries that would come, and help Molly set up.

Liza glanced at the gauzy floral dress that hung on the back of her bedroom door. She had set aside time to dress up for the wedding later in the morning but now wondered if there would be any use for that outfit at all.

WHILE Claire served the guests breakfast, Liza put finishing touches outside and throughout the inn and dealt with the flower delivery. She also found a moment to call the Bennets. Sylvia answered the phone.

"I'm just calling to see how everything's going," Liza said.

"No word from Kyle, which is what you're really asking," Sylvia said tartly. "If anyone knows where he is, they're not telling us," she added. "I'm ready to call the whole thing off. Why subject ourselves to the humiliation? But Jennifer insists on going through with it. So that's what we're doing. We'll be there by eleven, just as we planned."

"Thank you, Sylvia. I hope things change by then," Liza offered.

"Join the club," Sylvia said sadly.

Liza hung up the phone, feeling a pang of sympathy for her.

With all of Sylvia's concerns about Jennifer's

wedding day, Liza was sure the mother of the bride had never imagined this problem erupting. It made a water stain on the dining room ceiling look completely inconsequential.

Plus there was the added pain of watching Jennifer disappointed and yes, even humiliated in public, if Kyle actually left her standing at the altar.

The florist's truck was just driving away when Molly's vans arrived. Liza walked down from the porch to meet her in the drive as Molly climbed down and pulled open the side doors.

"Any sign of the groom?" Molly asked. She was dressed in a black top and slim black pants, as was the rest of her crew.

"I checked in with Sylvia a while ago. No word. But the Bennets say no change in plans."

"All right then. The show will go on. I give them a lot of credit," Molly added. "I'm not sure what I would do in their shoes."

"Me either," Liza agreed. She checked her watch. It wasn't quite nine. "We have a little over three hours. I guess Kyle could turn up by then."

Molly made a stack of white boxes filled with frozen hors d'oeuvres. "Yes, he could. I also know some great charities where we can donate all this food if the wedding is cancelled. Not that you need to tell the Bennets that right away."

"I understand," Liza replied. Molly wasn't exactly pessimistic. But she was practical.

Liza helped Molly get settled, then went upstairs and dressed. When she came back down again the wedding guests staying over at the inn were sitting in the front parlor, dressed in their finery. They seemed content watching the musicians who were to play during the ceremony unpack their instruments.

The Bennets soon pulled up in a long white limousine. Liza felt a clutch in her heart as they got out. Frank came first, followed by Sylvia and, finally, Jennifer, trailed by Meg and two young women in very similar dresses. They had to be the other bridesmaids, Jennifer's cousin, Elena, and her college roommate, Carrie, Liza realized.

Jennifer was wearing her glamorous makeup and a hairstyle that made her look like a fashion model. While the women walked toward the inn, Frank went to the back of the car and took out a big garment bag, which he carried with care, draped across his outstretched arms.

The sight was touching and Liza hoped with all her heart that all this care and preparation were not in vain. But time was running short. So short . . .

As Jennifer approached, Liza could see she'd been crying. She looked like a puffy-eyed, forlorn-but-determined princess.

Liza's heart went out to her.

"Good to see you, Jennifer." Liza gave her a

quick hug. She wasn't sure what else to say. "Come on upstairs. Your room is ready."

"Great. I'd better put the gown on. It's getting late," Jennifer replied.

"Yes, it is." Liza quickly agreed with her, then glanced at Sylvia. Jennifer's mother gave Liza a look and shrugged. Obviously, no one was willing to state the obvious: It seemed highly unlikely that the wedding would take place as scheduled—or that the wedding would take place at all.

Liza turned and led the way upstairs. She had prepared a suite on the second floor for Jennifer and her bridesmaids. The rooms and private bath were ready, complete with cold drinks, snacks, and bouquets of white roses.

Jennifer, Meg, and even Sylvia, all looked very pleased with the room.

Liza felt relieved. "If there's anything you need at all, just let me know."

"We will, Liza. Thank you. Time to get the bride dressed now," Sylvia said with a quick smile. She began to unzip the garment bag that held the gown.

Liza shut the door quietly, leaving Sylvia, Jennifer, and her bridesmaids to continue through the wedding rituals. As if by completing all the steps, it might somehow conjure the groom, she thought. An "if you build it, they will come" attitude. If only Kyle would heed the call.

She glanced at her watch. Perilously close to high noon.

As Liza came downstairs, she heard the sound of many voices and found the inn full of wedding guests. A young woman approached her, leading two little girls by the hand, one on each side. The woman bore a striking resemblance to Jennifer, what Jen might look like in twenty years or so, Liza thought. The little girls were also dressed for the bridal party. The flower girls, she realized.

"Jennifer and the bridesmaids are all upstairs, second door on the left," Liza told her.

"Thanks so much. The girls are getting a little overly excited down here. We could use some quiet time before the ceremony."

"Good idea," Liza agreed. She smiled at the flower girls as they passed by, their satin dresses puffed with crinoline, flower-covered headpieces trailing ribbons. They looked like two little angels, she thought. And they could all definitely use some help from that quarter right about now.

Claire and the catering helpers were ushering the guests outside. A few of the older guests balked at the cloudy weather and chose to remain in the sitting room and on the porch. The others were offered drinks and mingled on the back patio and in the garden.

Past the beds of roses, peonies, tiger lilies, and hydrangeas, rows of folding chairs had been arranged with a long aisle in between that led to the small wisteria-covered arbor where the couple would say their vows. The arbor was just large enough to cover the wedding party and the minister.

It was already a quarter to twelve. Many guests had taken their seats. Two of the groomsmen, dressed in tuxedos, were giving out programs to guests and helping them find seats. Liza guessed that Frank had instructed them on their duties since there had been no chance for a rehearsal.

She could hardly believe it but everything was in place and it all looked perfect. Just as perfect as all the pictures of weddings she had studied online and in magazines. The tent, the tables, the folding chairs with the tulle bows and fresh flowers. The arrangements of hydrangeas and roses, the tuxedoed bartenders and waiters at their stations, the musicians tuning up. The pleasant scent of food warming, the tinkling sound of glassware and silver trays clanking in the kitchen.

"Well, the wedding has begun. With or without the groom," Claire said, coming up beside her. "It would be hard to stop it now, even if you wanted to."

"Yes, it's really happening," Liza had to agree as she looked around. All the weeks of planning, researching, worrying were over. It had all come down to this.

Trying to stop it now would be like trying to hold back the tide. But if Kyle didn't show up . . .

Reverend Ben suddenly appeared. He walked out the back door of the inn and came toward her. "Liza, may I have a word with you?"

"Yes, of course, Reverend. Let's step over here, where it's quiet," Liza suggested. She led the reverend to the edge of the garden, knowing this conversation probably needed a private spot.

"I've just spoken to Jennifer and her parents and Kyle's parents, too." Liza had not met Kyle's parents yet but knew that they, too, were members of Reverend Ben's congregation. "No one has heard from Kyle. In fact, you seem to be the last person who saw him or spoke to him after he and Jennifer parted on the beach on Friday."

"I guess so. I had no idea at the time that their argument was going to be so . . . irrevocable. I would have made sure he waited for her. Or persuaded him to go find her."

"Of course you would have," Reverend Ben replied. "Who could have predicted this? I've advised the bride and her parents—and possible in-laws—to consider calling off the ceremony. It is just about twelve o'clock," he noted, glancing at his watch. "But they want to wait a bit. Especially Jennifer. I think you may have to announce a delay."

"All right, I can do that. And I'll do what I can to amuse the guests."

"Very good," Reverend Ben agreed. "I know you're in a difficult spot."

"Not as difficult as the spot that Jennifer is in," Liza said. "It might be easier if she would just accept that Kyle's not coming."

"She still has great faith in him," Reverend Ben replied. "It's hard for me to suggest that her faith might be misplaced. I'm going back up to talk to her. Would you like to come?"

Liza wasn't sure what she could do but decided she should see Jennifer and her family again, just to ask if they needed anything or wanted her to make any change in their plans.

She entered the inn and went upstairs with the minister. The ground floor of the inn was filled with guests, who all seemed to be having a fine time, largely unaware that there was a delay or any problem at all with the wedding.

Liza knocked once on the door to the bridal party's suite. "Jennifer? It's Liza and Reverend Ben. May we come in?"

The door quickly opened. "Come in, please," Sylvia said. Her glamorous glow was mostly worn away. She looked rumpled and exhausted. "Maybe one of you can persuade her," she added.

Liza took in the scene, Jennifer surrounded by her bridesmaids, her mother, two aunts, and her father. Everyone looked very frustrated and grim. Even the flower girls, who were lying on the floor in their beautiful dresses, coloring. One of them tugged on their mother's gown. "When can we go down and be in the wedding and throw the flowers?" she whispered loudly.

Their mother waved at them, signaling the little girl to be quiet.

Jennifer didn't notice the exchange. She wasn't looking at any of them. Her expression was stoic, resigned. She sat at the dressing table, looking into the mirror, trying to repair her tearstained makeup.

Megan sat next to her on the oblong stool, speaking softly and rubbing Jennifer's bare shoulder.

"Jen . . . please. You know I wouldn't say this if I didn't absolutely have to. I'm the last person in the world who wants to see you unhappy or disappointed. But I think you just have to accept it now. It doesn't mean that you'll never marry him," Megan hastened to add. "But probably not today. It's just better for everyone if we stop hoping and waiting. We just have to accept it now. I'm really sorry, but it looks like Kyle isn't coming, Jen."

Jennifer shook her head. "I know you all mean well. But I know Kyle will be here. He would never leave me at the altar. We had a horrible fight but . . . he just wouldn't do that to me. He still loves me. I know it. I know it in my bones, in my heart. In my soul. He'll be here," she insisted, looking around at the group. "You don't have to wait with me if you don't want to. But I have to wait. Because I promised him I'd marry him today, and I know he'll come."

The certainty in her voice was unmistakable, shocking under the circumstances, Liza thought. Still, she had to admire Jennifer's trust and the way she believed in the love she and Kyle shared, despite the facts right before her eyes. But Jennifer was looking at the situation with her heart, Liza realized. A quote came to mind, from *The Little Prince*, a book her aunt had shared with her. *It is only with the heart that we can see rightly. What is essential is invisible to the eye.* Liza hoped that Jennifer was seeing rightly and the rest of them were seeing only the mere, material facts of the matter. Though at this point, it seemed the material world was about to win out.

"Is there anything I can bring you? Or anything you'd like me to do now?" Liza asked Sylvia.

"I can't think of anything. But thank you," Sylvia said sadly. "Perhaps you should tell the guests there's a delay," she added. "That might be a good idea at this point."

"Yes, of course. I'll do that right away," Liza promised.

Liza left the suite feeling great sympathy for everyone in the family, especially Jennifer. But Sylvia was also shouldering her share of the disappointment. After all her fretting and fussing over every small detail, the party was ruined by a completely unpredictable turn of events, one that Sylvia had never expected and had no control over.

Liza went downstairs and sought out Molly, who had taken over Claire's kitchen.

Molly turned from checking a tray in the oven. "The groom is still MIA, huh?"

"No sign of him yet," Liza replied. "The family is trying to get Jennifer to call it off, but she insists he's coming. We need to amuse the guests with more drinks and appetizers. And I need to make an announcement."

"Whatever you say. We'll keep it coming," Molly told her. "Good luck with your announcement. Keep it short and simple," she advised.

Good advice, too, Liza thought. Once Liza was sure that the refreshments were flowing she went over to the musicians. They had set up for the ceremony near the arbor but were not yet playing.

"I'm going to say a few words to the guests, then you need to play something lively and cheerful. Okay?"

"No problem. Trouble in paradise?" the bass player asked.

"Is that the title of a song . . . or are you asking me what's going on?"

"A little of both," the trumpet player answered. "You go ahead. We'll take our cue."

He handed Liza a cordless microphone, and she

stared at it a moment, then realized she'd better use it if she wanted to be heard.

Liza smoothed her dress and stepped up to the front of the rows of seats, which were now filled with the guests. "If I can have everyone's attention a moment. There's been a delay in our proceedings today. We're not quite ready to begin the ceremony. Please enjoy some refreshments and—"

She was just about to say "music," when a huge gust of wind blew through the garden. The wooden latticework of the arbor shuddered, and the white fabric panels of the tent fluttered wildly. The wind blew through the dining area under the tent as well, knocking over wineglasses and blowing cloth napkins off the carefully arranged tables. A few of the bow-studded folding chairs toppled over, and a woman's silk scarf flew through the air and then snagged on a tent pole.

Another gust blew Liza's dress flat against her body and nearly pulled her hair from its careful, upswept arrangement. A startled cry went up from the guests. Most of them quickly got up from their chairs and started toward the shelter of the inn.

The sky grew even darker, as if an invisible curtain had dropped. Guests were hurrying now, the women clutching at their hair and handbags, the men holding down their ties. The folded programs flew about like seabirds, and more folding chairs fell in a chain reaction, like a row of dominoes.

The tent fabric snapped and flapped again with an ominous sound. Liza actually saw the entire tent rise up a bit, straining at the metal supports and cords that held it in place. Instinctively, she squeezed her eyes shut. When she opened them again, the tent was still standing, but she knew it wouldn't stand for long.

Fat raindrops began to fall, splattering everything, slowly at first, then falling in wind-driven sheets. Now the guests were in a frenzy, women screaming out in alarm, rushing to get inside as their high heels stuck in the soft grass. The men weren't much calmer. Everyone seemed alarmed by the shimmying tent.

"Please go inside. There's plenty of room," Liza urged the guests. "There's a door at the front of the house, too," she told them, noticing a logjam at the back door.

She heard a cracking sound somewhere behind her and saw that the wooden arbor was cracked, the old latticework falling apart, a few sections held together by the thick growth of wisteria. Liza couldn't bear to watch. The beautifully arranged party was being blown to bits.

She couldn't worry about it now. She had to get everyone inside. The musicians were the last to head for the inn, carrying their instruments covered by tuxedo jackets.

But as Liza headed for the door, she saw a strange sight. It was the bride, Jennifer, pushing through the herd of guests and running outside, into the rain.

What in the world was she doing out here?

"Jennifer, where are you going? We all need to be inside now."

"It's Kyle. I saw him. Is he down here?"

Liza reached for her and grabbed her shoulders. The poor girl was so upset, she was imagining things.

"No, Jen. He's not here. Please, go back inside."

"But I saw him. From the window," Jennifer insisted. She quickly twisted around, searching the garden, which was a whirlwind of rain and blowing debris.

Liza tried to hold on to her but Jennifer pulled away, grabbing up her wedding gown and running barefoot across the lawn. Liza saw Frank Bennet and Reverend Ben pushing through the guests to get outside as well. Sylvia stood in the doorway, her hand pressed against her mouth, her eyes wide with anguish.

Frank Bennet jogged past, slipping on the wet grass in his dressy shoes. "She thinks she saw Kyle," Liza explained as Reverend Ben followed.

"I know. We were with her in the bedroom upstairs when she said she saw him from the window. Just as it began to rain." He turned to her as he ran to follow Frank Bennet. "I'm going to help Frank. I might be able to calm him down."

"I'll come with you," Liza said.

Jennifer was a few yards ahead of her father and had pulled open the garden gate. She ran out on the long gravel drive, chased by her father, Reverend Ben, and Liza.

Liza ran the fastest of the three and soon passed both men.

The drive was empty. Everyone, including the catering help, had been driven inside by the rain.

Jennifer ran past the vans and stopped. She turned and pointed. "See . . . there he is. I told you he'd come."

Liza stopped, too. There was a figure standing at the end of the drive—or was she imagining it as well?

No, there was a man, tall and lean, wearing a hooded sweatshirt and jeans. He pulled off the hood and exposed a head of thick fair hair. It was Kyle. Liza had no doubt about it now.

"Wait . . ." Liza called back to Reverend Ben and Mr. Bennet. "It *is* Kyle. Look, at the end of the drive. He's here."

Frank Bennet caught up with Liza. He looked winded and amazed as he watched his daughter run the rest of the way down the drive to meet her errant fiancé.

Suddenly, he got his second wind, an angry look on his face. "I have a few things to say to that boy. He can't just ruin everything, then snap his fingers and have Jennifer come running."

Liza didn't know what to do or say. She was sure that Mr. Bennet's anger was justified, at least partly. But she was also sure that this was exactly the wrong time for him to interfere with his daughter and her fiancé. Not if he hoped that they would finally get married.

"Hold on a minute, Frank." Reverend Ben suddenly appeared and touched Mr. Bennet's arm.

Reverend Ben was breathing hard as well but managed to capture Mr. Bennet's attention.

"I think you need to just let her go," Reverend Ben advised. "It's between the two of them now. And God," he added.

Frank turned to the minister a moment, then looked back down the drive. Liza looked, too.

The exchange between the two men had taken just long enough for the rain-drenched bride and her runaway groom to slip out of sight.

All that remained was Jennifer's long veil that had fallen off during her run and was now blowing across the lawn, like a gossamer banner.

Chapter Fourteen

JENNIFER let Kyle tug her down to the beach. She felt herself getting drenched, the rain soaking into her hair and weighing down the many layers of her wedding gown. But she didn't care. She didn't care about anything except the feeling of Kyle's hand grasping her own.

At the bottom of the hill, they ran toward the cliffs. Jennifer held her gown bunched up against her chest, trying to keep the many layers clear of the wet sand, not entirely successful.

"There's a cave along here somewhere. Remember? Let's go inside until the rain stops," he called out over the wind.

Jennifer didn't bother to answer, running quickly to keep up.

Kyle found the opening in the cliff and led them inside. It was dark but not completely, Jennifer saw. It was dry at least, though certainly damp. She walked in warily, gazing around. The cave walls were high and hollowed out from the wind and waves. The wind off the water swept in and made a low whistling sound. Kyle pulled a small flashlight out of his back pocket. "Here, this should help." He turned it on and set it on a nearby rock. Then he looked down at Jennifer and took a step closer. He rested his hands on her shoulders.

"I'd give you my sweatshirt but it's sopping wet."

"That's all right. I'm not cold. Just a total mess."

"Not to me. You look absolutely beautiful, Jen," he said quietly.

Jennifer thought the same about him. All of her anger and hurt feelings evaporated at the mere sight of him. She was thrilled that he had returned to her. It seemed as if joy were washing over everything, like a great wave. She was feasting her senses on his nearness as he gazed down at her. It felt as if she hadn't seen him for years, though it had only been two days.

"Mad at me?" he asked quietly.

"Yes, I am. I'm furious," she insisted, though her tone of voice sounded anything but. ". . . but not about the fight. I got over that. Now I'm just mad at the way you kept me waiting. But I knew you would come," she added. "I knew you would."

"I knew I would, too. I love you so much. More than I can ever describe to you. That's one conclusion I came to. I had to be alone to think things through. But you were always with me, Jen. Deep in my heart," he admitted. "You're a part of me, no matter where I go or what I do."

"You're a part of me, Kyle. That's why I never doubted you'd come back. Sooner or later."

He paused, looking suddenly serious. "I've

done a lot of thinking. I stayed out on the beach the past two days, just walking and thinking. About you and me. About our future. I can see now that it was a mistake to spring that news about moving to New York on you. Of course you would react badly. You hadn't even considered the idea of it. But I'd been thinking about it for weeks, imagining us in New York—where we would live, the new friends we'd make, and all the things we'd do. But from your point of view, the whole idea just came out of the blue and sort of trashed all our other plans for the future."

"That's it exactly. After months of talking about living in Boston and where I'd find a job and how our life would be, all of a sudden . . . 'Wait, we're moving to New York City, Jen.' It blew me out of the water, Kyle. But I did react badly," she added. "I should have been a little more patient about it and not just pulled a tantrum on you."

His eyes widened at her last comment. "You said it, I didn't."

"Okay, I did act immature, and you had the perfect right to call me on that. I knew you were applying for that job. But the way you talked about it, I never thought you would be chosen. You said so yourself. You said it was highly unlikely," she reminded him. "So I felt I didn't even have to think about it, or take it that seriously."

Kyle ran a hand through his thick hair. "Yeah, I

316

did say that. But it wasn't because I didn't want the job, or even because I didn't think I was as good as the other candidates. I just didn't want to be disappointed if I didn't get it. So saying I'd probably miss out was a way of protecting my feelings, and saving face in front of you, too."

"But you were the one they picked, after all those interviews. I really am proud of you, you know. I'm not sure I ever said that."

"No, you didn't, Jen. And that hurt a little, too," he admitted. "I did try to talk to you about the job, but you were so wrapped up in wedding plans, I'm sure you didn't hear me. And I wasn't as direct as I could have been. I was afraid to upset you. I kept telling myself the same thing—that I might not get it, so why upset you?" he admitted. "I should have been more honest from the start. I should have told you how much getting that job meant to me, instead of downplaying it. Then maybe you would have understood better."

"I think I would have," Jennifer said. "At least I hope I would have. I'm sorry I reacted so badly, Kyle. I didn't mean to hurt your feelings—or sound like a spoiled brat. I was just so focused on the wedding, it did seem like it was coming out of the blue. But I've been thinking, too, and I understand better now. I know you want to take that job, and it will be good for our future. I can't deny that. And I don't have a job right now, so I have no real ties here. Except for our friends and my family," she admitted with a small catch in her voice. "And all the furniture we ordered. But furniture can be put in a truck and moved. And I can move, too," she added, trying to make him smile again. "So I think that's what we should do."

Kyle looked down at her in surprise. "What about your parents? Did you tell them what was going on?"

"I had to tell them what was going on when we had to cancel the wedding rehearsal. But I also told them I needed to think things through and work this out on my own. And yesterday, I told them that I would move to New York if that's what you still wanted. They didn't take it very well at first," she quickly added. "Especially since you had done your disappearing act. But I think that they understand now. Or at least, they're trying to. After all, it is our life and our decision to make."

"Yes, it is," he agreed wholeheartedly. "But are you sure, Jen? You seemed so much against it before. I don't want you to have to move to New York if you really hate the idea. I sort of lost my head, but there will be other promotions. The most important thing is our relationship, our marriage."

Jennifer felt something deep inside her relax. Kyle had just said the one thing she had desperately needed to hear, and it gave her the confidence to be totally honest with him.

"I can't say I'm not nervous or even intimidated a bit by the idea. But maybe it is for the best. Maybe we should start off someplace new. Someplace that we'll discover together. Maybe that will be good for our marriage. I can get used to New York."

"I think you can, too," Kyle said. "I think we can have a great time there. But I don't want to force you to do something that will make you unhappy, something that will make you resent me. A job isn't everything in life."

"No, it's not everything. I'm so glad you've seen the light," Jennifer teased. Then her voice grew serious again. "But I understand that this job is the kind of opportunity that might not come along again for a long time. I don't want to take that away from you. If you're willing to take on a challenge, I should be willing, too. I was thinking about what Reverend Ben told us, about marriage not being a fifty-fifty deal all the time, just fifty-fifty when you average it out. Sometimes it's seventy-five, twenty-five. And sometimes, one hundred percent, zero. There are going to be times in our life when I need you to take the smaller piece of the pie," she said wisely. "But this is my turn. I'm willing to give New York a try if that's what you want and you think it's the right thing to do."

The look on Kyle's face was all the answer Jennifer needed.

He seemed speechless for a moment, looking surprised and relieved and full of love and gratitude.

"Two days ago, I never thought you'd be able to say that to me, Jen. I thought you might agree to go to New York, just to hold things together. Just so we could still get married. I never really expected that you would be totally all right with it. But what you just said . . . you really are coming from . . . well, a mature, independent place. This is really a miracle of some sort. At least, it is for me," he admitted quietly.

"I don't know about that," Jennifer said with a small laugh. "You'll need to check with Reverend Ben on what qualifies as a miracle. I will say that there have been an awful lot of people praying for us the last few days, myself included. But I am sure this is what I want," she added with certainty. "And not just because you nearly left me at the altar, pal."

He smiled down at her. "I didn't leave you there, Jen. I never would have done that. But I did keep you waiting long enough." He pulled her close and they finally kissed. A long, deep kiss full of forgiveness for past mistakes and longing for the future.

"I hope we never forget what we've learned the past few days," Kyle said. "We have to talk to each other honestly. Our love is strong enough to stand up to the hard knocks, Jen. It's a bedrock that we have to believe in. If we'd been more honest with each other from the start, this would have never happened."

Jennifer looked around at the damp cave and grinned. "Somehow it's easy to be so open and trusting out here on our beach. But we have to learn how to carry this place deep inside, and come here together whenever we need to."

"You're right, Jen. No matter where our life leads us." They gazed out at the crashing waves, their arms around each other. Jen rested her head on Kyle's chest.

"But we can come back here sometimes, too . . . right?" she asked quietly.

He laughed. "Anytime you want." He kissed her again. "How about we make a pact now, that we'll come back at least once a year. Maybe on our wedding anniversary?"

"That sounds like a plan," Jennifer agreed. She leaned back and looked into his eyes. "Small detail. We just have to get married first."

"Good point," Kyle said with a self-conscious laugh. "Looks like the rain has almost stopped," he said, gazing out at the beach. "Are you ready to face the music?"

"I'm not sure the musicians are still there. And I'm a total wreck. But ready as I'll ever be," Jennifer replied. "I wonder if anyone is still waiting for us."

"As long as Reverend Ben stayed, I think we'll be fine. Let's go find out."

The couple ran out to the beach again, hand in hand, and made their way up the steep path to the inn. Jennifer felt as if she could have just floated up the sandy hill, her heart was so light and full of love. But she felt different somehow, too. Closer to Kyle, bonded with him in a new way, even though they were not yet officially married. She knew their love had faced a test and had come out on the other side, even stronger. She felt joined with Kyle deep in her soul, as if neither of them could ever take a step now without the other.

CLAIRE was the first to spot Jennifer and Kyle, emerging from the path to the beach on the other side of the main road.

"There they are. They're coming back," she told Liza.

Liza quickly looked up to see for herself. She and Claire had just come out to the porch and begun clearing up the mess the storm had made of the little bistro tables where guests had been congregating and enjoying refreshments.

"Yes, it's them, and they're heading for the inn. Thank goodness," Liza replied. "I'd better tell someone."

"Reverend Ben," Claire suggested. "Perhaps he should be the first to speak to them."

"Right. I'll go find him." Liza went inside and looked around for the minister. She knew he'd been sitting with Jennifer and Kyle's parents, offering his support.

Liza spotted him coming out of the dining room with a cup of tea. Everyone was so chilled from the rain, Molly had to suddenly switch from cold drinks to hot. But she'd pulled it off smoothly.

"Reverend Ben, the runaway bride and groom have returned," Liza told him. "Claire and I just saw them walking up to the inn. Maybe you should be the first to talk to them."

Reverend Ben's expression brightened. "Good. I'll go right out to meet them." He put his cup down and headed out the front door.

Liza saw him intercept Kyle and Jennifer on the front lawn and then they walked to the side of the building, heading up the drive to the back of the property. She closed the door and let out a long breath.

She was glad to see them back. They looked happy and were holding hands. But that still didn't mean they were ready to get married today. Liza just hoped they were at peace with their decision, whatever it was. And at least there would be a final answer soon.

Just about everyone who had remained at the wedding—or the almost-wedding—was inside, gathered in the front parlor and the dining room. Only about a third of the guests were still there.

Ironically, it was about the same number that Jennifer and Kyle had originally planned for, their closest friends and the immediate relatives of the two families. The others had made their apologies and slipped off, either unwilling to wait to see if the couple would come back or simply feeling too uncomfortable in their wet clothes.

Molly had been kind enough to sit and wait in the kitchen with her crew, though Liza knew she didn't have to.

"Not a problem. We're booked to stay until at least eight o'clock. And I want to see how the story turns out," she told Liza.

Liza found the Bennets and the McGuires in the sitting room, talking together. She was glad to see that the two families had no animosity toward each other. Reverend Ben had brought them together the last hour or so and had helped with that, Liza was sure.

She took a breath, preparing herself to tell the families that the couple had returned. But just as she approached the group, all eyes turned to the entrance of the sitting room.

Jen and Kyle stood there beside Reverend Ben.

"We're sorry to keep everyone waiting and to cause so much confusion," Kyle began. "This isn't the wedding day we had planned or dreamed of. But the way things worked out, we really had no other choice."

"But we are ready to get married, finally," Jen

added. "And we love you all and hope you will take part and celebrate with us."

"All I can say, is 'Amen,'" Reverend Ben said, making everyone laugh.

"Oh, Jen . . . I'm so happy . . ." Sylvia burst into tears, then walked up to her daughter and hugged her close. "Your beautiful gown . . . it's a mess. It's ruined," she said with a sigh.

"Don't worry, Mom. Let's go upstairs and make some repairs. I know you can help me," Jennifer said in a gentle tone. Then she turned to Kyle with a smile. "I'll be right back."

"Fine. But don't keep me waiting too long," he teased her.

Even Frank Bennet had to laugh with relief, hearing that.

THE rain had stopped and the sun was breaking through the clouds when Liza ran out the back door to survey the damage from the storm. She would have cried—if there weren't so many people around.

The folded chairs were a jumble, the beautiful little arbor had blown apart and sat in a heap, like a pile of large pick-up sticks. But the worst was the tent, which had come loose on one side and was now half-collapsed, folded over on itself like a deflated balloon.

Where could she even begin? The wedding would have to be inside now, she thought

325

frantically. But though two-thirds of the guests had gone, there were still too many to fit comfortably inside the inn to eat and dance and generally enjoy themselves.

Molly had come out along with the catering crew, and now they began to do what they could, turning chairs upright and wiping them dry. Liza headed toward the tent, wondering what disastrous sights awaited her under the folded canvas. But she turned when she heard the sound of a truck coming up the drive.

She looked over and saw it was Daniel's truck. She felt her heart catch as he parked and got out. He walked up to the gate, then toward the tent, looking around at the property.

Liza came out from behind the tent and faced him. She was unbelievably happy to see him but didn't know how to react.

"Wow, looks like a tornado touched down back here," he greeted her.

"You might say that. Things have been turned upside down today, in more ways than one," she said cryptically.

"I was working nearby and thought you might need some help. To tell the truth, I wasn't sure some of those quickie repairs would hold up with that wind," he admitted.

"I think your repairs held up fine. It's the rest of the place that fell apart."

Liza sighed and stared at him. So he was here to

help. She wasn't going to make too much of that, she promised herself. That must mean he still wanted to be friends. After all, they had started off as friends. No reason they couldn't go backward, was there?

She would take her cue from him and try. And she was certainly grateful for his help right now. Just having him here made her feel better about everything.

"If you want to help us clean up, I'd really appreciate it," Liza said honestly. "I don't know how we can get that tent up again. Maybe we'll just have to get some of the tables out from under it?"

He glanced at the tent that looked like a broken umbrella. "I think we can give it a try. Let me nab some helpers. Some of the groom's buddies maybe? By the way, how did it go? Did the storm interrupt the ceremony?"

"Not at all. The ceremony hadn't even begun. The groom made a late appearance. A very late appearance," she added.

She started picking up paper cocktail napkins and plastic glasses that littered the lawn, and Daniel automatically helped her.

Liza quickly told him Jen and Kyle's story and how they were finally going to walk up the aisle in a little while.

"Man plans, God laughs," Daniel reminded her.

"Wedding planners plan, God laughs," Liza added with a smile.

"Let's hope this wedding planner will have the last laugh today. We can get that tent back up pretty quickly—and even the arbor for the ceremony," he added. "As long as there's plenty of food and drink, the party will be fine. And a very memorable one, at that."

"It will be for me," she promised.

A tall, brawny member of the catering crew walked past and Daniel went after him, to enlist his help with the heavy work.

She watched as Daniel headed for the tent with his new recruit. Despite their serious talk and all her heartache and disappointment, somehow she and Daniel just slipped right back into their easy banter, she noticed. They had put aside romantic hopes but still maintained an effortless understanding of each other. It seemed they couldn't wish away, or talk away, their special connection.

Liza couldn't figure it out. She didn't even feel particularly upset with him anymore. Still a little wounded maybe. But there wasn't anything to be angry about except for fate or destiny or timing in life—whatever you wanted to call it. She could be mad at that, maybe.

And a lot of good that will do you. She had no time now to figure it out. She still had a wedding to pull together, one that had been blown apart at the seams.

The strong winds that had brought the storm

blew away the clouds just as quickly. The radiant sun beamed down on the garden while a fresh breeze helped Liza's efforts to prepare for the ceremony and party.

It was suddenly ideal weather, a perfect afternoon for a wedding, she realized, with a bright blue sky and a soft, cool breeze. With the help of the catering crew, and even some guests, the yard was soon set to rights. Folding chairs stood in neat rows again in front of the reconstructed, wisteria-covered arbor.

It slanted a bit to one side, but Daniel promised it was stable.

The tent had been raised and the tables underneath wiped down and set again with plates and glassware. The carefully chosen tablecloths had to be replaced, but Claire managed to find several good linen cloths with complementary colors and patterns that looked even more interesting and festive, Liza thought. There were far fewer guests so they didn't need to worry about nearly as many tables.

Finally all was ready once again for the bride to walk down the aisle. The musicians returned to their post, and the guests began to find their seats again.

Liza went inside to find Jennifer and Kyle. On her last trip up to the bridal suite, Jennifer had been reapplying her makeup and pinning up her wet hair. Her mother and bridesmaids were drying her gown with several small hair dryers that Liza kept in the guest rooms.

The plan had worked beautifully. The gown looked hardly worse for the wear and even her veil had been rescued from the lawn.

She was such a beautiful girl, it would have been impossible for her to look anything other than ravishing. A heart full of love and joy is the best makeup in the world, Liza thought.

Kyle looked very handsome in a black tuxedo, gray vest, and silk tie. His family had brought along the entire wedding outfit in the hope that he would finally arrive. Now he had the distinction of being the only one in totally dry, clean clothes.

The bride and groom were in the sitting room with Reverend Ben and both sets of parents. Liza felt as if she was walking in on a private conversation, but the door had been left open. "Everything's ready," she announced. "The guests are taking their seats again."

"Wonderful," Reverend Ben said. "We'll be right out. Kyle wanted to speak to everyone first, though. He has something important to say."

"I'll just wait outside," Liza offered, backing toward the door.

"No, that's all right. You can stay, Liza. I want you to," Kyle said. "I need to apologize to everyone, and I've certainly made your life difficult the last few days."

That was certainly true, though Liza didn't

want to admit it. Before she could say anything, Kyle continued. "Mom and Dad, Frank and Sylvia, I want to apologize to all of you for disappearing the way I did. I've already explained this to Jennifer," he said, glancing at his bride-to-be. "I probably shouldn't have run off so dramatically. But I really needed to think some things through. Totally alone, too. I know it seemed crazy and even immature. But if I hadn't done that, maybe I wouldn't be here right now, ready to get married to the most wonderful, beautiful woman in the world."

Jennifer shook her head, blushing at his lavish praise.

"I think you all know I was offered a position in New York, and it would be a big jump for me," he went on. "I think you also know Jennifer and I had a big argument about moving there. What you don't know is that we've figured it out and decided that I will take the job and we will make the move." He turned to Jennifer and took her hand. "We'll miss you all, but we're excited to start our life together someplace new to both of us, a real adventure. We know this is a sudden change in plans and a bit of a shock. But we hope you can all wish us well and share in our excitement and happiness."

He paused and looked at his parents first. They didn't seem surprised, Liza thought. Kyle had probably told them about the job interviews so they expected this. His mother did look a little sad at the news, but Kyle's father looked proud.

Then Kyle looked at Frank and Sylvia Bennet. Sylvia was forcing a smile but actually crying. She dabbed at her eyes with the edge of a tissue. "I guess my mascara didn't have a chance today. I don't know why I even bothered," she murmured. She laughed a bit and everyone else did, too.

Jennifer sat beside her and put her arm around her mother's shoulders. "Oh, Mom, I'm sorry. But Kyle and I talked it all out, and we think it's the right thing to do. I'm sure of it."

"Yes, I know, sweetheart." Sylvia touched Jen's cheek. "I'm just being selfish. I hate to lose you so . . . totally."

Liza's heart went out to her. It had to be hard to part with your beloved daughter, an only child no less, and send her off to a whole new life, out of your care. Jennifer's marriage signaled a new stage in Sylvia's life, too, Liza realized. In her shoes, Liza wasn't sure she'd do any better.

"I won't be dishonest and say I'm happy about this," Sylvia continued. "But you're a married woman now, or about to be. And you need to make your own decisions. You're not my little girl anymore," she admitted.

"Oh, Mom . . . as if there's any chance of that ever happening," Jen replied in a loving tone and gave her mother a squeeze.

Sylvia smiled at her. "Letting go is not my strong point, I know. I just want you to be happy. That is my strong point, don't you think?"

"Absolutely. I know you'll understand—once you have time to think about it. And we'll be back up here all the time," Jennifer promised. "And you can come down to New York and we'll go shopping and—"

"More shopping? Your mother promised me that after this wedding she'd never go shopping again," Frank piped up. "Isn't that what you said, Sylvia?"

"Oh, Frank . . ." Sylvia managed another small smile. "He'll miss you, too, Jen. He's just acting tough."

"I will miss you, darling. With all my heart," Frank told his daughter. "But being a parent is a long process of letting go. I figured that out a long time ago, from when you were a baby in my arms and suddenly crawling and stumbling and then running away from me. This is your life, yours and Kyle's, and no one can tell you what to do. You need to make the decisions that feel right and live with the consequences. You both know that you'll always have us, your family, to come home to if there's ever a need. And may God bless both of you, wherever you go."

Liza glanced at Reverend Ben. He seemed pleased but also ready to move the families on to the main event. "Well, if everyone's ready now, I think we can go outside and take our places. Kyle . . . Jennifer . . . are you ready to get married?"

"Without a doubt," Kyle answered for the both of them.

A few minutes later, a beautiful piece of classical music drifted over the garden, which was bathed in late-afternoon sunshine. Liza stood at the back of the seated guests alongside Claire, watching to make sure everything went smoothly.

Kyle stood up at the head of the aisle, flanked by Reverend Ben and his best man. The two flower girls drifted down first, sprinkling rose petals.

"Aren't they adorable?" Claire said. "And no one is noticing the color of the petals," she reminded Liza.

How true. How she worried about that for no reason.

Escorted by the groomsmen, the three lovely bridesmaids, Jennifer's cousin Elena, her college roommate Carrie, and then her matron of honor, Megan, followed.

Finally, Jennifer came down the aisle on the arm of her father. Her expression was radiant with joy and a certain settled, peaceful air that made her look a bit older, Liza thought, and even more lovely.

Frank lifted his daughter's veil, kissed her on the cheek and gave her a hug.

Then Kyle took Jennifer's hand and led her to Reverend Ben. They turned and gazed into each other's eyes. Liza knew then for certain that her aunt had been right—they loved each other truly and were meant to be together, for all time.

"Don't they look perfect together?" Claire whispered.

"Yes, they do. It makes you hope that the legend of the island is true, and that all marriages performed here are forever blessed by angels," Liza whispered back.

"Yes," Claire agreed. "Especially this one."

The couple read their vows, and the traditional prayers were said. Then Reverend Ben asked them to state their intentions and both answered in loud clear voices. "I do."

Finally, Reverend Ben gazed down on them and said, "Kyle and Jennifer, I pronounce you man and wife. You may kiss the bride," he added with a small smile.

Kyle did not wait to be told twice. He pulled Jennifer close in a sweet, tender kiss while the crowd of happy guests—and even the catering crew, who was watching from the back rows—applauded.

"I love doing a wedding," Molly told Liza as the couple came down the aisle. "It always gives me such a happy, romantic feeling. I want to just run home and hug my husband."

Liza laughed at her.

"Don't worry," Molly added. "I'm going to stay until the last hurrah. I can always hug him later."

Liza was grateful for that. Molly was so experienced and capable, Liza felt she didn't have a thing to worry about from here on in. Now that the ceremony was over, a huge burden had been lifted, and it suddenly seemed possible that she could actually enjoy herself at this party.

The long wait and suspense before the ceremony had served to make the guests even more jubilant and joyful once the couple was officially wed. Daniel had been right, Liza realized. As long as there was music, good food and drink, and such a beautiful setting, the guests were happy to do the rest. Most of all, a beautiful bride and a handsome groom so much in love set the tone of the celebration.

Despite the storm's havoc, the party was still lovely and elegant, Liza thought. Everyone seemed to be thoroughly enjoying themselves as the party progressed from cocktails and appetizers to dinner and dancing.

The sun slowly sank into a rose and lavender sky and the glow of tiny white lights, strung through the wisteria and illuminating the tent, mixed with soft candlelight on each of the tables. It was an intimate setting for a small but lively group of close friends and family. The bride and groom and both of their families seemed genuinely happy. That's what mattered most.

During a short break in the music, Frank Bennet raised his glass and began to make a toast, his wife looking on in quiet approval and affection.

"Sylvia and I are very grateful to all of you for coming from near and far to help us celebrate the marriage of Jennifer and Kyle. Words can't express the fullness of my heart right now. I can only ask your help wishing this wonderful young couple great happiness and health and every blessing in their life together. To the bride and groom . . ." he concluded, raising his glass of Aunt Elizabeth's wedding punch.

Everyone cheered and clinked their glasses. Liza had found a glass and raised it in the air as well. Suddenly, from out of nowhere, someone tapped a glass to hers.

"To the bride and groom. I wish them well." She turned to see Daniel standing right next to her, sipping now from his cup. "Hmmm. This is good. One of Claire's creations?"

"My aunt's famous wedding punch," Liza explained. She took a sip of her drink. It was good, a subtle blend of flavors. "I squeezed the oranges," she added with a smile.

"Nicely done," Daniel teased her. He peered into his glass. "I haven't found one orange seed so far."

"You have to be very detail-oriented when you run a wedding," she explained.

"Oh, you excel at that, Liza, no question. So,

are you pleased with the end result? The bride and groom had you jumping through hoops for a while," he observed with a quiet laugh.

"They did, didn't they? Flaming hoops, you might say. But here we are. Not bad, all things considered."

"Not bad at all," he agreed. "I'd say, all things considered, you've done a remarkable job."

"Thanks, I'm glad you're enjoying it," Liza said. His compliments still meant a lot to her.

"I am enjoying myself, even though I'm crashing the party."

"Don't be silly. We need you here, in case anything collapses again," she teased him. "Besides, you've been hearing me go on about it for weeks. You must feel like you know the couple as well as I do."

"Well . . . not exactly. But almost," he agreed. "So, as an unofficial guest, I have a question for you."

"Yes?" Liza tipped her head back, catching his glance and wondering what this could be about.

"Would you dance with me?"

The question was surprising. The nicest surprise she'd had all day.

"I'd be happy to," she said, trying hard not to show how happy she really was at the invitation.

He took her hand and led her to the dance floor, which had turned out, after all, to be the somewhat bumpy brick patio under the wisteria that had bloomed just in time for the party.

"So you went with the brick dance floor anyway. No hazard signs posted, I noticed." He glanced around theatrically. "Dance at your own risk? No lifeguard on duty?"

"I did take out some extra insurance," Liza confided with a grin.

"She thinks of everything." He smiled and glanced down at her, then was suddenly quiet.

By some strange coincidence, the band was playing the very same song that Daniel had been humming the day that Sylvia had caught them on that very spot, pretending to be dancing.

She wondered if Daniel realized the serendipity of the moment. She glanced up at him, but she couldn't tell. She still couldn't remember the name of the song but that was not surprising. She could hardly remember her own name, distracted by his nearness and the feeling of his arms around her as they gently moved together to the music.

They danced without speaking. Liza was glad he didn't try to talk to her. She didn't really want to talk. She just wanted to focus on all the feelings and sensations of this moment and store them away in her memory.

She still felt so much for him. So much beyond mere friendship. It was going to be hard to let go of that. If she ever could.

When the song ended, Daniel stepped back. "Thank you, Liza. It was better with real music instead of my humming, don't you think?"

"It was lovely. What's the name of that song? I can never remember."

"I'm pretty sure it's called 'At Last.'"

"I think you're right," Liza replied unable to meet his gaze. "At Last." Of course that was the title. She knew she would never forget it again.

THE hours flew by and before Liza realized it, the bride and groom were departing for their honeymoon night at the Ritz-Carlton in Boston. They would take a day's rest in the city and leave for their honeymoon on Tuesday.

Jennifer hugged Liza close to say good-bye. "Thanks for everything, Liza. The wedding was wonderful, even better than I ever imagined," she said.

"I'm so glad you're happy, Jen. With the wedding—and with everything else," Liza replied sincerely.

"Thank you, Liza," Kyle said. "We appreciate all you did and all your patience and help. Now more than ever, I think there was a reason why we *had* to be married here. I'm not sure we would have made it if we'd planned to get married anyplace else."

"Oh, I didn't do that much," Liza said lightly.

"Maybe there were some angels watching over you, though," Claire added with a smile. "God bless you both and keep you forever in His sight."

Claire had been hovering in the background of

the party all night, Liza had noticed, spending a lot of time in the kitchen, too, though Molly had everything under control. Liza hadn't even noticed that she'd emerged until she stepped forward to offer her good wishes.

Then they were off, flying down the road in Kyle's sleek black car. Jennifer had promised to stay in touch and visit when she came back to the area. Liza hoped that she would. She knew that their story was just beginning, and she wanted to keep up with every new chapter.

Chapter Fifteen

IT took Liza several days after the wedding to recuperate and get the inn back in order. On Wednesday morning Molly dropped by to pick up some chafing dishes she'd left behind. Liza was on the porch, having an extra cup of coffee. She brought one out for Molly, and they sat together in the bright morning light and cool, fresh air.

"Ready to do it again?" Molly asked brightly.

"Not quite," Liza said with a laugh. "Give me a few more days, at least."

"You're getting rave reviews all over town. You know Sylvia. She doesn't hold back with her opinions."

"Good thing she was pleased with the results," Liza said.

"Better than good. It's like Internet gossip

going viral. I've already had two brides call and ask if they can move their wedding to the inn."

Liza felt her jaw drop but couldn't help it. Was Molly teasing now?

"You did . . . really?"

"Really, I did. One family has signed a contract. But the other wedding is just in the early planning stage. Would you like to meet with them?"

"Yes . . . yes, of course I would. I appreciate this, Molly. Not to mention all the help and coaching you gave me to pull together the Bennets' reception."

"My pleasure. I think we make a good team," Molly added. "And I love working at the inn. There's something special about this place," she added, gazing around.

Liza couldn't argue with that. She had always felt that way about the inn, coming here to visit her aunt and uncle. But now she saw it differently and knew it was even more unique than she'd fathomed as a child.

After Molly left, Liza finally had time to call her brother, Peter, and give him a full report. She only hit the highlights, not wanting to worry him about the blown-down tent or other potential insurance liabilities. He was alarmed enough at the mention of a storm and the bride nearly left at the altar.

"—but they finally came up from the beach when the rain stopped, and the ceremony and reception went on pretty smoothly after that," Liza concluded.

"I'm glad to hear the story has a happy ending. And the family was pleased?" he asked.

"Very pleased. They've already recommended the inn to other brides. There could be a second wedding here very soon."

"That's great news. Sounds like you're building a nice extra stream of income for the inn, Liza. Good work," he commended her.

Peter liked to talk about streams of income, as if money flowed along on little pipes in some cosmic, financial plumbing system. Liza tried not to laugh.

"Yes, weddings can be profitable, no question. But I was also really happy to see them finally get married and start their new life."

"Well, that's good, too, I suppose. But maybe that was just because it was your first wedding. Maybe you won't get that emotionally involved after this," her brother suggested.

"Maybe," Liza replied. "But I hope I do." Getting to know Jennifer and Kyle, and even Sylvia had been the best part of the experience, she realized.

After talking to Peter, Liza realized she had checked in with just about everyone close to her with the post-wedding wrap-up. Everyone except Daniel.

She hadn't heard a word from him since the

wedding and wondered now if she had merely imagined their romantic moment dancing together. Or was he in hiding again because of it? They were just friends, she reminded herself. He had made that very clear.

But deep down, that was not what she really felt or wanted.

She missed him and missed the feeling of falling in love with him. That part was real. Could they just wipe that all away, like chalk from a board, and start again? Liza didn't think so.

Perhaps it was best not to see him for a while. She couldn't win either way. If he acted cool and distant, she would feel hurt, and if he acted interested and attracted . . . well, she would feel even more confused.

She heard Claire come out on the porch and quickly turned to face her.

"Mrs. Ripley just called to confirm her reservation for this weekend," Claire reported. "I noticed there are several couples coming in."

"Yes, three couples coming on Friday," Liza confirmed. "Time to get back to business," she said, rising from her chair.

"High time, I'd say. I just started some cooking," Claire agreed with a smile.

Liza never failed to marvel at Claire's abundant energy and cheerful attitude. You would never know the older woman had worked so hard before, during, and after the wedding. Liza was in awe of her.

"Do you need anything from the store?" Liza asked. "I can run up now, before it gets too warm for the bike."

"If you don't mind, I do need a few things," Claire replied. She slipped a folded sheet of paper from her apron pocket. Liza had to smile, noticing Claire was already prepared.

Liza scanned the list. "Looks like some classic clam chowder is on the menu," she remarked. "And some scones?"

They had come to have a little game: Liza guessing the dishes Claire planned by the clues on the shopping list.

"You got the chowder, but that one is easy. I wasn't planning on scones. I was thinking of popovers, but maybe scones would be a good idea."

"Whatever you make will be delicious." Liza knew that for a fact. She tucked the list in the front pocket of her jeans and headed inside to get her cell phone, wallet, and a knapsack to carry the groceries. The bike had a basket, but it filled quickly.

A few minutes later, Liza was pedaling along toward the town center, the inn disappearing around the first bend in the main road. She passed the Gilroy Goat Farm and other neighbors. It was not even noon but already hot and sticky. Summer was here, no doubt about it. About halfway to the village center, she decided to take a break, maneuvering her bike into the shade of a large tree on the side of the road.

She took out her water bottle and took a long drink, her attention drawn by the brightly colored wildflowers that bloomed in the tall grass all around her.

She suddenly heard the smooth whiz of bikes far fancier—and more efficient—than her own and turned to see a group of cyclists flying up the hill she had just crawled along. They were soon swooping past her, like a flock of birds flying in formation, their legs pumping rhythmically at top speed.

One of the riders waved to her as he pedaled past. Liza smiled and waved back.

A cloud of sandy dust rose in their wake, and Liza watched it settle back to the road in the shimmering heat.

She wiped her mouth on the back of her arm, stored her water bottle, then took her bike up on the road again. She didn't mind traveling at her own pace, especially in this weather, and was glad she hadn't been on the road when that group passed. They were taking no prisoners.

Liza reached the island's little cluster of shops a short time later. She saw a bunch of sleek new bicycles parked in front of the General Store and realized that the cyclists who had passed her on the road had arrived—some time ago, by the looks of it. Several had come out of the store, toting snacks and cold drinks, and were ready to go again.

Liza found a space for her own bike and went inside. Marion Doyle spotted her quickly and trotted the length of the deli counter. "Hello there, Liza. We hear you had quite a shindig at the inn on Sunday."

Shindig? Liza wasn't sure when she had last heard that word. She struggled to hide her amusement. "It was a very nice party. We had a few challenges with the weather. But it turned out fine."

"I'll bet it was." Marion drew closer, practically whispering. "But I heard the groom went AWOL, and Frank Bennet had to chase him down the beach almost a mile in the rain . . . in a dune buggy," Marion concluded. She looked at Liza expectantly, waiting for her to confirm or deny the information.

A dune buggy? How did people come up with these embellishments?

"Oh, no, it was nothing like that."

Of course, there was gossip about the wedding. Especially on the island. It hadn't been the typical ceremony, that was for sure, and people were bound to tell stories. But this one seemed totally beyond belief.

"There was a delay," Liza confirmed, "but the couple was thrilled to be married. Happiest I've ever seen," she stated sincerely.

Marion leaned back and stuck her hands in her apron pockets. "That's very nice to hear. I knew that story couldn't possibly be true."

Though that hadn't stopped her from repeating it, Liza thought with an inward sigh. "It was a very happy day," she assured Marion, "happy for everyone." Liza picked up a basket to collect her groceries, then took out the list, written in Claire's neat, even handwriting. "Do you have any littlenecks today?"

"Sure do. How many are you looking for?"

"Let's see. The list says five dozen," Liza told her.

"Sounds like Claire's cooking a batch of chowder," Marion remarked. She headed toward the back of the store, where the fish was stored in a walk-in refrigerator.

Liza heard the shop door open and turned at the sound. A cyclist entered, still wearing his helmet. He was red-faced and sweating, his eyes bulging.

Liza stared at him curiously. "Is something wrong?"

"There's been an accident. Up the road, at the turn. Just as we were leaving town . . ." He was breathless and could hardly speak.

Marion came forward. "What happened? Do you need an ambulance?"

The young man nodded, unable to speak.

"Did you try the medical center? It's just a few doors down," Liza added. She dropped her basket and headed for the door. "Come with me, I'll show you. . . ."

The cyclist followed as Liza ran across the small square toward the storefront marked by a red first-aid cross.

Luckily, other riders in the group had noticed the sign and were already coming out the door.

"He's just down the road, not too far," she heard one of the cyclists say.

Liza stopped in her tracks when she saw who followed them.

It was Daniel. He ran out of the clinic behind the bikers. He suddenly glanced over at her and met her gaze for an instant. Then he turned and ran after the cyclists again.

Marion came out of the store and called to Liza. "An ambulance is coming. From Cape Light."

"Thank you," called back the young man who had come into the store. Then he turned to Liza. "I don't know why I missed that clinic. I ran right past it."

"You were upset. It's understandable."

"I guess. I'm going to follow them, see if I can help."

"Me, too," she said suddenly, and began to run alongside him.

It had turned into a hot day. The sun beat down mightily as they ran. But Liza soon spotted the cluster of cyclists gathered at the edge of the road, just past a sharp turn.

Daniel was crouched down beside the fallen rider. When he saw Liza approach, he glanced up and said, "Liza, I need your help."

Daniel looked so serious, she knew at once the man was badly hurt.

"My truck is parked in front of Daisy Winkler's shop. Here, take the keys. You'll find a black medical bag on the floor, behind the driver's seat. Bring it back as quickly as you can."

Liza nodded. She knew this could be a life-or-death matter and she ran off at full speed, back up the hill to the town center.

Marion was still in the doorway of her store and called out to her. "How bad is it, Liza? Is he conscious?"

"I'm not sure. Tell the ambulance where we are," Liza called back without stopping.

She pulled open the passenger side door of the truck and grabbed the bag. Then she slammed the door shut and ran back down the hill.

The bikers were so quiet when she approached that Liza feared the worst. *Please let him be all right,* she found herself silently praying.

Daniel was kneeling beside the injured rider, who was stretched out on his back. Someone had removed his helmet and Liza saw his eyes were closed. He looked bruised and limp, and his breathing was labored. Liza wondered if he was even conscious.

She quickly handed Daniel the medical bag.

He grabbed it and yanked open the zipper without even looking at her.

"What's wrong with him? Can you tell?" she asked quietly.

"He said his chest hit that rock." Daniel nodded toward the large boulder next to them. He looked down at the injured man and spoke in a quiet, steady tone. "It's hard to tell without an X-ray, but it looks like your trachea is pushed to one side and your lung has collapsed," he explained. "We need to release the pressure right away or you'll go downhill fast."

"D-do it," the man struggled to say.

Daniel had already taken a long needle from the medical bag. He wiped down the cyclist's collarbone area with alcohol. The injured man seemed to be fighting for every breath now, and he looked agitated.

Daniel glanced up at the other riders. "Can I get someone to hold him steady?"

The biker who had run into the store quickly knelt down next to his friend, on the same side as Daniel. Liza was on the other side.

Liza glanced down at the man. His face was pale and drenched with sweat.

"Ready?" Daniel asked. Liza and the other helper nodded. The injured man closed his eyes.

With a quick, sure movement Daniel inserted the long needle just below the man's collarbone.

Liza felt the man flinch and in the same second she heard a rush of air quickly come out. The man's body sagged with relief, even before Daniel withdrew the needle.

Everyone turned at the sound of the ambulance siren getting louder and louder. Daniel wiped the man's forehead with a clean, damp cloth. "The ambulance is here. You're going to be all right," he assured him.

His patient nodded and closed his eyes again. "Thanks . . . thanks a lot . . . I think you saved my life."

Daniel shook his head, but Liza could see he was moved by the man's gratitude.

The ambulance pulled up and the emergency medical technicians jumped out. One of the technicians took Daniel aside and spoke to him about the man's condition, while the other checked the man's vital signs.

Moments later, the injured rider was loaded into the ambulance, which quickly drove off, headed for Southport Hospital.

The rest of the cyclists seemed stunned. Gradually, they picked up their bikes and rode off—at a much slower pace than the speed at which they'd come, Liza noticed.

Daniel and Liza walked back up to the General Store.

"Will he be all right?" Liza asked.

"Yes, I think so," Daniel said.

"That's good. It all happened so fast. It was pretty exhausting," Liza admitted.

They had reached the benches where Liza had left her bike.

"Want a lift back to the inn?" Daniel offered. "I could toss your bike in the back of the truck."

"Thanks, that would be great," Liza said. She steered her bike over to the truck, and Daniel lifted it into the bed and closed the gate. Then they both climbed in, and he started the engine.

They drove along in silence for a while, both lost in their own thoughts. Liza felt shaken by the event but she guessed that Daniel was even more shaken, taking charge in such a stressful, traumatic emergency.

"So . . . what was wrong with the guy again? You said it so quickly, I didn't really understand," Liza admitted.

"When he was thrown off his bike, his chest hit that big rock. You'd call that blunt trauma. Like being struck with a heavy object. That caused his lung to collapse, but more importantly, air was coming into the lung space from a small leak in his chest with each breath, which it normally shouldn't do. That caused his trachea, his windpipe," Daniel translated, "to shift to one side. When that happens the extra pressure on the lung doesn't let the body get enough oxygen, and you asphyxiate. And very quickly, too," he added.

"He would have died right there," Liza said,

understanding. "Which is why you had to treat him so quickly."

"Exactly. Pneumothorax will sometimes be very minor and resolve itself spontaneously, but a tension pneumothorax needs immediate care. Needle aspiration, or aspiration with a tube inserted into the chest. Sometimes surgery," he added.

He spoke in an automatic tone, sounding as if he were reading out of a textbook he had memorized. A medical textbook, she realized.

"Do all EMTs know how to do what you just did?" she asked, turning to look at him. "I mean, diagnose that man on the spot like that and then treat him so quickly—for something that seems pretty rare, too."

"Probably not," he said quietly. "I guess it was just lucky I was at the clinic."

She could tell he was trying to sound offhand about the matter. But Liza wasn't ready to let it go. They were nearly at the Gilroy farm and would soon be at the inn, she knew, and it might be a long time before she would have another chance to talk to him.

"He was lucky," Liza agreed, "lucky that you're not the typical volunteer EMT. You're a doctor, Daniel, aren't you?"

Liza saw Daniel's entire body tense at her question. For several long moments he didn't answer. He just drove, his eyes fixed on the road ahead. Liza was beginning to wonder if he'd heard her when he said, "Yes, I have a degree in medicine."

Liza waited for him to say more, but he didn't.

"That's all right. You don't have to tell me anything more if you don't want to. I've had time to think about things, Daniel. I've decided that I don't want to lose your friendship over this. If that's all it can ever be, then so be it. I'd rather be friends with you than not have you in my life at all. So if you need to keep your privacy about certain parts of your life, that's just how it has to be," she said finally.

Daniel turned to her. "Oh, Liza . . ." He swallowed hard and looked back at the road. "I've been thinking, too . . . and I've been an idiot. About a lot of things."

He pulled the truck over to the side of the road and turned to her. "I don't want to lose you from my life either. The last few weeks, trying to stay away from you, has taught me that," he admitted. "And when I saw you today, when I came out of the clinic, it seemed like more than a coincidence. It felt like you'd been sent there to help. You, out of everyone I know," he said quietly. "The procedure I did wasn't easy—the needle has to go in at exactly the right place, and I haven't done it in a long time and didn't know if I could. But having you there helped," he admitted. "It probably helped me save that guy's life. And since you were there, you figured out what I couldn't tell you. Well, at least part of it."

Liza felt a quiet thrill at his words. She had given him strength to do something important today, and he had missed her. He didn't want to end their relationship.

Suddenly the truck cab seemed far too small a space to contain the happiness and hopeful feelings rising up inside her.

"Why don't we go down to the beach and take a walk? I need to clear my head a bit," she said.

"Good idea." They hopped down from the truck and Daniel came around to her side. He took her hand and they soon found a path down to the shoreline.

Though it was a hot day, there was a strong breeze off the ocean that felt immediately refreshing.

Daniel glanced down at her. "No more questions for me?"

Liza shook her head, determined not to push. After what they'd just been through, she was happy just to walk with him like this and just . . . be.

If he wanted to be closer to her, he would have to come in his own way, in his own time. If he wanted to open his heart, he was the only one who had the key.

"Well, I have one for you," he said. "How have you managed to put up with me? I was defensive and hurtful to you, disappearing and not being honest. You didn't deserve that, Liza. I'm truly sorry for acting like that."

Liza was surprised by his apology. "Thank you for saying that. But it's all right now, honestly. In fact, I have a feeling you don't want anyone else to know what you told me, that you're a doctor. Don't worry. I can keep a confidence."

"I'm sure you can. You're the only one on the island who knows," he told her. "I've never told anyone, not even Reverend Ben. It's hard for me to talk about. There are things that happened I'd rather forget," he added.

Liza had guessed as much. She glanced at him but didn't reply.

"I did think about telling you, Liza. A million times. I even wrote you letters—but ended up throwing them all away."

He stopped and turned, gazing out at the water. "The problem was that I was always afraid that once you heard the whole story, you might not think that well of me anymore." He turned and looked at her. "I'd like to tell you now. I want you to know, but . . . "

Liza understood. He was still afraid that the truth would drive her away. She answered the only way she could. "I think you have to take that chance, and give me a chance to try to understand."

Would she think less of him? Would the story

357

diminish him in her eyes? She truly hoped not but part of her was truly afraid to finally hear what he had to say.

Once you've found love, you want to protect it, Liza realized. Even if it means being less than honest with the one you cherish. But then it isn't authentic. It hasn't stood up to the tests. So how can you really say you love that person? she reminded herself.

Because she did believe now that she loved Daniel. Or could love him. If she knew all of him, not just what he chose to show her.

"All right . . . here goes," he started. "I did go to medical school and earned my degree. But I wasn't lying to you about working construction jobs while I was in college, that part was true," he added. "Anyway, I put myself through med school and became an emergency room doctor at Mass General, in Boston. It was hard to be in a serious relationship while I was in training, but once I finished my residency, I did start dating and got engaged. But a few months before we were supposed to get married, it started to become clear to me that I had rushed into this commitment and we really didn't see things the same way—or want the same things in life. We were arguing all the time. It was taking a toll on me. It was hard to concentrate on my work. I wanted to go into counseling, but she wouldn't do that. She insisted that it was all my problem—my long hours and the demands of my job. She wanted me to leave the hospital and start a private practice. . . .

"Well, one night we had our last argument. A real blowout. I knew it was over and I just walked out. All I wanted to do was walk. I walked for miles. I must have walked around the entire city that night. I walked until I was completely exhausted. I got back to the apartment after midnight. My fiancée—or ex-fiancée, actually—was gone, along with a lot of her stuff. That hit me hard, too, and all I wanted to do was just drop down on the couch and sleep. But I realized that I had never checked my messages, and when I did, there were a few from the hospital. They needed me, right away. A multicar accident." He paused and took a breath. Liza could see how hard it was for him to tell this part of the story.

"I knew my judgment was totally off, but I went in to the hospital anyway. 'Hey, I'm a doctor,' I told myself. 'I've trained for situations like this. I can handle it.' You know, the real macho code. But I couldn't handle it. I had no focus, no mental clarity." He drew in a long breath, then went on. "I was treating one of the accident victims and ordered the wrong procedures. The man went into a coma for three days. Fortunately, he survived. But there was brain damage, a loss of faculties. There's no telling if the outcome would have been the same just from the accident, or if the treatment was the cause. But I knew that what I'd done was wrong. It was selfish and self-indulgent. I should have just admitted I wasn't capable of being a doctor that night, but at the time, it felt like a terrible humiliation on top of everything else I'd been through that day. My ego was too big to stand back."

Liza could hear the deep regret in his voice, his self-disdain.

"Did you get in trouble afterward? Is that why you left?" she asked quietly.

"Amazingly . . . no, I didn't. Though I should have. But you know how doctors stick together," he said with a note of bitterness. "The family filed a complaint, but they never filed a lawsuit. My performance was reviewed by the board and I was reprimanded. But my job was never on the line and I never lost my license. I had to mete out my own punishment. I knew in my heart that I'd made a huge mistake. It was a weak moment and another life was damaged. I couldn't continue practicing. I tried, but I just couldn't. I left the city and I came out here—at first, just to take a break and pull myself together. After a while there didn't seem a reason to leave."

"I know the feeling," Liza said with a small smile. The ending of his story was pretty much part of her own.

They started walking again. This time, Liza

took his hand. Daniel had made a terrible mistake, a life-altering mistake. But she wasn't going to stand in judgment of him. Daniel was doing a thorough job of that on his own.

"You did make a mistake," she said finally. "Maybe you even hurt that patient. But it doesn't change the way I think of you. A person is more than a single moment in their life, or a single act. And you can't let this one mistake define the rest of your life. You're a good person, Daniel. You do a lot of good in the world. I know that much about you."

He glanced down at her. "I appreciate you saying that, but I don't feel like a good person all of the time. Not when I think about that night. I suppose, living out here, I don't have to think about it that much. There are no real reminders, not like there would be back in the city. This place is like another world. It's . . . somehow healing."

"It is," Liza agreed.

But she also knew at a certain point, the healing is done. Was that what Daniel was trying to tell her when they'd had their serious discussion before the wedding? When he'd said he was thinking of leaving the island?

"But are you finished here?" she asked. "Are you ready to go back? Or go someplace else?"

He took a deep breath and stared out at the water. Liza wasn't sure if she even wanted to hear his answer, but she knew she had to hear him out. She had to know the whole truth.

"I feel like I've come through something. That staying here, I've finally worked something out. But I can't see myself going back to my old life in Boston. That wouldn't work anymore. Maybe I've finally learned that I can't keep pretending the past didn't happen. Sooner or later, you have to own up to everything. You have to face it and accept it. And trust someone else to see and accept the whole picture, too. You showed me that, Liza."

"By being so relentless about it?" she asked with a smile.

"Not exactly," he admitted. "But men do need to be nudged. We have thick heads. Believe me, I know this. I'm a doctor," he said, making her laugh. "I finally got the message that you really cared about me—enough to know everything, even if it wasn't entirely good news." He paused and turned to her. "As hard as it was to tell you the truth, part of me wanted you to know. Wanted you to know all of me. I haven't let myself get this close to anyone in a long time. I haven't wanted to. I thought, what the heck, I can leave here and start over someplace new, no problem. Then I realized I could leave the island, but I couldn't get away from my own feelings. I'm falling in love with you, Liza. That would stay with me, wherever I ended up."

Liza was speechless. She wondered for a moment if she was just imagining this conversation. She'd imagined it so often in her daydreams.

She didn't exactly know what to say. But her surprised reaction had clearly pleased him.

Daniel pulled her close, his strong arms holding her tight. She could tell he was going to kiss her and finally, he did. A long, sweet, soulful kiss, expressing his love as no words ever could.

When she finally lifted her head away, she felt dazed and overwhelmed. "I love you, too," she said quietly. "I think I have for a long time."

Then words didn't seem necessary. She felt so close to Daniel now. All the curtains had been lifted, the barriers between them swept aside. Their hearts were open to each other now, and anything was possible.

Finally, they decided it was time to return. They walked back along the shore, their arms twined around each other. Liza stared out at the blue sea and sheltering sky. "There is something special about this place," she said quietly. "Something mysterious, even."

Daniel pressed his lips to her hair. "It brought us together. That's special enough for me."

This recipe is so easy, even Liza can make it. It's a wonderful treat in the spring, when fresh berries first appear at the market. But you can whip it up during any season, using peaches, plums, apples, or pears, or a mixture of your favorite fruit. Serve it with whipped cream or a scoop of vanilla ice cream for an extra delicious touch.

Blessings,
Claire

Claire's Mixed-Berry Crumble

For the fruit filling:
  6 cups berries, a combination of blueberries, blackberries, and raspberries (or use just one kind of berry if you prefer)
  2–3 tablespoons fresh lemon juice
  1–2 tablespoons finely grated lemon zest
  2 tablespoons granulated sugar
  4 tablespoons dark brown sugar
  1 tablespoon all-purpose flour

For the crumble:
  2 sticks cold, unsalted butter
  ¾ cup all-purpose flour
  ½ cup granulated sugar
  ¼ cup dark brown sugar
  1 teaspoon cinnamon
  ¾ teaspoon nutmeg
  ¾ cup chopped nuts of your choice

Preheat oven to 350 degrees. Lightly butter a 9x13 baking dish. Set aside.

Rinse berries. Let drain and/or pat dry. They'll give off a lot of juice as they bake, so you don't want to add extra moisture in this step. Place the berries in a large bowl. Gently toss with lemon juice and zest.

In a small bowl, combine the white and brown sugars and the flour. Sprinkle over the fruit and toss gently to combine. If your fruit seems extra juicy, add a little bit more flour. Pour the fruit mixture into the baking dish and set aside.

Cut the butter into small pieces and place in a large bowl. Combine the flour, sugars, cinnamon, and nutmeg in a small bowl. Add to the butter. Using your dampened hands, blend until crumbs form. The butter will be stiff at first, but will warm up slightly as you work it with your hands. When all the dry ingredients are incorporated, add the nuts. (If you have family members and/or guests with nut allergies, old-fashioned rolled oats are a good substitution here.)

Sprinkle crumb mixture over the top of the fruit, squeezing the crumbs together to form clumps as large as you like.

Bake for 20 to 30 minutes, until the crumb topping is crisp and golden and the fruit is bubbly. Serve warm with whipped cream or ice cream.

Center Point Publishing
600 Brooks Road ● PO Box 1
Thorndike ME 04986-0001 USA

(207) 568-3717

US & Canada:
1 800 929-9108
www.centerpointlargeprint.com